The Last Light of Home

Sophia Luxe

Twisted Ink Press

Even in the dark, there is hope.
Keep fighting for the light.

Chapter One

THE STARS SHONE BRIGHTLY over the ruins of the Twin Cities. They twinkled and flickered like diamonds against the darkest blue velvet— a beautiful yet foreign sight that served as a reminder of a world that had moved on without humanity.

Once, the stars were barely visible in the city, hidden by light pollution. The streetlights and neon signs lit the sky so bright that the stars could not compete against the modernity of civilization. But civilization had since collapsed, and nature, patient and relentless, was reclaiming its dominion.

Trees split the pavement. Ivy strangled steel. The wind whispered through hollowed-out buildings, telling stories of abandonment and life after people. Maybe the world was better off now. Maybe the plague and the solar flares had simply corrected the balance.

George pulled her coat tighter, the chill of autumn creeping into her bones as she finished the evening's chores. The sheep were fed, the horses blanketed, and the gas supply checked— still enough to last the week. The old Ford pickup remained their lifeline, a relic from a time before cars relied on fragile circuits and fickle networks.

When it failed, and it would, she and Ana would be left with nothing but their feet and wits. The thought gnawed at her, an ever-present whisper of doom she tried to ignore. For now, they were surviving.

For now, they were lucky.

She stepped inside, basket of eggs in hand, sealing out the bitter wind with the weight of the old wooden door. The house, built in the 1880s and repurposed into a bed-and-breakfast sometime around 2002, had proven to be their salvation. It was designed for efficiency in an era before electricity was taken for granted, and that made all the difference when the world went dark. The firelight cast long shadows across the walls, warm yet restless. The heat was a comfort and warning; without it, the cold could take them as easily as hunger or disease.

Disease was a cruel and unforgiving force. The outbreaks snaked through cities like wildfire, a monstrous thing that thrived in desperation and close quarters.

People crammed into makeshift shelters, grasping for safety, only to find sickness waiting instead. Two-thirds of the Twin Cities' population had been wiped away, coughing and fevered, with no modern medicine left to save them. And that was only what they had seen. The world had gone quiet, but silence didn't mean survival. If anything, it meant the opposite.

They had been fortunate. Others had not.

The early days had been chaos... sirens, riots, desperate voices over failing radio stations. And then, nothing. Neighbors vanished, some seeking a better chance elsewhere, others choosing not to fight at all.

George had stopped wondering about them. The weight of it all threatened to crack something inside her if she let it. There was no room for grief. Not when there was still work to do, not when winter was coming, not when survival was a fragile, fleeting thing.

She entered the house through the back door, trying her best to stay out of Ana's way in the kitchen. Ana had many skills, but was a try-hard magician with a pot and a ladle, creatively turning even the most inelegant ingredients into a somewhat edible feast. It wasn't Michelin-star worthy, but they wouldn't go hungry. George carried the basket of eggs like a prize to the counter, salivating at the savory aroma of warm food, as she watched Ana apply the final additions to rabbit stew.

The promise of sustenance after along, exhausting day in the cold made the meal even more appealing. She deposited the bounty of eggs on the counter and navigated toward the snug breakfast nook Ana had set with bread and cutlery.

"Smells good," George complimented as she removed her coat and gloves and placed them on the bench beside her.

Ana tucked a wisp of blonde hair behind her ear and ladled the stew into two bowls. "Remember when you could just refrigerate leftovers and eat them later?"

"Yeah," George replied.

Ana plopped the bowls down on the table. "I miss them. Cooking everyday sucks."

It had been years, yet they found something they missed from the old world every day. The time before wasn't perfect, but it had some advantages.

Hell, if disease hadn't destroyed so much of the population in quick succession with repeated solar flares, they may have gotten the infrastructure the world once had back sooner. Instead, they were living in a version of the world that had more in common with Midwestern plains life in the 19th and early 20th century, rather than the 21st century they were in.

George broke off a chunk of bread and dipped it into the dark stew. She slipped it into her mouth, the smoky flavor melting on her tongue as she chewed. "It's good," she said, her mouth full. "You get a break starting tomorrow. It's my turn to cook for the next week. Though it won't be as good."

Ana chewed and swallowed a spoonful of stew. "I delivered Sabrina's baby. Elliot agreed to an extra favor to keep it quiet, considering his wife is also pregnant. Guess he's worried about his wife finding out about the mistress. Not like anyone else cares. They just reelected him to the mayor role."

It was down to brass tacks. They rarely did more than talk about work anymore. Once upon a time, George and Ana gossiped as they worked on chart notes and chatted about the plots of shared favorite television shows. Now, there was nothing so exciting. Every day was more of the same. And the cataloging of goods and favors was a necessity of survival.

However, with Elliot, it was more personal. The fucker had been a thorn in George's side for years, entitled and ungrateful. Once, she had tried to like him— when they were kids. But that notion was long gone. She'd learned to settle for tolerance.

Knowing that Elliot had nothing of value to barter with beyond a favor to be called upon later, George said, "Good. I like having my stepbrother by the balls. Don't forget tomorrow is inventory day."

Ana rolled her eyes. She hated doing inventory. It was tedious and time-consuming. George didn't mind it, preferring the predictability and order, even if it was depressing to know how few medications they had left. They had to make it last. After that, it was a matter of reverting to folk remedies and letting nature take its course.

While some herbal medicine and folk remedies did work well, it didn't replace the advancements of having more sophisticated medicinal compounds. Using books from the university and their limited chemistry knowledge from their undergraduate days, George and Ana were working on trying to recreate some drugs from the natural botanical forms.

It'd be faster if the remaining chemists in the city weren't so focused on getting people high, since their knowledge far eclipsed anyone else's. But they couldn't fault them, though. Everyone was doing what they needed to survive, and there was very little room for anything else.

"I have a couple of house calls to make, so you'll have to do it without me," Ana said, her tone indicating she was practically giddy at being able to avoid the monotonous task..

George got up and filled her bowl again. It was no use eating sparingly. The stew wouldn't hold without refrigeration. "I gave the Warner boys' mother a wheelchair and some pure CBD oil for her chronic pain. They'll keep us stocked with wood and oil this winter, and their sister will supply candles and soap to pay us back. It'll take some of the load off us."

Once upon a time, the economy was based on paper backed by metal. These days, those things were worthless. If you had something to trade— a product or service— then you had wealth. In the case of George and Ana, they had the knowledge and skills to trade, and so many people owed them.

"I hate winter," Ana muttered as she cleaned up after herself.

George couldn't agree more.

After dinner, Ana went upstairs to bed while George finished the rest of the kitchen cleaning. It was their way. One cooked while the other did the dishes and cleaned the kitchen afterward. She went into the closet where the hot water heater was hooked up and turned it up a little so she could bathe. Thank goodness the gas still worked, but like everything else, could not be taken for granted. Even the tiniest luxuries were scarce.

George made her way up the narrow back stairs to the house's second floor. Only one occupant slept in the rooms they reserved for patients; by tomorrow, they'd be gone. The patient only needed monitoring after accidentally ingesting unknown mushrooms. Turned out they weren't poisonous, after all.

George checked in with the patient, taking their temperature, blood pressure, and pulse. Out of habit, she recorded it in a notebook that served as the medical chart and bid the patient goodnight.

Alone, she stripped out of her clothes and started a bath, throwing an extra log on the fire in the fireplace in her adjoining room. The flames flickered and danced, casting a soft glow and shadows around the room. The Victrola was in the corner, tempting her to crank it and play a record, but the noise would wake Ana, who'd throw a royal bitch fit if she were disturbed from her beauty sleep. She settled for softly humming the tune to *I'll Be Seeing You* to herself as she entered the bathtub and soaked her weary body.

The hot water seemed like a treat as she felt all the tension of the day seep away from her muscles. George reclined against the back of the porcelain tub and remembered her days as a nurse and eventually nurse practitioner at the University Medical Center.

In the ICU, her patient load was small and complex, but the work was still rewarding. In her last months there, before the world went to shit, there was a patient— John Doe— whose story was almost too sad to bear. They'd found him in the Mississippi, barely breathing, with no identification. The police checked missing persons' reports, releasing information and photos on the news. Still, no one came to claim the comatose, late twenties to early thirties man. No one.

George worked the 7 p.m. to 7 a.m. shift and tended to have more time on her hands in the wee hours of the morning. Just so he wouldn't be alone, she'd spend her downtime charting in his room, singing to him, and chatting about the latest news. George shaved him every night she worked, on the off chance that someone would come for him eventually, wanting him to look his best and deepening their one-sided bond.

He graduated off a ventilator fairly early in his stay. It was like Doe was sleeping— a sleeping beauty. He was a handsome man, after all. When the blackout happened, she knew that patients who needed ventilators and more critical equipment would die, but she hoped the man would wake. It was possible to continue his parenteral tube feedings without the pumps, but eventually, that too would become difficult as supply chains were disrupted, and hospitals eventually went dark and staff-less. In those days, she prayed he wouldn't starve to death, trapped in a dreamless slumber, alone in the dark.

George pushed the thought out of her mind. There was no sense in worrying about someone who was more than likely dead. Every time she thought of him, a twinge of sadness took over, and she felt almost guilty that she never tried to go back to the hospital. How could she? She and Ana had to live, and in the beginning, it was a battle against chaos to start over.

In those early days, George's careful planning got them through. That same planning put them as one of the people at the top of the food chain now and kept them there.

George exited the bath and dressed in the wool pajamas Ana made for her. She loathed the texture of wool against her skin, but they were practical, especially since she wouldn't wake in the middle of the night to put more wood in the fireplace.

The oil lamp near herbed brightened the room enough for her to sit and write at her desk. It'd become a habit to chronicle her thoughts, practical experiences, and new remedies she'd discovered or heard from older people, hoping it could serve as a record for an apprentice later.

Eventually, the world would go back to the way it was. Her legacy wouldn't be the work she did now. It'd be the notes she left behind. At least, that's what history had taught her.

Almost as though she had no control of her hands, she ended every entry with: *Thought of John Doe again.*

The house was quiet by the time George got out of bed and made her way downstairs. Ana must've been out already making her rounds of house calls, and the patient may have still been asleep.

The silence was familiar now, seeming to creep into every facet of life these days. The contemporary world wasn't as noisy as it'd once been and, in some ways, it was good. Less overwhelming, but there were days when she missed former annoyances like the sound of morning traffic.

People used to talk about having quiet mornings and doing crosswords, but that was every morning now, as she had her black coffee and toast before starting her day.

George carried a bowl of oatmeal up to the patient with a small glass of orange juice. As she entered, the woman sat up fully dressed in bed, smiling. She looked much better than she had when she came in now that the anxiety of danger had passed. George set the oatmeal and milk down on the bedside stand and began her assessment while the woman started eating.

"You're doing God's work, Georgianna," the patient said as she ate. She'd known George as a kid and was one of the few people who still called her by her given name rather than her preferred one.

George finished documenting in the medical record notebook. While there was immense pleasure in healing, she didn't do it for purely altruistic reasons. It was a necessary trade. She had the knowledge and skill, and treating people gave her access to things she needed. It was capitalism by way of trade.

"Stay away from wild mushrooms, Ms. Betty, and you should be fine."

The woman grinned. "I've learned my lesson. Guess I'd better invest in a book on mushrooms." She paused. "Is my husband here yet?"

George glanced up from her notes. "Or just stay away from mushrooms altogether. You don't need them unless you grow them. I did see Mr. Calvin's truck pull up on my way up here. Sounds like it needs a new serpentine belt. Finish your breakfast, and you can go home."

Ms. Betty finished her meal and got out of bed; George accompanied her to the door. "How should we pay you, Georgianna?" she asked, voice kind.

George smiled sweetly. "Consider this a favor. I always do favors for my friends, just as long as they reciprocate when I need one." Favors were just as valuable as currency in the new world order. They could get you just about anything and then some. And George kept a careful accounting of who owed her favor and had yet to pay up.

Ms. Betty nodded and went outside to join her husband. George went into the study, to the writing table, and wrote in her ledger: *Ms. Betty Ambrose, One.*

Onto the next one, she thought, tossing Ms. Betty's medical record notebook onto the pile waiting to be taken to the basement and filed to maintain continuity of care.

The day was more of the same. They'd built a clinic on the first floor, turning an empty parlor into a suitable environment for outpatient medical care. The former solarium had been turned into a surgery, where they could perform mostly minor procedures.

First, she saw a prenatal patient. Without an ultrasound, she had to listen for the fetal heartbeat with her stethoscope and a special bell device that she'd managed to obtain from a medical museum. Most of their current toolset was a combination of more modern tools and antiques that were used before technology became so electronic.

Then there was a kid with strep throat, a woman with a urinary tract infection, and George removed a splint from a broken arm.

By noon, she'd finished her scheduled clinic patients for the day and set about doing the physical work of fixing the smokehouse. George laid out the wood and began measuring where to cut. *Measure twice*, her grandpa used to say on the farm where she grew up. *Always measure twice; when you're ready to cut, measure a third time to be sure.*

The house and surrounding grounds had many benefits, but the tradeoff was a lot of maintenance of the house and surrounding structures. It reminded her of the farm she'd grown up on and the hours she and Elliot spent helping her grandfather to maintain the property in the summers when they'd visit. Though they moved to Minnesota when she was in high school, many of the lessons her grandfather had taught her came in handy now. For anything she didn't know, she was fortunate enough to find books on fixing things from the 1950s and '60s in her travels around the city.

George made the first cut and remeasured the wood, comparing it to the measurements she'd written yesterday. When she was satisfied, she moved on to the next piece and the next, singing as she worked.

Today, the musician of choice was the Backstreet Boys. Of all the things she missed, besides the internet, she missed music. Some of it was still available... just the stuff they made into vinyl records. Hand-cranked record players still worked. Most of it was gone.

Ana came back in the old pickup truck. She parked just outside the workshop and got out of the truck, carrying her backpack in her hands rather than slung over her shoulders. "Have you done the inventory yet?" she asked.

George tucked her pencil behind her ear and set her ruler on the table. "Nope. I was waiting for you."

Ana sighed. "Shit. And here I thought I'd missed all the fun." Her tone dripped with sarcasm.

"It's boring but necessary. How else can we keep up with our supplies? It's not just for the patients, you know."

"It's depressing. Once upon a time, you got sick, and you got some medicine. When we worked in the hospital, if someone needed something, we popped into the supply cabinet or the med cart and got it, no concern over making it stretch. If something was out, we just called someone, and it would be there in an hour or two. Now you get sick, and someone— namely us— has to decide if you are worthy enough of medicine."

George shrugged. "It keeps the status quo."

"It's playing God," Ana countered, raising an eyebrow at her.

"There is no God," George retorted with a scoff.

Ana sighed and shook her head. Despite her assertions that there wasn't a God in the early days, she still clung to her lifetime of Lutheran upbringing. George realized it was just Ana's way of coping, and far be it from her to debate theology.

If there was a God, why could so many people be allowed to suffer, including the innocent? The Bible talked about suffering God's tests, but it seemed unnecessary.

George had never been sure about what force ran the universe, but now she was certain it was all just some random chaos. What kind of a great being who was supposed to be loving would do this, unless they simply enjoyed chaos?

Still, she wouldn't argue with Ana. They were both in a strange land that looked like it used to, somewhat, but would never be home again.

"I know there is no God. I'm just saying..." Ana stopped and sighed, as if she were trying to talk herself out of her faith.

George put a hand up. If faith gave Ana hope, then that was good enough. "I guess we can do it later," she said. "The smokehouse still needs repairs. I'd rather do that so we can smoke meat for winter."

Ana smiled. "Thanks. You know, venison would be nice."

"Who's going to go out to the woods? You? The urban deer are too good at hiding."

"I'm not even a good shot," Ana laughed, walking into the house.

It wasn't implausible to go to the woods. After all, they were full of plants that could be used for medicine making. George had been learning more about the apothecary properties of certain plants, trying to familiarize herself with what could be found in the wild and grown in her garden.

Once again alone with her thoughts, George returned to work. Judging by the weather, snow was only a few weeks away. Of course, it was Minnesota, where they had the saying, "Don't like the weather, wait five minutes." It could all change tomorrow.

She changed her mind about the Backstreet Boys and went to an oldie but goodie: The Big Bopper's *Chantilly Lace.*

Good music to work by.

Chapter Two

THE SHARP SOUND OF breaking glass jolted David from his restless sleep. He sat up and reached for the gun under his backpack on instinct.

"Don't fucking move, or you'll get a load of buckshot in your chest," shouted a man partially hidden by shadows that clung to the small shop's walls.

David slowly raised his arms and sighed. Damn his sense of self-preservation.

"I don't want any trouble," David mumbled. He looked at his bag. A week's supply of food lay in there. There was no way he was just going to let them have it. It was hard enough to find supplies when you were a nomad.

He thought back to his military training. He'd have a chance against the guy if he could find something that could be used as a weapon without overtly reaching for his gun.

Cautiously, he said, "I'm just going to stand up."

"Do it slowly. Keep your hands up," replied the man.

David got to his feet. A broken pvc pipe was just a few feet ahead of him. It wouldn't pack the same wallop as something metal, but could be somewhat effective if he swung it right. David took a step forward, trying his best to seem harmless.

"I said don't fucking move!" There was a tremor in the man's voice. Was it fear?

David took another step forward. The man didn't shoot, which meant either he'd never killed someone before, or it wasn't loaded. Maybe it was both, but he was willing to risk the gamble.

Emboldened by the idea, David continued forward and grabbed the pipe. The man with the gun charged at David and hit him in the chest with the butt of the rifle. He stumbled back as a dull pain blossomed above his sternum. Despite this, the adrenaline in his body kicked in and David continued forward, swing the pipe at the man.

He managed to hit the attacker with the gun twice in the face, the impact of the swing combined with the hard plastic forcing the man to the ground, blood trickling from his mouth. David stood above him, ready to swing again. Then he heard it.

A rattling noise came from behind where David stood, drawing his attention away from the man in front of him to a mousy-looking kid hurriedly stealing his supplies.

The kid couldn't have been more than fourteen or fifteen. If he'd been a man, David would have attacked without hesitation. But he was a boy, and despite being in survival mode, David didn't want to hurt a kid. But he couldn't let him take his pack, either.

The kid looked to his accomplice, eyes flashing in fear. David peered back at the man, bleeding and spluttering on the floor, then back at the kid.

It would be easy enough to subdue him, even without a weapon. He was scrawny enough. David dropped the pipe and moved fast. He wasn't about to beat on a teenager, but he couldn't lose a week's worth of supplies.

David grabbed one of the straps of the backpack, struggling to wrench it from the kid's grasp. They wrestled for the bag, both tumbling to the damp carpet of the skyway office.

Pain, deep and stabbing, radiated from David's thigh up to his hips, causing him to cry out and lose his grip on the strap. Warmth blossomed from the initial stabbing sensation and slowly seeped into his pants.

David grabbed at his leg, focusing on the cut that went from the top of his thigh to the middle of it, deep and oozing with blood. He looked up at the kid, who paled while holding a bloody knife in his hand. The teen scrambled to his feet and joined his accomplice, who stood over David with a mix of dry and wet blood covering his mouth and chin, holding his rifle tight in both hands.

He knew what would come next, because it was what he'd have done. Incapacitate the enemy. David raised his bloodied hands to protect his face.

The rifle's butt smashed into his hands and the top of his head, where he'd failed to cover. It was an agonizing blow, only adding to the pain he was already fighting through from the cut on his leg. Both his head and legs burned, and his ears began to ring, dulling his other senses.

The man delivered forceful kicks to David's side over and over again, as though he meant to kill him or at least ensure David wouldn't get up again. It felt like bones were snapping under the repeated weight of his boot.

David willed himself to not lose consciousness, but his body disobeyed. Under the excruciating pain, his vision went blurry before the world was black.

Bitter cold chilled David, stirring him awake. The fire had finally gone out, and the bastards hadn't even had the decency to leave him his coat.

David glanced out the window of the once small-time attorney's office to a sky slowly turning from dark blue to light. It was nearly dawn. He attempted to stand but was hindered by the gash in his leg, face twisting in pain.

"Fuck," he gritted out, willing himself to work through the pain. Survival depended on it.

Near a forgotten coat rack was an old wooden cane in an umbrella stand. Suddenly, he was grateful he didn't use it for firewood like he'd originally planned.

David crawled to the stand and grabbed the cane. Using the door handle and the cane, he managed to pull himself to his feet, careful to minimize the weight on his injured left leg, lest he pass out again from pain. Staying at the abandoned office in the skywalk was impossible with its broken windows and no supplies or coat. He'd die of starvation or hypothermia.

The immediate need was a more secure shelter, food, and clean water. Then he could attend to his injury. He wouldn't last long without basic necessities, nor would he be able to fight off any infections from the wound. As reluctant as he was to venture into the dark, the skywalk was safer than the streets, and he could at least get somewhere more secure. At least in the skywalk he wouldn't have to worry about packs of wild dogs.

Navigating the maze of skywalks was slow going with only one good leg. The large windows helped him get his bearings. Even if it was mostly crumbling and desolate in the streets below, enough landmarks remained to give context to which streets he was crossing over.

Some of the glass was still broken from jumpers in the early years. After the grid went down, some people committed suicide, and others were killed during riots. Disease, aided by the ravages of climate change, took care of most of the rest. The population had dwindled to a fraction of what it once was. A large, centralized government had been replaced by a multitude of smaller locally run communities lacking many services that were once taken for granted.

Not that the apocalypse had done all the work of ending centralized governance. The erosion began long before that when democracy became little more than idealized words. At the same time, fascism slowly seeped into the United States government, helped along by ignorance and mass media bending the knee to a series of authoritarian leaders and oligarchs.

Down on the streets, the pharmacists were just starting to open shop, selling drugs to despondent souls who wanted to forget where they were. They specialized in compounding formulas to help people obliterate their misery and the desperation of a hard life. It was far more lucrative to create blends of shit to get people high rather than healing. And they'd found a niche in a world where it was adapt or die. He couldn't fault people for earning a living. It'd always been the way of the world.

David rounded a corner near the old U.S. Bank building. This corridor was a familiar one as he often found clothing in the best conditions if he ventured down one level to a defunct sports memorabilia shop. Trixie, a woman he knew and helped out on occasion, lived here in an old candy shop— *Lily's Candy*.

He imagined when the young woman chose the shop to set up house in, she may have been a kid. What kid didn't want to live in a candy store?

But that would have been years ago. There was no candy left in *Lily's*. Just Trixie, who was a young woman now, worn by the ravages of survival like the rest of them. She was still sweet, though. Still someone that he didn't mind running the occasional errand for or sharing meat with from his hunting.

"David, you're bleeding." Trixie's voice was melodic and light, sounding like a teenager's, emphasizing her youth. Trixie stood in her doorway, clad in a ragged flannel robe, just as a client slinked past her. He tucked his shirt into his pants and hurried past David.

"What happened to you?" she asked.

"Thieves," he said through clenched teeth, the pain in his legs settling into a steady, pulsing throb as he hobbled to her door.

The robe loosened, giving peeks of bruised pale flesh on her chest. Trixie wrapped her robe tighter around herself and tied the sash. "Come in. We've gotta get that cleaned up before infection sets in."

When they were both secure, she locked the shop door and closed the fabric she'd hung to make a privacy curtain.

The room was lit by candles and decorated with scarves and panels of mixed fabric. A bed of pillows was on the floor in the middle of the room, the blankets disturbed by recent activity. Off to one side was a small table and two chairs next to a long counter with a case that would have once held ice cream.

Small tags still clung to the glass indicating flavors like spumoni, pistachio, chocolate, and rocky road. Trixie helped him to the table and sat him in one of the chairs before going to the sink just behind the counter. She filled a kettle of water and set it on a gas camp stove before reaching under the long shop counter and producing a handle of vodka. She grabbed a couple of rough-looking fabric strips and returned to him.

"How'd they get the jump on you?" she asked.

"I was asleep... for once," he replied gruffly.

Trixie undid the button on his jeans. "We have to get these off so I can wrap the wound."

David nodded and stood long enough for her to roll his pants down over his hips before collapsing back in the chair. He scratched his beard and rubbed his chest. Everything hurt. More than hurt, it *burned*.

The kettle screeched moments later, and Trixie grabbed it off the stove. She turned the burner off and poured the water into a bowl, depositing a rag in with it and adding just a splash of cold water.

She lightly touched his side, and David suddenly felt weird being half naked in front of Trixie. Sure, she saw men naked all the time, but he'd never been with her like that, nor had he even thought of her in that way.

Her auburn hair fell forward, some falling into her face, emphasizing her youth and for the briefest of moments hiding the world weariness of her gaze. Trixie, despite turning to prostitution to stay fed, was a vulnerable woman. She needed to be guarded from the evils of the world and cared for properly, but that was a role he couldn't fulfill.

Looking out for anyone but himself was not something he was accustomed to before the blackout and especially not now that survival depended on being selfish.

Trixie was only twenty-two or so she'd once told him. Ten years younger than himself. In a different world, she would've been listening to music on her phone, chatting with friends on social media, and grumbling about schoolwork. If times had been different, she'd be worrying about her career after college. But that wasn't anyone's life anymore.

The sting of the alcohol on his wound brought him out of his thoughts as Trixie meticulously poured the liquor directly into the gash. "Ow. Goddammit!" he cried out.

"Sorry," Trixie muttered, her lips twisting in a grimace. "But this is better than gangrene."

She was right. Even so, it still hurt like a son of a bitch.

Trixie soaked a long scarf with the vodka and wrapped his leg with it. She used a second scarf, the same red as the muscle underneath, to cover the first and absorb more blood. "That ought to do it for now. You really should see the clinicians," she said.

"I'll be fine," David murmured, picking up the handle and taking a swig. The bathtub hooch burned going down.

Trixie frowned. "I'm worried about you, David. It looks pretty deep. You might need stitches or somethin'."

"Trixie, I'll be fine." His tone was firmer this time.

She didn't argue further. Instead, she rolled her eyes and put her long dark hair into a ponytail. "Well, what are you going to do now?"

"I've got to find some food and supplies. Bastards took the whole weeks' worth, along with my coat and gun." He took another swig of the vodka, hoping it'd work some magic and help with the pain. No such luck.

She looked thoughtful for a moment. "I've got food and water to spare. You can stay here until you're healed up enough to find a new place."

David got to his feet, the effort to stand making him woozy. The room began to spin, and the slight ringing in his ears was maddening now that he was no longer fighting to get somewhere safe. As much as he hated to impose, there was no way he could get any further tonight. Trixie's was safe enough, and he could at least trust that she wouldn't kill him in her sleep.

"Thankyou," he sighed, deciding that the only smart choice was to sit. "What about your business?"

Trixie pointed to a narrow door at the back of the shop, next to another door with a unisex bathroom plaque. "There's a storeroom in the back. You can sleep there."

He sized up the room. It'd be cramped, but was better than nothing. As soon as he could get around decently, he'd find something more permanent to get through the winter, secure it, and stockpile supplies. It seemed like each winter was colder than the last, and it'd be better to get settled before the first snow. "Thanks, Trixie."

"I still think you need to see a clinician." She was right, but he was stubborn.

David shrugged. "They don't work for free. I've got nothing to pay them with."

"They trade favors," Trixie argued.

"I'd rather take my chances than be knee deep in debt to someone."

She crossed her arms over her chest and huffed. "They're not that bad."

"Have you ever seen them?" David asked, drinking more of the alcohol. Even to him he sounded like a child, but it was better to live free of obligations. Seeing the clinicians would saddle him with a debt he wasn't willing to pay.

"George helped me with a little situation this past spring. I didn't have much to give either, so I traded a favor."

"Have they collected?"

Trixie nodded. "They had me put them in contact with Aces Wild."

He couldn't keep the skepticism out of his voice. "That's it?"

Yup." Trixie began to remove blankets from one of the shelves under the cabinet. She carried a couple to the storeroom and set them up on the far wall of the cramped space. "They're not monsters, David. They're just doing what the rest of us are."

He rolled his eyes. "I beg to differ. They're taking advantage of people who are vulnerable and need their skills."

"They have to make a living, David. I'm not going to argue with you. I don't see anything wrong with it. I do the same on my back, or with my ass, or on my knees. We all have to use what we've got to get what we need." He watched as she attempted to make it somewhat hospitable in a room meant for boxes.

"People pay you in actual items," he pointed out.

She shrugged. "If I had any way of ensuring they'd repay favors, I would take those too. It's a very different world we live in now."

David looked up from his bottle. Every time he allowed himself to think of Trixie as a kid, she'd say something that reminded him that she existed in the same harsh reality they all lived in. She wasn't naïve. And she knew how to survive.

"I think I should lie down now," David said.

Trixie grabbed a can of something from one of the shop cabinets. "You need to eat something first. Food and then bed."

He decided not to argue with her. His best chance at a speedy recovery was rest and sustenance.

Trixie started the camp stove again and opened the can. She poured the lumpy contents, which he assumed was chili, into a pot and set it on the stove. The cooking chili smelled faintly of dog food, not at all appetizing, but it was hot.

The aroma took him back to the days immediately after he'd woken up alone in a dark hospital room. He'd wandered the streets, acclimatizing to the new world. Death seemed to be everywhere as he tripped over bodies in bags or lying exposed in the streets.

During those days, he *did* eat dog food or cat food— anything he could find. He needed to get strong again and it seemed that dog and cat food were the only things not looted on convenience store shelves. Being indiscriminate kept him alive until he could find something better... until he had enough strength to forage for real food and shelter.

It wasn't a taste he was in a hurry to remember.

Trixie returned with the heated chili in a bowl and a glass of water. "Thanks." A spoon was already standing straight up in the thick sludge as he took the bowl from her. David suppressed a gag and shoveled some in his mouth, quickly following it with water.

Trixie set two white pills on the table. "Percocet," she said.

David raised his brows suspiciously.

She shook her head. "Don't look at me that way. I had some left from when I had my molar pulled. Go ahead. Take them."

"I'll sleep too hard. I'll be useless until it wears off." He'd be helpless, a feeling he loathed.

Trixie shrugged. "I don't see the problem. You need to rest. You're basically useless until that gash heals."

Of course, Trixie was speaking from common sense, but that didn't mean he had to like it. His body was working against him. The pain was slowly becoming unbearable, making the pain-killer sound better by the moment.

Trixie went to the bathroom while David finished eating. He downed the water and pills, then used the now cold water in the bowl to wash his face and clean up the extra blood.

Standing proved difficult. Every ounce of strength seemed to have left him as he tried to get to his feet. His entire body radiated with pain from being kicked, beaten, and stabbed. His torso hurt so much that he was sure a rib or two was broken.

With a grunt, he hobbled to the small room using the cane. Trixie had outdone herself trying to make a cozy bed for him on the floor. The blankets were clean and neatly arranged the best she could in the small space. It was very thoughtful of her. The poor kid was taking better care of him than she did herself.

David slowly lowered himself to the makeshift bed, listening to Trixie in the bathroom next door humming an indecipherable tune. She stepped out of the bathroom moments later and sauntered to a nearby baker's rack full of silver trays where she kept her clothes and chose something to wear.

Before dressing, Trixie paused in front of a mirror on the wall, examining herself in the nude. Purple and yellow bruises blossomed on her alabaster skin in random patterns. Some fresher ones lay right above the thick crest of curls between her legs.

Was she trying to get his attention?

For a long time, Trixie had made little secret of her attraction to David. Once upon a time he'd have been considered handsome, and he knew it. Now he was just a scraggly, bearded man. What she saw in him, he didn't understand. Maybe it was some sort of misguided angel complex. Perhaps she wanted to save him.

He was beyond saving.

And even though she was a woman, he just didn't see her that way.

He stopped watching her and eased himself into a lying position, closing his eyes. Sleep, he decided, would be the best remedy for his current situation.

The soft sounds of Trixie's off-key humming, while soothing, weren't as soothing as the woman who used to sing to him. Even in his perpetual sleeping state, he heard her voice, a lullaby that made him envision the angel of mercy who cared for him in the hospital. Sometimes he wondered if he'd just dreamed her up and that his memories were false coping mechanisms. Other times, he remembered the smell of the soap on her skin and the exact pitch of her voice as she talked to him.

When he slept, David imagined what she looked like. Sometimes she was beautiful and young. Other times she was motherly and mature. Either way, she was his angel. The one person who made him believe he could atone for his past sins.

"David, are you asleep?" Trixie whispered.

He stopped fantasizing about the singing angel and opened his eyes. "Not yet."

"I was just going to tell you, I have a client coming in a few minutes. I'll shut the door, but if you need anything, just holler."

He nodded.

Trixie appeared to want to say something else for a moment, but she didn't. She left, shutting the door behind her. David closed his eyes once more and quickly fell asleep.

Chapter Three

A GREAT PLUME OF smoke curled upward in the air like an ominous black cloud. David stood on a hilltop, surveying the village below. Stone and wooden structures made up the vast number of residences, a contrast to the city four hours away from this remote village.

His orders were simple: observe and do not intervene. They were supposed to study the Libyan rebels and collect intel, not give away agent positions.

He curled his hands into tight fists, feeling utter disgust and despair as he watched the flames from the church grow higher, reaching the cross that stood on the roof. People had gathered to pray for an end to the rebels' reign of terror in the region. For their sons to remain home and not be made into child soldiers.

And as they prayed, the rebels barred the doors and set fire to the church. Even with the distance he maintained, the screams seemed to carry on the wind to his position, fuel for nightmares to come.

The people inside were facing a gruesome fate. First, they'd become overcome by the smoke. Then they'd lose conscious-

ness as their body became starved for oxygen. They were usually dead long before the burns got too bad. Even if the pain-in-
duced screams were so gut-wrenching, they were nearly palpable.

He swallowed hard, his stomach a churn of guilt and rage.
Orders. Always orders.

David cursed the generals and politicians safe in their ivory
towers, issuing commands without ever seeing the blood their
decisions spilled. He was supposed to observe. Observe and
survive. But what kind of man could stand by while people
burned?

Not that he could do anything. Not against seventy-five
armed men. Not alone. If he broke cover now, he'd be dead
before he reached the door.

When this mission was over, he'd walk away. No medals. No
pension. Just his conscience, blackened and worn.

A sudden boom shattered the air, jerking him back to the
present. The ground trembled violently beneath his boots,
nearly throwing him to his knees. Another explosion, then another. The rebels weren't content with a single atrocity. They
were erasing the entire village.

David scrambled back, instinct taking over. Debris rained
down around him— wood, stone, shrapnel, even smoldering
leaves. A jagged beam struck the ground mere feet away, kicking up a cloud of dust and ash. He forced himself to focus, to
slow his breathing. Panic was a death sentence.

Voices shouted in the local dialect, sharp and commanding.
David only caught fragments, but the meaning was clear: move

fast, clear out, leave nothing standing. He slid into a ditch, pressing himself against the damp earth to avoid detection until he could time his escape just right.

Then the world went eerily quiet. His body trembled as adrenaline ebbed. When he opened his eyes again, he wasn't in the village.

He was lying in the back of a car, every bump in the road jarring his bruised and battered body.

And the heat. Why was it so hot?

"Where—?" His voice came out in a croak. His throat was dry, his head pounding. Heat radiated off him in waves.

"You're burning up," said a familiar voice. "I know you said no doctors, but I couldn't just let you die."

Trixie.

Libya dissolved into nothingness. He wasn't in that hellscape anymore. It had been a dream. Just a dream.

But as he struggled to sit up, confusion clawed at his mind. Trixie didn't own a working car.

"Remember our deal, Trix," a hoarse male voice said.

Trixie nodded. "I remember. You'll get your payment."

The car stopped, and Trixie climbed out. Moments later, she reappeared with another woman. The stranger's frown was as sharp as her tone. "What the hell happened to him?"

"Thieves," Trixie replied, keeping her voice steady. "I've been trying to keep the wound clean."

David swallowed the lump in his throat, frustration brewing. He wanted to yell, to demand an explanation. How the hell was he going to pay for this? He had nothing to trade and no favors left to offer.

"Let's get him inside so I can take a better look," the woman said, her voice brisk and commanding.

A man appeared to help, and together they maneuvered David out of the car. He clenched his teeth against the pain, each step an unbearable jolt to his fractured ribs and injured leg. They carried him into the house and up a narrow staircase, finally lowering him onto a bed layered with hastily placed towels.

"I'll pay for him," Trixie blurted, worry etched across her features.

David opened his mouth to protest, but the woman cut him off with a sharp look. "Take it easy. Just relax." She turned back to Trixie, her expression softening. "We'll talk about it later. You should get home before dark."

Trixie nodded. "Thank you, George." She hesitated, looking at David. "I'll see you later."

The man ushered her out. David's chest tightened. He hated this— being helpless. A burden.

George disappeared briefly into another room and returned with a damp rag, cool and soothing as she pressed it to his fevered forehead. "Let's see how bad those ribs are."

She gently lifted his shirt, her touch surprisingly careful as she examined his chest.

He winced when she traced the bruises and felt along his ribs. "At least one's fractured," she murmured. "Nothing major, but it's going to hurt like hell for a while. Now, let's look at that leg."

With sudden clarity, David realized that beneath the blanket around his waist, there wasn't much preserving his modesty. He tensed as George snipped away the scarves, her lips pressing into a grim line when she saw the wound.

"I'll be right back," she assured him.

As she left, silence crept in, broken only by the faint rustle of leaves outside the window. David's thoughts churned, restless and chaotic. That's when he heard it— a voice, soft and melodic, humming an old ballad that tugged at the edges of his memory.

George reappeared, singing under her breath as she carried an IV bag and a med kit. Her rich and haunting voice froze him in place. He *knew* that song.

She moved with practiced ease, preparing the IV. "You're going to feel a small pinch," she said, pausing her melody. The needle slid into his vein, and moments later, the chill of the fluid coursed through him.

"I wish you'd come sooner," she muttered, her voice tinged with frustration. "You wouldn't have this infection."

David's gaze settled on her face, his breath catching. She wasn't the woman he'd imagined— the nurse from his dreams. This woman was real, her caramel complexion glowing in the dim light, almond-shaped eyes focused intently on her work.

Her hair was tied back, highlighting the graceful lines of her face. She was beautiful, but appeared tired, like the world had taken its toll on her as much as the rest.

"Do I know you?" he croaked, his voice hoarse.

She didn't respond, her attention fixed on stitching his leg. Her humming returned, the tune resonating with painful familiarity. David clenched his jaw, biting back cries of pain as the needle pierced his skin.

When she finished, George covered the wound with gauze, taped it in place, and administered a shot. "Tetanus," she explained, her voice softening.

"Thank you," he rasped.

She smiled faintly, offering him two pills. "Lortab. For the pain."

David swallowed them with a sip of water, his body sagging into the pillows she adjusted behind him. For the first time in years, comfort found him, even if only briefly.

"What did you do before the blackout?" he asked.

George paused, sorting supplies. "I was a nurse."

"At the university hospital?"

She nodded. "Yes." Her eyes flicked to his face, studying him. "Would you like me to shave you? You don't seem like the type for a beard."

David nodded, too drained to argue. She returned with a towel and shaving kit, her movements deliberate as she lathered his face with foam.

"What was that song you were humming?"

"*I'll Be Seeing You*," she replied. "Billie Holiday."

"It's nice."

George said nothing, her focus shifting to the razor as it glided across his skin. Her fingers, deft and precise, left his cheeks smooth. She hummed again, barely audible, but the melody tethered him to her, grounding him in this surreal moment.

When she finished, she wiped his face clean. Her hand paused, her eyes widening as she took a step back.

"What is it?" he asked in alarm.

She sat down beside him, her voice a whisper. "John Doe."

The words hit him like a thunderclap. His pulse raced, memories flooding back. "You remember me?"

Her hand brushed his face, tentative and searching. "No one ever came to claim you."

"There was no one," he admitted, his voice breaking. "Hello, I'm David Andrews."

Her lips quirked in a bittersweet smile. "Georgianna Harris," she replied softly. "But everyone calls me George."

"George," David repeated her name as though it were a spell.

She switched her attention to the IV bag, checking a knob in the tubing. "I'll be back to check on you later," she said, making a hasty retreat.

That hadn't gone how he'd imagined. Though, if he was honest with himself, he wasn't entirely sure how he'd imagined it. For the first time since waking up in this stupid world, he didn't want to be alone. He wanted to be near *her*. To learn who she really was... not just the fragments he'd pieced together from her one-sided conversations while he was unconscious.

It was strange, wasn't it? He'd spent hours by her side, knowing her but not *knowing* her. Her voice had been his anchor, her soft chatter breaking the endless quiet of his mind. She'd had a fiancé once, he remembered. Left her for a life in Los Angeles. At least, that's what he thought she'd said. The details were hazy, but the regret in her tone wasn't.

David shifted as much as his battered body allowed, angling for a better view out the window. George was outside again, this time speaking with a blonde woman. He studied the scene for a moment until the blonde glanced up at the house, her gaze brushing against his. Flustered, David pulled back.

Why should he feel embarrassed? Looking out a window was perfectly normal, especially for someone bedridden. But knowing that didn't stop the heat crawling up his neck.

It didn't help.

He wanted to thank George properly— for her care back at the hospital— and now, for patching him up yet again. She'd gone above and beyond, saving his sorry ass despite his protests. He owed her, but he owed Trixie, too. And while Trixie would never ask for anything, maybe he could hunt her a rabbit or something when he was back on his feet.

Turning to the window again, he caught sight of George moving into a coop to collect eggs. The blonde woman was gone.

"It's not polite to stare, you know."

David nearly jumped. He turned to find the blonde standing just inside the door, watching him with a wry smile.

"I wasn't staring," he said quickly.

"John Doe..." She strolled closer, her tone laced with amusement. "We used to hide out in your room and talk." She checked his IV, tilting her head slightly as if counting the drops. "George says your name is David."

"It is," he replied warily. "And you are?"

"Ana Hilk." She tugged lightly at a corner of tape, inspecting George's handiwork. "She's always been good with a needle. Still, it's going to leave a scar."

"I'm not too concerned about scars," David replied with a shrug. "The girl who brought me here, Trixie, she made a deal with you?"

"Not me. George," Ana said with a small smile. "Trixie's always trading in favors."

"Well, I'll pay," he said firmly. "I settle my own debts."

Ana's lips quirked into a faint O, like she was surprised anyone would willingly take on that responsibility. "You ought to be careful with a statement like that. Besides, I don't know what kind of man you are. Are you a man of means, or a man of character?"

David's jaw tightened. "I don't have much," he admitted. "But I have skills."

"So not a man of means then," she said, her tone teasing. "Still doesn't tell me if you have character."

"I said I'll settle it," David repeated, his voice low and steady.

Ana tilted her head, studying him. "You're going to need food, board, medical care— not to mention supplies. It'll take weeks before you're back on your feet. That's a lot of debt you're racking up."

"He owes us nothing," George said firmly as she entered, carrying extra blankets and a set of men's clothing.

"I don't need charity," David shot back, his voice edged with defiance.

"George, need I remind you—" Ana started, her tone laced with warning.

"I said, he owes nothing." George placed the items down on the dresser with a decisive thud.

"George…" Ana's voice dipped low, a quiet challenge.

George didn't rise to it. Instead, she turned to David, her focus steady and unwavering. "Shouldn't you start supper?"

Ana hesitated, tension crackling in the air, before she stepped back with a tight smile. "Nice to meet you. I hope you like chicken." Her footsteps echoed as she disappeared down the stairs.

Silence followed, thick and heavy.

"I'm going to bathe you," George said abruptly, breaking it.

David bristled. "I can do it myself."

"It may hurt."

He shrugged. Pain was nothing new to him. "If you handle my back, I can manage the rest."

"Okay." George nodded, grabbing a porcelain wash basin from the nightstand and retreating to the bathroom.

She returned with the basin filled and a folded pair of wool pajamas balanced on her arm. "It gets cold here at night," she said simply, setting the clothes aside.

David exhaled, exasperated by her walls. "Are you always this good at making small talk?"

Her lips twitched slightly, more acknowledgment than smile. "I'm actually terrible at it. Most of the time, I hate small talk."

"How do you talk to patients, then?"

"I don't," she said, handing him a wet rag. "I can do that, if you'd rather."

"I don't prefer it," David muttered, taking the rag. He began scrubbing his face, the cool water a relief against layers of grime and sweat.

George helped him maneuver out of his shirt, threading the IV bag through carefully, then moved to his pants, preserving his modesty with a sheet. Her hands were clinical and deliberate, and she avoided looking at him as he dunked the rag into the basin again and began washing his arms and chest.

When he reached his crotch, she turned her back, staring at the door as if to give him some semblance of privacy.

David worked in silence, the awkwardness gnawing at him. He was terrible at small talk too, at least about himself. Lying? That was his specialty— a skill honed through years of necessity. But talking about *David Andrews*? He hadn't practiced that in years.

He searched for something neutral, something safe. "Remember Starbucks?"

George glanced over her shoulder, eyebrows raised. "One on every corner," she remarked. "For a while, it looked like they were going to be the McDonalds of coffee shops."

It was a start. "Yeah," he said, clearing his throat. "Loved their blended drinks. Hated their drip."

She shrugged. "It was too dark for my tastes. I used to order the iced tea."

The corner of his mouth tugged upward. Just like that, the tension started to thaw.

And for a few moments, they simply talked.

Dinner was simple and hearty: half a chicken, a squash dish of some sort, and thick slices of fresh bread. They'd even given him a microbrew porter, which was surprisingly good and leagues better than plain water. The bitter tang of the beer lingered on his tongue when George entered, balancing two plates of pie and forks in her hands.

She handed him a plate. "It's pumpkin. I made it yesterday."

David sank his fork into the creamy, spiced dessert and took a bite. It was better than any pumpkin pie he could remember, though the bar wasn't set high. Store-bought pies had been the extent of his experience. The smooth, rich filling made him hum in appreciation, and he dug in with eager bites.

"This is much better than..." He stopped himself before finishing the sentence, catching the potential embarrassment just in time.

George chuckled, a sound that warmed the room, and for the first time, the smile reached her eyes. The transformation was startling. Her face, so often guarded, seemed younger, her features softened by humor.

"It's okay," she said, amused. "Ana's not exactly Julia Child, but she's pretty good, considering what we have. I'm more useful outdoors, so we agreed she'd handle the cooking and cleaning while I take care of the animals and yard work."

David set his empty plate and fork on the nightstand. "I meant what I said earlier about paying my debts."

George took a bite of her pie, chewing thoughtfully. "And I meant it when I said you owe nothing. Would you like more pie?"

He nodded, and she handed him her plate without hesitation.

"I know you don't do something for nothing," he said, his tone edged with insistence.

George raised an eyebrow but didn't rise to the bait. "We don't advertise it, but sometimes we do freebies."

David frowned. She wasn't going to budge, clearly determined to let him off the hook. Providing medications and food couldn't have been easy for the two women, and he hated feeling like a freeloader.

He decided to pivot. If one tactic failed, another might succeed. That's what he was trained for. *Adjust the approach until you get the outcome you want.*

"Ana said it'll be weeks before I'm fully healed," he began, testing the waters.

George nodded, setting down her fork. "Healed, yes. But we'll start you walking tomorrow with a cane. It's important to keep you moving, or that leg and rib won't be our only problems."

"But I won't survive out there on my own, will I?"

George's lips thinned, and she drew a slow breath. "No. Not with winter coming."

Her honesty settled heavily in the room. "When you woke up, how did you survive?" she asked, her voice quieter now.

David had expected the question but was surprised it had come up so soon. That afternoon, their small talk had meandered from coffee to politics to global warming and animal husbandry. But this felt heavier, more direct.

"I woke up in the dark," he said, the memory sharp and vivid. "There were noises from the hallway outside my door—wild animals, maybe, fighting over scraps. At first, I called out, but then I realized I had tubes in me." He hesitated, swallowing hard. "The whispers I thought were dreams started making sense. I was in a hospital."

George's gaze never left him, her expression unreadable.

"I pulled the tube out of my nose, the IV out of my arm, and grabbed a plastic bedpan to use as a weapon." He smiled faintly at the absurdity of it. "Not exactly threatening, but I didn't run into anyone. Found scrubs in a locker, shoes on a dead man, and lived off canned peaches from the cafeteria until I could move better. After that, it was dog food for a while."

He grimaced at the thought. If he never saw another canned peach, it would be too soon.

George checked the dressing on his leg again before gathering the plates from the nightstand. "I'm glad you made it," she said softly. "I often wondered if you did." She turned to go.

David reached out, his hand catching her arm. She looked down at him in surprise but didn't pull away.

"I can be useful," he said earnestly. "Fix that back fence in the garden, or whatever else you need. I can't just let you take care of me."

Her expression softened, though her voice remained steady. "You're going to need a place to stay for the winter. We could use help around the property, that's true. I don't know what I was thinking, trying to handle it all with just the two of us."

David's heart drummed faster with excitement. "So, I can stay? Earn my keep?" For some reason, he knew he just wanted to be near her. It was a sensation he hadn't felt before.

She nodded. "Sounds fair." George reached the door, then paused and turned. "You know anything about cars?"

David shook his head.

"Tomorrow, I'll teach you. We've got to keep the jalopy running. It's a beast, and I can't risk damaging my hands. I'm no good without them." She gave him a lingering look before walking out.

After she left, David glanced at his arm where the IV had been. A bruise was already forming, violet against his skin. Not the worst he'd seen, but a reminder of how fragile he was.

He thought back to the first day he woke from the coma, legs useless from months of disuse. Standing had felt like scaling a mountain, and it had taken hours to find the strength to move around the hospital.

Come on, David.

Gripping the bedpost for leverage, he swung his legs over the side and attempted to stand. Pain shot up his leg and into his ribs, sharp and unforgiving, and he collapsed back onto the mattress.

I'm not giving up. Even if it takes all night.

David huffed, worn from the exertion, then placed his hand on the bedpost once again. He kept trying, through the night and into the early hours.

Chapter Four

ELLIOTT MICHAELS CARRIED HIMSELF with the kind of self-importance that seemed woven into his very being. It had been there since he was a boy, this unshakable belief that he was meant to be noticed, that his presence in a room should command attention.

When he spoke, he expected people to listen. Not just to his words, but to the authority behind them. It was no surprise, then, that when the former mayor of Minneapolis had cracked under the weight of the crumbling world, Elliott had stepped into the role without hesitation. Not that anyone else had been eager to take it.

The de facto title of mayor was little more than a formality now, a hollow badge in a city where real power belonged to the underworld and the shadowy networks that had risen to control the new order.

But Elliott didn't mind. He had always carried a chip on his shoulder, and this was just another way to prove he was meant for something more.

George began carefully arranging her tools on the night-stand, her hands steady as she prepared to examine Kate, her pregnant step-sister-in-law. Kate, as always, was gracious despite being confined to bed. Her voice had the easy lilt of someone who could charm their way out of most things, and she chattered on, peppering George with half-questions and attempts to glean gossip.

From the room next door, Elliott's voice rose, persistent and sharp, the tone of a man used to wheedling his way into agreements. He sounded like a desperate salesman, his words spilling out in rapid succession, determined to close the deal.

"Who's in there with Elliott?" George asked, pausing mid-motion to glance at the wall.

Kate exhaled, the sound more labored than it should have been, as though her lungs struggled under the baby's weight. "Some guy from Aces Wild. He's been here twice this week. Elliott always gets like this when they come around." She waved a hand lazily toward the shared wall.

George pressed her lips together in a tight line. "I'll wash my hands, and then we'll start." She left the room before Kate could say more.

The bathroom was across the hall from Elliott's home office, and the door stood wide open. George caught sight of Elliott, his pale face flustered, red with effort as he gestured animatedly at Brennan, Aces' general manager. Brennan, calm as ever, leaned back slightly, his expression unreadable except for the faintest hint of irritation.

Brennan rose as George finished drying her hands. He tipped an imaginary hat to her with a casual grin. "Doc."

"Brennan," George replied, her tone dry but warm. "Fancy seeing you in the 'burbs. Thought you hated it out here."

"Just wrapping up a meeting with the mayor," Brennan said, his grin widening. "He's full of crazy ideas."

"They're not crazy, are they, sis?" Elliott's voice cut in from the doorway, slick with faux charm. George turned to find him smirking, the same predatory curve of his lips she'd seen too many times as kids. He still had that look, the one that promised trouble if she didn't play along.

"The mayor wants the faction leaders to cede control," Brennan interjected, his voice flat. "Ain't gonna happen."

"Not cede control," Elliott corrected, stepping forward. "Collaborate. Centralize trade with the other cities. It's efficient."

George looked between the two men, her stomach tightening. Too much power corrupted the corruptible, and Elliott was nothing if not corruptible. At least with Aces Wild and Roberta, George knew what to expect. They weren't saints, but they were predictable.

Elliott? He was chaos with a smile, and chaos didn't mix well with control.

"I don't know a thing about politics," she said finally, keeping her tone light. "I keep my head down and people healthy. If you'll excuse me, I've got an exam to finish."

Kate had repositioned herself by the time George returned, surrounded by pillows that tried their best to cushion her large frame. "I thought for sure he was going to yap your ears off," Kate joked, a twinkle in her eye.

"Nope," George replied, smoothing her features. "I don't do politics. But I *can* see how you and this little one are doing."

George began the examination, her movements deliberate as she palpated Kate's abdomen. Her fingers traced the contours of the baby but then paused. Two distinct forms.

Her stomach dropped.

How had she missed this before? Maybe one baby had been tucked behind the other, but there was no mistaking it now—twins. And with Kate's history, twins were anything but good news.

Masking her concern, George moved to the table and flipped through Ana's notes, scanning for any mention of multiple fetuses. Nothing. She added her findings to the notebook, hands steady despite the knot in her chest. She needed confirmation.

"How's it looking?" Kate asked, her voice hopeful. "Am I ready to pop yet?"

George forced a smile as she reached for her stethoscope. "Let's take a closer listen."

Elliott entered then, crossing to Kate's side with a sweetness George didn't expect. He kissed her cheek, murmuring, "How are you?"

Kate chuckled softly. "Trying to find out if I'll be able to get out of this bed anytime soon."

George adjusted her stethoscope. "You still have a mucus plug, so you've got some time yet."

Placing the stethoscope against Kate's abdomen, George listened intently. The mother's heartbeat thundered loudest, but under it came the faint, rhythmic pulse of not one, but two heartbeats.

Her blood turned cold.

George lowered Kate's dress, hiding her unease behind a careful smile. Kate's fragility was an open secret, one Elliott exploited as much as he nurtured. How could George tell her that this pregnancy was more dangerous than she'd realized?

"Everything's fine, right?" Kate asked, catching on to her unease with a frown. "It's all going to be okay?"

George swallowed hard, the lie already bitter on her tongue. "Everything's going as planned. But your blood pressure is higher than I'd like. You're officially on bed rest for the rest of your pregnancy. Ana was right."

Elliott smirked, his hand brushing Kate's. "Don't worry, Georgie. I'll keep her in bed."

"None of that," George scolded, packing her equipment with brisk efficiency. "Her pulse doesn't need *that* kind of exercise, at least while I'm here. We all know how babies are made."

Elliott's grin faltered as she strode past him, her voice crisp with authority.

"I promise not to make her pulse spike," replied Elliott.

George smirked. "Then you aren't doing it right, Lelliot," she teased, using his childhood nickname. "I need to talk to you about something. We should let Kate get some rest. It's a lot of work making a new human."

He frowned at the mention of that name. George felt a sense of satisfaction that she could still get a rise out of her stepbrother even in their adult years. It was as though there was still some semblance of normal in a world that was anything but.

Elliot followed George back to his office and crossed to his desk. He sat on the edge of the fine, antique wood, which had once belonged to her grandfather. She hated that it was his ass that sat on the tabletop with such little reverence.

"You aren't saying something," he said, brows furrowed.

George squeezed the bridge of her nose with her thumb and forefinger and sighed. How could Elliot have been so stupid? She'd warned him about this. "She's carrying twins, Elliot."

He smiled. "That's great news."

God, he was thick.

George counted to three before she spoke, lest her exasperation come through in her tone. "Elliot, I told you not to get her pregnant. I warned you about the danger."

"Don't be silly, Georgie." His tone was the patronizing one of patriarchy. He loved his wife, but he was still a man who could never understand or experience the intensity of childbirth or labor. And he didn't seem to want to either. He continued, "Women have been giving birth without doctors or modern medicine for millennia."

"They've also died from untreated high-risk conditions or complications related to birth for millennia," she pointed out.

Elliot's pencil-thin lips tightened. "What are you saying?"

"She had a C-section when Abigail was born before the blackout. She has a history of preeclampsia. Plus, the babies don't seem to be in the birthing position yet. That's a bad sign this late in the pregnancy and usually an indication for a C-section."

"Is that an option?"

It was. It could be. Ana would have more practice than her at it, but Elliot would never let her anywhere near Kate for a surgical procedure. He tolerated her during obstetrical visits, but that was it. Ana had a way of being too blunt and didn't buy into his bullshit anymore than George. Elliott was just used to dealing with George, and oftentimes, George kept her mouth shut not to worsen things between them. Though occasionally, she did enjoy getting a rise out of him when he was being an absolute ding-dong.

George leveled her gaze at him. "Ana would be the best one for the procedure, so it's an option, but it's not a good one. Not with our limited means for dealing with possible complications. Then if she makes it through, Kate may risk infection, anemia due to blood loss-- and I hate to remind you, but it's not like we can do a blood transfusion— fetal injury... the list goes on."

"It's risky. I get it," Elliott said flippantly, "Kate wanted another baby."

George took a deep breath and stood up straight. She glared at her stepbrother. How dare he put her in this position? "There's a reason why doctors used to make people choose in the Victorian era and before."

"Georgie..."

"If there's a complication and we can't save them both, I want you to be ready to choose who we prioritize. Do you leave the daughter you already have without a mother, or do you disappoint Kate? Those are your options if something goes wrong. I'm going to watch her, and Ana is going be closely involved and you'll let her. She's the one with the most labor and delivery experience. Hopefully, the babies both turn into the right position, and she can give birth vaginally."

A small voice cut through the room. "Daddy?"

Elliot's eight-year-old daughter, Abigail, burst into the office, her blonde hair bouncing as she ran. She looked like a miniature version of Kate, all rosy cheeks and bright eyes, the kind of child who seemed plucked straight from a Scandinavian postcard. Elliot, Kate, and Abigail were the billboard versions of the perfect northern Minnesota family.

George watched the scene from across the room, a familiar pang tugging at her chest. She and her father had always been the odd ones out, misfits in a world of Nordic perfection. Her father's roots traced back to Tangier, and her mother was African American.

Elliot's mother, though kind enough, had never truly understood George's challenges growing up. How could she? Her life and privileges didn't allow for that kind of understanding.

Abigail threw herself into her father's arms, her laughter ringing out as Elliot hugged her tightly and whispered something in her ear.

When the girl caught sight of George, her face lit up. "Auntie George!"

"Hey, Abby," George greeted, smiling despite herself.

Elliot patted his daughter's back, his tone soft but firm. "Honey, why don't you head downstairs and wait for me? Your Aunt George and I need to talk about some important things."

Abigail nodded dutifully and scampered off, her small footsteps fading down the hallway.

Elliot turned back to George, his expression shifting to something more deliberate. He picked up a stack of papers from his desk, the pages creased and marked with the unmistakable imprint of an old typewriter. He handed them to her with an air of triumph.

"What's this?" George asked, flipping through the pages, the faded ink smudged in places.

"My vision," Elliot said, his voice practically vibrating with excitement. "A united Twin Cities under one leader. We start with trade agreements and work toward centralized government."

"And that leader would be... you," George surmised.

"Naturally. I came up with the plan." His grin was wide and unrestrained, the kind of smile that belonged to someone who thought he'd already won.

George stifled a groan. This was the last thing the Twin Cities needed— Elliot in charge of everything. He was a lot of things, but a selfless leader looking out for the greater good wasn't one of them. She could see this for what it was: a blatant power play. Elliot didn't just want unity. He wanted control to satisfy his authoritarian leanings.

"Why are you showing me this?" George asked, her expression guarded.

"I need your support," Elliot said earnestly, though she could see through it. "They listen to you, Georgie. They trust you. If you back this plan, they'll fall in line."

"I don't have any power, Elliot," she sighed, even though she knew it wasn't true.

From the earliest days, George and Ana had solidified their positions as the unseen architects of survival. They were the ones who held the keys— access to medical supplies, knowledge, and treatment. The faction leaders knew it and avoided crossing the two women at all costs.

If you controlled life itself, people tended to listen. The whole situation left George and Ana enmeshed in a strange facsimile hierarchy while allowing them to remain outside of any real confrontation.

"Let me read it," George said at last, holding up the papers in resignation. "I'll let you know what I think."

"That's all I'm asking." Elliot moved closer, placing a hand on her back in a gesture that felt more calculated than affectionate. "I trust you'll see the wisdom in my plan."

George shrugged him off, her movements deliberate. "I'll let you know when I'm done."

Elliot escorted her to the front door, the house around them a strange blend of the past and present. Abigail now slept in

George's old bedroom, a detail that never failed to twist her gut with a mix of nostalgia and unease.

The master bedroom, where Kate now rested, still carried the ghosts of their parents. The furniture was unchanged, the air thick with memories George tried to avoid. She couldn't help but wonder if Elliot had even bothered to replace the mattress their parents used to share or if he simply ignored the weight of the past, as he always did.

The door creaked as George stepped outside, clutching Elliot's so-called vision in her hands. The chill of the autumn air bit at her skin, but she didn't mind. It was easier to breathe out here, away from the suffocating weight of his ambitions.

She hated coming here. Returning to the memories of happier times and of the tragic day she discovered her parents. Elliot had been there and seemed less disturbed by the loss of their parents. He'd even volunteered to bury the bodies, so she didn't have to.

George swung herself onto her horse, the leather saddle groaning softly under her weight. The cold air bit into her cheeks, sharp and relentless, and she could feel the horse shiver beneath her, its breath curling into the frosty air like wisps of smoke. The world was hushed, save for the rhythmic crunch of leaves beneath the horse's hooves as they moved steadily from Miriam Terrace Park toward her home off the East River Parkway.

She tugged her gloves on, the wool rough against her skin, and urged the horse into a brisk trot, eager to outpace both the chill and the restless thoughts nipping at her heels.

By the time she reached the carriage house, her fingers were stiff with cold, and the horse's coat glistened with a fine sheen of sweat. She led him inside, the familiar scents of hay and leather wrapping around her like a comforting embrace.

After settling him in his pen with fresh water and a handful of oats, she lingered for a moment, her hand resting on the horse's neck as he nuzzled her palm, his breath warm and steady. The quiet of the stable was soothing, but the warmth of the house called to her, and with a final pat, she turned and headed inside.

The kitchen teeming with life and warmth, a stark contrast to the stillness outside. A shaggy, dark-haired boy, Pedro, one of the neighborhood kids, sat on a stool by the counter, his hands busy shucking corn as he regaled Ana with tales of his latest escapades. His voice was animated, his gestures exaggerated, and Ana listened with a rare smile, her hands moving deftly as she prepared jars for canning.

"Hello, Miss George," Pedro said, glancing up as she entered. His grin was wide, his cheeks flushed from the warmth of the room.

"Hi," George replied, her voice awkward and clipped.

Kids always left her feeling off-balance, their boundless energy and unfiltered curiosity a mystery she couldn't quite unravel. She didn't know how to talk to them, didn't know how to bridge the gap between their world and hers. Even Abigail made her feel awkward at times.

"Good, you're back," Ana said, cutting through George's discomfort with her usual efficiency. She handed George a thermos and a plate with a thick sandwich, the bread still warm from the oven. "Take this out to David. He's in the garden."

George hesitated, her fingers tightening around the thermos. The sooner she could relay the news about Kate, the sooner they could formulate a plan. "Ana, I need to talk to you."

"Not now," Ana said, her tone firm. She turned back to Pedro, who had begun hacking at the corn with more enthusiasm than skill. "Not that way," she chided, taking the cob from him. "Let me show you." Her hands moved with practiced ease, stripping the kernels cleanly from the cob, as Pedro watched with rapt attention.

George stood there for a moment, caught between the warmth of the kitchen and the task waiting for her outside. David made her nervous in a way she couldn't quite explain. It wasn't the sharp, gut-deep unease she felt around people she didn't trust. No, this was something else entirely— a fluttering in her chest, a heat that crept up her neck whenever he looked at her. It reminded her of middle school, of the awkward, breathless crush she'd had on the boy who sat two rows ahead of her in math class. She hated it.

Ana glanced up, her sharp eyes catching George's hesitation. "Go on," she said, her voice brooking no argument. "If you insist on keeping the man around, you can't starve him. Now go."

With a deep sigh, George turned and headed toward the back door, the thermos and plate clutched tightly in her hands.

David had been living with them for a month now, and she still hadn't figured out how to act around him.

When he was in a coma, it had been easy. She'd talked to him for hours, her words spilling out in a steady stream as she worked. But now that he was awake and looking at her with those piercing eyes and that infuriatingly charming smile, she couldn't seem to string two words together without stumbling.

It didn't help that he was, objectively speaking, ridiculously good-looking, with that tousled hair and the kind of smile that made her stomach do somersaults.

David was in the winter garden when she found him kneeling among the rows of broccoli with his cane propped against a nearby planter. His hands moved carefully, checking the temperature of the black-painted water jugs he'd placed strategically around the cauliflower, spinach, and broccoli.

The plastic cover of the garden rustled as he adjusted it, his movements slow but deliberate. His legs trembled slightly when he stood, and he reached for his cane to steady himself. Then he turned, and his eyes met hers.

Damn. He'd caught her staring.

"Ana said to bring you some lunch, "George stammered, holding out the plate and thermos like a shield. Her voice sounded too loud in the quiet garden, and she cringed.

David took them with a smile, his fingers brushing against hers for the briefest moment. "Thanks," he said warmly, walking over to the low retaining wall and sitting down, placing the plate beside him. He unscrewed the thermos and took a sip, his eyes never leaving hers. "I was wondering," he said, his tone casual, "my hair's getting a little long. Do you think you could trim it for me?"

George froze, her mind racing. Trim his hair? She wasn't a barber. She wasn't even particularly good at small talk. But the way he looked at her, with that quiet, hopeful expression, made it impossible to say no.

"I... I guess I could try," she agreed, her voice barely above a whisper.

David's smile widened, and George felt the tension in her chest ease just a little for the first time in weeks. Maybe, just maybe, she could figure this out.

George walked over to the wall and took a seat next to him. "Why the sudden care for your appearance? All you do is work around here all day." She resisted the itch in her hands to run her fingers through his golden-brown strands.

He shrugged and drank from the thermos. "I just don't like to have long hair, that's all."

George glanced at the smoke house she'd left unfinished. David had fixed that, too. He was good. "Okay. I can do it for you whenever you're ready. Why not ask Ana, though?"

"I don't think she likes me much."

She couldn't help but smirk. Ana could be abrupt, but that was just her way. "Ana is fine with you. She's like that with everyone, and I think she's just worried about the winter and having another person to feed."

"Winters are lean," he commented.

She nodded. "That they are."

They sat in silence as David ate the sandwich. Finally, George stood.

"I'd better get to sewing. I promised Ana I'd make some new pillowcases." She headed back to the kitchen door, then stopped and turned. "David, do you like music?" That was a stupid question. *Who doesn't like music?* she thought.

"Yes." Was that eagerness in his tone?

"I mean, the old stuff. The stuff that came on vinyl," George clarified, her voice trailing off as she gestured vaguely toward the past.

"Some of it," David replied, his tone casual but his gaze sharp as if he were trying to read her.

George licked her lips, suddenly aware of how dry her mouth felt. "Well, I've got an old record player. It works by cranking it. Sounds like shit, but it does the job. Um... maybe tonight you can come to my room, I'll cut your hair, and we can listen to it." The word stumbled out before she could stop them, and she immediately regretted how awkward they sounded.

One side of David's mouth curled into a smile, slow and knowing. "I'd like that."

George nodded, her cheeks burning, and she quickly returned inside. Ana was at the counter, skinning corn off the cob with practiced efficiency. She looked up as George entered, her expression a mix of amusement and exasperation.

"You wanted him here, and now you can't say more than two words to him," Ana said with a laugh. "Georgianna Harris, the woman with the gift of gab, has nothing to say. That's just rich."

George frowned, crossing her arms over her chest. "Leave it, Ana. We have more important things to talk about."

"Like what?"

"Kate is carrying twins, and I know they can be delivered naturally, but I'm worried with her history—"

"That she'll need a C-section," Ana finished, not missing a beat. She didn't stop her work, her hands moving deftly as she stripped the kernels from the cob. "It's likely, but there have been women who successfully give birth vaginally after a C-section. Any other complications?"

"Hypertension and her history of preeclampsia."

Ana paused, her knife hovering over the cob. "She's more likely to bleed out if we cut into her. How's everything else look?"

"I'm worried because she's not dilating as well as I'd like."

"And the babies?"

"At this point, they're still in breech position from what I felt."

Ana nodded thoughtfully. She swept the corn kernels off the counter and into a bowl, then dumped them into a pot on the stove, adding a dash of salt. "Elliot doesn't like me," she remarked.

"I've already told him you're going to be helping with this one," George said, her voice firm. "You worked L-and-D longer than me, and before all this, you were only a semester away from being a qualified midwife. Delivering babies is…"

She paused, catching the sharp breath Ana took. How insensitive of her to phrase it like that. "You're better suited for it than me."

Ana stirred the pot, her back to George. Whether or not there were tears, George couldn't tell. Sometimes Ana cried, sometimes she didn't. "I'll stop in for her next visit," Ana said finally.

"Thank you," George breathed in relief. "Do you mind if I play some music tonight?"

"No. You go on ahead." Ana turned to face her, her expression unreadable. "Can you go down to the root cellar and get me a few potatoes?"

George nodded and opened the door on the other side of the wall, descending the stairs carefully. She counted each step, her hand brushing the rough stone wall for balance. More than once, she'd missed a step and stumbled in the dark. She hated wasting candles or lamp oil when the dim light from the afternoon sun provided just enough to see the potato bin.

A rustling sound came from the corner, followed by a hazy shadow of movement. George froze, her heart pounding. She searched the darkness for something, anything, she could use as a weapon. Her fingers closed around a crowbar, and she moved forward cautiously, her pulse racing.

I should've fixed that broken window, she thought, her grip tightening on the crowbar. *Let it be rats.* She rounded the corner, the crowbar raised high with both hands.

"Jesus Christ, Ralph. What the hell?" she shouted, relief washing over her when she recognized the man on the other side of the shelves. He used to be a cop, but these days he was a harmless junkie and vagabond, strung out on whatever new synthetic he could afford to pay a pharmacist for.

"I'm sorry, George. I just—"

George took stock of the potatoes in his hands. "You were hungry."

He nodded, his eyes downcast and skin yellowed from the likely damage to his liver.

She sighed, the tension draining from her shoulders. "Go on and take those, but don't ever come into my house without permission again."

Ralph stepped out from behind the shelves. Once, he'd been overweight with a gut; now, he was gaunt and frail. Any day now, he'd stop coming around and be found lying among the hundreds of other corpses that turned up every year. "You're a good lady, George. I don't care what anyone says about you."

"Thanks, Ralph," she said, her voice softer now.

He headed toward the stairs, his movements slow and un-steady.

"Ralph," George called after him. He stopped. "I mean it. Don't let me catch you here again. I'll kill you if I do."

Ralph scurried up the stairs, and George grabbed a few potatoes before following him back up. David was at the sink, washing his hands, while Ana kneaded bread at the counter. George set the potatoes down and turned to David. "You think you can help me fix the window at the back of the house tomorrow?" she asked

He dried his hands with a towel and shrugged. "Don't worry about it. I'll take care of it."

"I kind of want to do it. I need to learn how to properly install a window."

"Where'd you learn to be so handy?" Ana asked curiously.

He glanced at her. "My dad was a carpenter by trade, but kind of a jack-of-all-trades. He built the house we grew up in on the farm."

Ana's eyes lit up. "Really? You know, George grew up on a farm too."

David looked at her in surprise. "Did you?"

George nodded, her eyes dropping to the ground. She could feel his presence like a physical thing, warm and solid beside her. Her entire body seemed to react to his proximity, a quiet ache building in her chest. She wanted to touch him, to feel his hands on her, but she shoved the thought aside, her cheeks burning.

Taking his cane in hand, David stepped closer to her. His eyes were aquamarine, deep and unreadable, like oceans hiding secrets. With his light brown hair and pale skin, he was like a German-Irish Adonis, all sharp angles and quiet strength. "I look forward to spending time with you tonight," he said, his voice low and smooth, like satin on bare skin.

"It's just music and hair cutting, "George replied, her voice barely above a whisper. She could feel the blush spreading across her cheeks.

"Still, it'll be a welcome change to George Bernard Shaw," he said, his lips curving into a small smile. "I'd better wash up before dinner." He left the room, his cane tapping softly against the floor.

Ana turned to George after he vanished down the hall, her smirk widening. "Oh, just fuck him already," she exclaimed with equal parts exasperation and amusement.

George rushed forward, her eyes darting around to make sure David wasn't nearby. "What the fuck, Ana? He's a patient."

"Don't give me that crap." Ana rolled her eyes. "He stopped being a patient the moment you stopped having conversations with him longer than two words. You *like* him. And newsflash, he likes you too. You both walk around this house staring at each other like dogs at table scraps."

"David..." George trailed off, her defenses crumbling.

Who was she kidding? She'd been attracted to him before, when he really was a patient. It was easier then. He was comatose, and the lines were strictly drawn. Now, things were messy and complicated.

"I just figured he might like to hear something. That's all. I mean, he's been living in downtown."

"Uh-huh," Ana said, her tone dripping with sarcasm. "Just tell me one thing."

"Hmm?"

Ana raised an eyebrow. "Should I be sleeping in a different room tonight?"

"You can rest assured there will be no rousing sexual noises," she scoffed.

"A pity. Maybe if you got laid, you'd stop being so uptight."

George didn't respond. If she brought up that she was just doing what it took to survive, it'd start a fight. Ana had time for extracurricular activities, after all. Instead, George decided to go make sure her room was tidy and free from insidious underwear carelessly strewn on the floor.

Chapter Five

DAVID STOOD OUTSIDE GEORGE'S door, his hand hovering just shy of knocking. He ran through a dozen possible openers, but none seemed right. Everything felt either too stiff or too casual, and the thought of stumbling over his words left his stomach in knots.

He glanced at the hall mirror, smoothing the front of his shirt. The shave had gone surprisingly well, with no nicks from the straight razor. His hair, though still longer than he liked, was combed into some semblance of order. It seemed absurd to comb it only to get it cut, but it gave him something to do while his nerves frayed.

David blew into his hand and sniffed. Minty enough. He nodded at his reflection, steeling himself.

Before he could knock, the door swung open. George stood there, her hair loose, wearing long pajamas that managed to look both effortless and alluring on her. "I was just going to grab some scissors. Go ahead and make yourself comfortable."

She brushed past him, leaving behind the faint scent of lavender and soap. He stepped inside, taking in the space. Her room was vast, like someone had knocked out a wall to create a suite. There was a sitting area with a writing desk, bookshelves lined with novels and medical journals, and the kind of lived-in charm that made it unmistakably hers.

On top of one shelf, a photo caught his eye. He moved closer, leaning his cane against the wall. In the picture, a teenage George, who appeared no older than fifteen, smiled brightly, her arm around an older man with a warm, proud expression.

"I've got the scissors." George's voice startled him, and he turned to find her standing in the doorway, scissors in one hand and a small towel in the other. "Do you want me to wash your hair first?"

Caught, he gestured toward the photo. "Is that your dad?"

She nodded, her expression tightening.

"Where is he now?"

"Dead." The word was clipped, as though keeping emotion at bay was the only way to say it. "So is my stepmom. My Mom died when I was young. Cancer."

"I'm sorry," David said softly. A platitude that seemed to ring hollow.

For a moment, George's gaze lingered on the photo, something unspoken flickering behind her eyes. Then she straightened. "Take your shirt off if you want to save it. And is there any particular type of music you want to listen to?"

"I'm open to whatever you have."

He set his cane aside and tugged his shirt over his head. George crossed the room to an old record player and turned the crank. The soft crackle of an old jazz song filled the space.

"What's this?" he asked, glancing at her.

"*Paper Moon.*"

George disappeared into the bathroom, and the sound of running water followed. David stood in the doorway, watching as she gathered supplies from the counter, her movements efficient and unhurried. She tested the water with her fingers before glancing back at him.

"You should feel this," she said, sitting on the edge of the tub. "Tell me if it's too hot."

David crouched, dipping his hand under the stream. "It's fine."

George helped him to his knees, her touch steadying but light, and he ducked his head under the faucet. Her fingers threaded through his hair, massaging his scalp as she lathered soap into his locks.

Her voice came softly at first, humming along to the music. It was becoming a habit of hers, one he didn't mind in the slightest. She had a warm, rich tone, perfectly in tune, and the melody wrapped around him like a soothing blanket.

The music shifted. Billie Holiday's *I'll Be Seeing You* began to play, the first few notes pulling at something deep inside him. It was their song— or at least, it was his song for her. It had been the soundtrack to the strange connection they'd shared before they even met, the thread that had tied his scattered thoughts to her.

George sang along, note for note, her voice blending seamlessly with Billie's. It wasn't just humming this time. She sang with practiced precision, as though she'd been performing this song her entire life.

"Did you always like these old songs?" David asked, spitting as soap slipped into his mouth, leaving a bitter tang.

George laughed, grabbing a towel to dab his face. "Don't talk with soap in your mouth, rookie."

David chuckled, leaning back as she rinsed his hair. He let his eyes drift shut, savoring the warmth of the water, the pressure of her hands, the way her voice lingered in the air like something sacred.

She didn't answer his question right away, and he didn't press. For now, it was enough to sit there, letting her care for him, allowing her voice to fill the space between them.

"Yes," George replied after a beat, a flicker of fondness in her tone. "My grandmother got me hooked on old movies. Seems like you can't be a fan of classic cinema without falling in love with the music. Convenient, really. The old stuff's all you can get now, and no one seems to want it."

She turned off the faucet and reached for a towel, wrapping it around his head with practiced ease. "Don't dry it too much."

"Yes, ma'am," David said with a hint of teasing as he patted his hair gently. He settled into the chair she'd set up in front of the mirror.

"How much do you want off?" she asked, her fingers combing through his damp hair.

He closed his eyes briefly, savoring the simple pleasure of her touch. "Just a little. An inch or so," he replied.

George picked up the scissors, her expression flickering with... hesitation? Or was it something else?

"It's only hair," David said, smiling to reassure her. "It'll grow back."

She didn't reply, but he could feel her focus sharpening as she began snipping. There was something endearing about how tentative she was, so unlike the capable, decisive George he'd come to know. Watching her now, he felt like he was glimpsing a side of her that rarely surfaced. A softer, more cautious side she'd tucked away long ago.

It made sense, though. He knew all about hiding parts of yourself. In his old line of work, adapting quickly and convincingly was survival. You read the room, became what was needed, and kept moving forward.

"Did you own this place before?" David asked, closing his eyes again. Her fingers moved through his hair, steady and deliberate, as the unruly strands fell away.

"No," George said. "I found it."

"It was abandoned?" He pictured the grand house falling into disrepair. A place like this, with its wide, welcoming rooms and bed-and-breakfast charm, shouldn't have been left to rot.

Her silence stretched, her hands slowing just enough for him to notice. Whatever the answer was, it weighed on her.

David opened his eyes and turned slightly to meet her gaze. "Sorry. I don't mean to pry."

George hesitated, then resumed cutting, her voice quieter when she finally spoke. "No, it's fine. In those early days, everything was chaos. We stayed in my one-bedroom apartment as longas we could, but with all the supplies I managed to gather while everyone else was looting useless crap like TVs and laptops, we ran out of space fast."

Her words hung in the air, and David's mind turned over what she wasn't saying. The way her shoulders stiffened as she worked. The way her jaw tightened, just slightly, like she was keeping something at bay.

He treaded carefully. "You and Ana..."

"Not like that," George said quickly, shaking her head. "She used to have a husband and a kid. And I just don't like girls."

Relief hit him, though he hoped it didn't show. He would've felt like an idiot chasing after someone who wasn't interested in men.

George continued, her voice gaining momentum. "We were at a concert when it started. The power went out first. We walked downtown to her car, but it wouldn't start. Then there was this flash of light across the sky, like an aurora borealis. I knew what was happening— I'd just read about it in *National Geographic*. It was like what happened in Canada back in the '80s. Only this time, the lights didn't come back on. Three solar flares back-to-back. HAM radios worked for a while, people saying it was global, massive. Then even they went silent."

David leaned forward slightly, drawn in despite himself. "So how did you two become the gatekeepers of medicine?"

George's lips quirked into a faint, humorless smile. "We walked to a Target. On the way, we found an old Chevy truck restored by some car enthusiast. I hotwired it."

"You hotwired a car?" David asked, surprise slipping into his voice.

She nodded, her expression unreadable. "I picked the locks at Target, too. One of my brothers was... let's just say, not exactly on the right side of the law. He taught me things that turned out to be pretty useful after everything went to hell."

"What happened next?"

"We loaded up. Food, water, blankets, clothes— everything we could think of. But the pharmacies were the real priority. We raided every one we could find before dawn. When we finally got back to my apartment, it felt like we'd barely scratched the surface of what we'd need."

Her voice grew softer, the words weighted with memories she'd rather not revisit. David could see it in the way her shoulders tensed, the way her gaze seemed to drift somewhere far away.

She didn't have to say it. He could see the burden she carried, the way the weight of those early days had left its mark. From the moment George had reentered his life, one thing was clear: she was a survivor. Her strength wasn't just in her ability to adapt; it was in her resolve to keep moving forward, no matter how much the past tried to pull her back.

David smiled faintly. "You're full of surprises, you know that?"

George glanced at him, her lips curving into something softer, something almost vulnerable. "You have no idea."

Then she cleared her throat.

"You should probably rinse your hair again, just to get the loose stuff out," she said, rinsing the scissors in the sink.

Storytime was over, and David still didn't have the full story about the house. He crouched by the tub, letting the warm water run over his scalp, rinsing away stray hairs. Afterward, he patted his head dry with a towel and turned to find George sweeping the floor with quick, deliberate strokes.

"What happened to the owners?" he asked, his voice careful.

She paused mid-sweep, her grip tightening on the broom handle. "I found them in the backyard. They'd been bludgeoned to death days before I got here." Her voice was steady, but her gaze turned distant. "First people I ever buried."

David froze, towel forgotten in his hands. She didn't flinch as she said it, but her eyes betrayed her. He could see the shimmer of unshed tears.

Before the coma, David had lived a life built on burying truths— his own, other people's. He'd disposed of secrets with cold efficiency, convincing himself that every piece of his soul sacrificed on the altar of duty was for the greater good. That lie had been easy to believe, until the blackout stripped it all away.

The first winter, starving and desperate, he'd beaten a man to death for a box of stale rice. The memory didn't haunt him the way it should've. It was survival, nothing more. The man didn't need the rice. Or the coat David had stolen off his body.

But George? She buried them. Honored them. Even now, the weight of it lingered on her face.

He placed the towel on the chair and grabbed the dustpan, kneeling silently as she swept the hair into it. For all his flaws and sins, she made him feel like something else. *Someone* else. The nightmares that had plagued him for years had vanished since he'd come to her house. Sleep was dreamless, peaceful. Her light had chased away his darkness.

He emptied the dustpan into the trash and turned back to see George standing at the sink, rinsing her hands. When she faced him, her lips pulled into a faint smile, but it didn't quite reach her eyes. Whatever he'd stirred up, it was still there, haunting her.

David cursed himself for it. Of all people, he should've known better than to dig up the past.

"What do you think?" George asked, motioning toward his hair.

He stepped closer to the sink and tilted his head, inspecting it in the mirror. "You did a good job, Miss Harris."

She stepped closer, running her fingers through his hair, testing the length. "It's not salon quality."

"It's great," he said. Turning to face her, he lifted his hand, cupping her cheek. Her skin was warm and soft beneath his roughened fingertips.

George's lips parted, her tongue darting out to wet them— a small, unconscious gesture that sent heat surging through him. It would be so easy to kiss her. All he had to do was lean in.

And he wanted to. Desperately.

It wasn't just her beauty, though she had that in spades. It was her strength. George wasn't someone he needed to protect; she was someone who would stand beside him, someone who could take care of herself— and probably save his ass if he was ever cornered.

But she was also the woman who washed his hair, who swept the floor and carried the weight of memories without crumbling. She was softness and steel, and she was everything.

Fuck it.

David dipped his head, stopping just short of her lips. Their breaths mingled, and for a moment, he felt the same rush of nerves he'd had as a kid before his first kiss. His heart raced, and when George didn't pull back, he closed the gap.

Her lips were warm, soft, and exactly as he'd imagined. She parted them just enough to let him deepen the kiss, and he tangled his hands in her curls, pulling the elastic tie free to let her hair fall around her shoulders. It was deceptive; coarse at first glance but silken in his fingers.

What started as tentative grew urgent. He wanted more. No, he *needed* more. Her hands slid around his waist, tugging him closer, grounding him even as his head spun.

When he finally pulled away, breathless and dazed, he rested his forehead against hers. His pulse thundered in his ears, his body humming with energy.

George brushed her fingers across her lips, staring at the floor.

"I'm sorry," he said quickly. "I don't know what came over me."

"Don't be." Her voice was quiet, but she looked up, her eyes meeting his. "I liked it."

His lips quirked into a soft smile. "I liked it, too."

The moment hung between them, charged and fragile. David bit his lip, stepping back. "I should go to bed. We've got to find a window in the morning."

George nodded, her voice low and husky. "You're right."

He lingered for a moment, unable to tear himself away. "Goodnight. And thanks for the haircut. And the... kiss."

"Anytime," she said, a flicker of humor softening the tension.

David left her room, his thoughts a whirlwind as he made it back to his own. He let the grin spread across his face only when the door was safely closed.

Sleep was out of the question. Grabbing his coat and scarf, he slipped outside into the cool, black night. The streets were quiet, the only sound his steady footsteps against the pavement.

By the time he reached the river, the moonlight shimmering on its surface, one thought echoed through his mind.

Georgianna Harris is going to be the death of me.

The thought didn't bother him at all.

Chapter Six

"**WHAT YOU'RE GOING TO** do is pry the siding away so we can get at the nails," David said, handing George a cat's paw and a hammer. His gaze lingered on her a moment longer than necessary, his protective instincts at war with her calm determination.

They were closer to downtown than he liked, but George seemed unfazed. She'd reminded him, with a touch of exasperation, that she often came into downtown to deliver care to the sick. Still, unease prickled at him. The open space, the slow light of dawn creeping in— it all felt too exposed. Darkness gave cover to those who wouldn't hesitate to kill for the clothes on their backs.

"I'm going inside to separate the window from the casing," he added, his voice tight.

David moved toward the side door, his eyes scanning the street one more time before he broke the glass. The sharp crack echoed, a sound that made his nerves spike despite the quiet of the morning. He reached through, unlocked the door, and stepped inside.

The stench hit him immediately, a nauseating mix of fetid garbage, decay, and mildew. He wrinkled his nose and muttered a curse under his breath. There was no telling what he'd find in here. Animal or human, the house could easily harbor death in some form.

"You okay, George?" he called, keeping his tone even.

A muffled, "Yeah," came from outside.

"I'm going to have a look around, see if there's anything else we can use."

His body shifted into high alert, every sense sharpening as he moved further inside. His training took over, and his steps were deliberate, almost soundless. The hairs on the back of his neck stood on end. Something wasn't right.

The house was supposed to be abandoned. That's why George had agreed to take the window in the first place. A faint skittering echoed down the hallway— too heavy to be a rat. His jaw tightened. He'd be damned if someone got the jump on him again.

Shrugging off his coat and sweater, David left himself in a plain white undershirt, freer to move. His options for weapons were limited: an old X-Acto knife in his pocket and his cane. It would have to be enough.

The reassuring creak of wood outside told him George was still working, the rhythm of her efforts steady. He'd made her take the hammer, and she'd insisted on bringing the rifle as a backup. She hated wasting bullets, but if a shot rang out, he'd know she needed him. Not that he worried about her. George was tough. A survivor, like him.

He edged around the kitchen island, the faded linoleum peeling beneath his boots. The carpet in the living room muffled his steps as he hugged the wall, inching closer to the hallway.

"If there's anyone back there, I need you to say something," he said, his voice calm but firm. "We don't want any trouble."

Silence.

Then the telltale *click* of a revolver's hammer being pulled back.

David's heart slowed to a deliberate, steady beat. His body hummed with adrenaline; every nerve attuned to his surroundings. The world seemed to contract, each second stretching into eternity.

He needed a plan. And fast.

His gaze darted to the side table near the wall. A ball, small and scuffed, sat abandoned on its surface. He reached for it, fingers curling around its surface as he calculated his move.

Whoever was on the other side of that wall wasn't counting on him hearing the hammer. That gave him an edge. One chance to get it right.

David rolled the ball to his left, letting it bang against the opposite wall.

The sound broke the silence, drawing a faint curse from the hallway. Footsteps followed, hesitant but moving.

He tightened his grip on the cane, shifting his weight slightly as he prepared for what came next.

Two hands holding a gun appeared first. Instinct took over. David swung his cane hard, the sharp crack of metal meeting bone echoing in the still house. The gun clattered to the floor, and in one fluid motion, he twisted, elbowing the person in the face before striking their throat with the cane.

The figure collapsed onto the white carpet, gasping and choking.

David moved without thinking, his body in full control while his mind stayed quiet, detached. Eliminate the threat—that was the only objective. He grabbed the person's head, his grip sure, ready to finish it.

But then he froze.

It wasn't a man.

It was a teenage girl. Her short hair, likely a practical choice, had fooled him. Small, delicate features. No more than fifteen or sixteen. Alone. Squatting in an abandoned house to survive.

Her chest rose and fell in frantic, shallow bursts, and she squirmed weakly, her hands clawing at her throat.

Fuck.

He'd crushed her windpipe. Death was inevitable, but it wouldn't come quickly. It would be slow, torturous.

David cursed under his breath, dropping to his knees. His hands trembled as he reached for her head, steeling himself for what had to be done. A sharp twist, and it was over. The girl's body stilled, her labored gasps silenced.

He dragged her into the bedroom, laying her on the bed and covering her with a blanket. She looked small, fragile beneath the worn fabric. Later, when George and Ana were busy, he'd come back to bury her— if the dogs didn't get to her first.

In the bathroom, he scrubbed at the blood on his hands, the red streaks swirling down the drain like a stain he couldn't erase. He forced his breathing to slow before heading back to the kitchen.

George greeted him with a warm smile, the sight of it hitting him harder than he expected.

"Find anything useful?" she asked.

He shook his head, not trusting his voice, and turned his attention to the window casing, slicing into the wall.

They worked in quiet efficiency, removing the window and loading it into the truck, cushioning it with blankets. George let him drive, her hands firm on the frame to keep it from sliding. He avoided every bump and pothole, his focus sharp, though his thoughts were anything but.

When they reached the carriage house, George hopped down and began sliding the window off the truck bed.

"Let me help you," David said, stepping forward. He stopped short when he noticed the tiny speck of blood on the back of his hand.

"It's okay, I've got it," she assured him, adjusting her grip.

David swiped the blood onto his pants, checking to ensure it was gone before stepping in. His fingertips brushed hers as he grabbed the window. The contact lingered longer than it should have, sparking something he longed to act on.

But the memory of the girl stilled his hand.

He didn't deserve this. Not her, not the light she brought to his life. Not when there was a body waiting to be buried.

They carried the window into the house and set it down gently. "I'll grab the caulk so we can get this installed," he said gruffly, needing an excuse to step away.

George nodded, already cutting away the old casing, her confidence shining through. His lessons had stuck.

The shed was dim and smelled of damp wood and rust. David leaned against the workbench, letting the guilt wash over him. His eyes fell on a mallet nearby, and before he could stop himself, he hurled it across the room. The crash was loud, shattering jars and scattering nails across the floor.

It had been too easy to kill again. That calm, detached state had come rushing back, and his body had moved without thought. No hesitation. No remorse in the moment. Just action.

"David?" George's voice cut through the haze, calling from outside.

He straightened, shaking off the mess of emotions and grabbing the caulk and gun. By the time he stepped back into the crisp autumn air, his smile was back in place— a lie he wore like armor.

"You're doing great, George. You'll be better than me soon," he said, loading the caulk into the gun.

She looked up, her smile lighting up her face and sending a pang through his chest. It was rare, her genuine smiles, but when they came, they lit up the world.

"You're a good teacher," she said softly.

David lingered too long, caught in her gaze. When her smile faded, he cleared his throat to cover the awkwardness. "Why do you go by George? Georgianna's a pretty name."

"I had two brothers— well, one was my stepbrother— and no female cousins. Guess I was always trying to keep up with the boys." She shrugged.

"Do your brothers call you anything besides George?"

She wrinkled her nose. "Elliot calls me Georgie. I freaking hate it. My other brother sometimes called me Gianna. I don't know where he is now. He moved somewhere out West as soon as everything happened. He was scared of facing a Minnesota winter without electricity."

When she talked about her other brother, there was a sadness in her eyes.

They framed the window and hung it carefully. George brushed her hands together. "Job well done, Mr. Andrews."

"Thank you, Miss Harris."

The butterflies stirred again, an unwelcome reminder of how much she made him feel. He wanted to be the man she deserved, but the blood on his hands made it hard to believe he ever could.

"So... I saw a flyer for a dance at Yannerlly's," he said, testing the waters.

"It's just people dressing up in impractical clothes and pretending life's normal," she replied, dismissing the idea with a wave of her hand.

There went that plan.

David sighed. "Want me to paint the window?"

"If you want to," she said, her tone indifferent. "I don't care about the color."

"I just thought... if this is your home, you might want it to feel nice."

George grinned, swinging the hammer. "As long as it's safe, warm, and dry, I'm happy."

He shook his head, a soft chuckle escaping. "You're painfully practical. Has anyone told you that?"

She moved closer, handing him the hammer. "What do you want from me, David?" Her voice was low, teasing, but the way her gaze held his made his mouth go dry.

He hesitated, fumbling for the perfect response that never came.

The moment broke when Ana stepped out. She whistled at the sight of the new window. "Nice work, you two. But that window could use a coat of paint."

"I'll handle it," David muttered, grateful for the distraction.

As George disappeared into the kitchen, Ana turned to him, a smirk on her face. "She just gave you an in, Einstein. You really should just ask her out like a normal person."

"I was trying to," replied David. Why was this difficult? In another life he was charming and slept with women on the regular. He didn't want to have a love-'em-and-leave them life anymore.

He wanted George.

Ana sighed. "I'll get her there, lover boy. You just make sure to sweep off her feet."

David looked at Ana for a moment, trying to decide how to thank her, before deciding that painting the window was the best option.

Just before she went back inside, Ana added, "You really should spend more time off that cane. It'll mess up your gait if you don't."

Before he could reply, she slipped inside and shut the door.

Ana sat at the sewing machine, squinting in the dim lamplight as she tried to thread the needle. Each failed attempt earned a muttered curse, the frustration palpable. Across the room, George looked up from her book, a chuckle escaping her lips.

"No wonder seamstresses in Edwardian times went blind," teased George

Ana grumbled but finally managed to thread the needle. Triumphantly, she began feeding a length of sea-foam green satin under the presser foot.

"That can't be for sheets," George commented, setting her book aside.

Ana pressed the pedal, the machine coming to life in jerky movements. "It's not. I found a Vogue pattern from nineteen-fifty-two and I'm giving it a try."

"Waste of fabric, if you ask me."

"Well, I didn't. Besides, what else am I going to do with satin?"

George got up from her chair and crossed the room. "I don't know. Make underwear."

Ana smirked, pausing her sewing to glance up. "While I'm sure I could craft something sexy for a certain suitor upstairs..." she trailed off meaningfully, her eyes twinkling as George flushed. "I'm making this instead."

George turned her face away, fighting a smile. The playful tone didn't entirely mask the worry bubbling under the surface. It was dark now, and David had been gone since after dinner.

His new nightly routine of long walks gnawed at her. A week had passed since he'd mentioned the dance, and while their relationship hadn't changed on the surface, she felt stuck. It wasn't like he was avoiding her, but she couldn't shake the anxiety that something— dogs, gangs, or worse— might catch him out there. Who even walked at night anymore?

"He's not a suitor," she said finally. "One kiss hardly qualifies."

Ana raised an eyebrow. "Has he tried to make any other moves?"

"No."

"Pussy."

George laughed despite herself. "He's not a pussy. There's no point. He's leaving anyway."

Ana's smirk softened. "George, you should just march into his room, straddle him, and ride him till the sun comes up. No sense looking for forever. I did that once and look how it turned out."

The air thickened, Ana's words landing heavily between them. George winced, her voice a whisper. "I'm sorry."

"Don't." Ana shook her head, resuming her sewing. "I blamed you for a long time, but I see it now. It was John's fault. He panicked." Her voice wavered, stopping short of the full truth. Some wounds refused to close, even when spoken aloud.

George stared at the floor, guilt wrapping tight around her chest. She'd been the one to convince Ana not to leave that day, to stay until the chaos subsided. When they finally returned to Ana's home, it wasn't safety they found— it was senseless carnage.

"I'm going to check on the animals," George said abruptly, her voice thick. She grabbed her coat and stepped into the night.

The carriage house was cool and damp, but it offered her the solace she needed. She ran a hand along the horse's flank, tossing a blanket over its back. The steady rhythm of its breathing soothed her frayed nerves.

"It's a little cold for you to be out here."

She turned quickly, startled to see David leaning in the doorway, mud streaked on his boots and a shovel resting against the wall.

"Same could be said for you," she replied, attempting a smile, but it faltered.

David crossed the room in a few quick strides, his expression instantly concerned. "What's wrong?"

"Nothing," she lied.

"Bullshit." He stepped closer, his voice low but firm. "I've figured you out, George. When you're really happy, your eyes light up. But when you smile for someone else's benefit, it looks fake."

He was too perceptive for her comfort. His lingering gazes, the way he noticed every detail, it was infuriating and endearing all at once.

"Ana was talking about her family," George admitted at last.

David's expression shifted, a flicker of understanding crossing his face. "That's never easy for her, is it?"

"No." George's voice wavered. "Remember how I said she used to have a family?"

He nodded. "Yeah."

Her throat tightened, the weight of her confession threatening to choke her. "It's my fault she doesn't anymore."

David's brow furrowed. "How could that possibly be your fault?" he asked softly.

"I kept her from them," George said, the words spilling out in a rush. "When everything went to hell, I didn't want her to leave. I couldn't handle the thought of being on my own, so I convinced her to stay. I told her we'd find them when things calmed down."

David's silence urged her to continue.

"When we finally went back, they were already gone. John had..." Her voice broke, the memory too raw.

David didn't push. He reached out instead, placing a hand on her shoulder, his touch grounding.

"You made the best choice you could with what you knew," he said softly. "It's not your fault."

George shook her head, unshed tears glistening in her eyes. "I'm not sure Ana sees it that way. And honestly, neither do I."

The horse whinnied softly, and for a moment, the quiet stretched between them. David didn't offer hollow reassurances. He just stayed by her side, his presence speaking louder than anywords could.

George nodded, a heavy sighescaping her lips. "Little Ella was the second body I ever buried. John was thethird. He killed their daughter, and it's my fault. Ana wasn't there to protecther baby because of me."

"If she'd been there, he would've killed them both," David said gently.

"I know that," George replied, her voice cracking, "but I denied her the chance to be with Ella in her last moments because I didn't want to be alone. I'm a horrible human being."

The tears came unbidden, spilling over her cheeks, hot and relentless. George hadn't wanted to cry, hadn't meant to, but now there was no stopping them. David reached out and pulled her close, wrapping his arms around her like he could shield her from the weight of her guilt. She buried her face in the crook of his neck, inhaling the warm scent of musk and honeyed soap.

She let herself hold him back, clutching at his shirt like a lifeline. It was wrong to cling to him like this, but she couldn't stop herself. He'd leave eventually, and all she wanted in this moment was to hold onto him.

"It's hard to survive alone," David murmured. "There's no way you could've done what you have without her."

George pulled back slightly, enough to look at him but not enough to break the embrace. "She was useless at first. I brought her here, and all she did was sit in her room or tend the garden near her daughter's grave. She wouldn't even talk to me, not that I blame her."

"And you kept her alive," he pointed out. "You kept both of you alive. Wasn't it easier to keep moving knowing someone else needed you to be strong?"

Her eyes searched his, the question hanging between them. "You sound like you know."

"I do," he admitted.

"From this life or the one before?"

He smiled softly. "I like how you call it a previous life."

She shrugged, the corner of her mouth tugging upward. "We were all something else before. What were you, besides a John Doe?"

"A lot of things," he said with a wry chuckle. "More than a few exes called me an 'emotionally unavailable asshole.'"

George broke free of his arms, shaking her head with a smile. "Seriously."

David's grin faded, replaced with something more thoughtful. "I was a government man. Worked for Uncle Sam. That was my whole life. No time for anything, or anyone, else. That's why no one came to claim me."

"No family, no friends?"

"No lovers or girlfriends longer than a few months. They all wanted something I couldn't give them."

George reached out and touched his face, her hand lingering against his cheek. "Must've been a lonely life."

"It was," he admitted, his voice quiet. "But it was a life. I wouldn't want to live it again. After I woke up, I spent so much time surviving on my own. It was hard. Then I came here, and I saw how you and Ana work together. Even when life is shit, you make it through."

"It's been years," she sighed. "We've had to rely on each other. We're friends, but... there are still days when she looks at me, and I know she's thinking I should've let her die. I know some days she hates me."

David tugged on the edge of her coat, coming away with water droplets. "I don't think that's it. I think you like to punish yourself."

"You don't know me."

"No," he agreed, letting her coat go. "But I see glimmers of you. Just like you don't know me, but we've got time to learn."

Her heart skipped. "What are you proposing?"

"Nothing," he said, stepping back and gesturing toward the house. "But we should get you inside. You're no good to anyone laid up in bed."

He placed a hand on the small of her back, guiding her to the house.

At George's door, David shoved his hands into his pockets, hesitating. "Ana's probably asleep. She's not going to like me playing music," she said.

He nodded. "Probably not."

Where do you go when you walk at night?" she asked suddenly. "It's not safe."

"I just walk," he said, his gaze dropping to the floor. "Sometimes I find it hard to sleep."

"Without the cane?"

"Yeah. I'm strong enough now. Still can't walk as far as I'd like, but I'm getting stronger."

"You'll probably still have a nasty scar, though."

He smiled faintly. "I'll take scars over death. You did a pretty good job stitching me up. How'd you learn to do it so well?"

"I trained to be an acute care nurse practitioner," she explained. "I was studying for the test before the blackout."

"Why a nurse and not a doctor?" he wondered.

"I like taking care of people," she said simply. "Besides, look who turned out to be the most useful. The doctors trained for diagnoses and modern tech. They lacked basic skills. There are a few left, but they've found other trades."

"Survival of the fittest."

"Exactly."

She glanced down the hall. Ana was peeking from her door, watching them.

David caught her in the hall mirror and smiled. "We've got an audience."

George laughed softly. "Pleasant dreams," she said, slipping into her room.

She shut the door, leaning against it as her mind raced. *Pleasant dreams?* What the hell was that? For someone who prided herself on being quick-witted, she felt remarkably inept when it came to him.

George hummed as she went to the bathroom and ran a bath, stripping out of her wet clothes. A knock at her door interrupted her solitude. George grabbed a towel and wrapped it around herself to preserve her modesty.

She opened the door to Ana. "What's up?"

Ana was dressed in jeans and a sweatshirt, like she'd dressed in a hurry. Her hair was still wet from her shower. "It's Pedro's grandma. She's started coughing up blood-tinged mucus. He says she is gasping like she can't get the air in."

"I'll get dressed," said George with a frown.

"You don't have to, I'll go."

George shook her head. "You don't speak Spanish. Pedro's grandma understands far more of it than English. I'll go. You hang out with Pedro."

Ana shrugged. "Fine. Meet you downstairs in two. I'll have your gear packed. Pedro is here, by the way."

His abuela must have been really bad for the kid to have the balls to go out after dark. George held the towel tight as David walked down the hall. "All right. Keep him here, ply him with food or cake or something. "

George closed the door, shut off the faucet, and found something clean to wear. She threw on a pair of yoga pants and a t-shirt with a coat. Then she headed downstairs, still smoothing her curls back into a bun. Pedro was in the kitchen with Ana, clearly upset, shaking at the counter while Ana prepared hot cocoa.

David grabbed the keys to the truck off the counter and had the shotgun in his free hand. "You ready to go?" he asked, glancing at her.

"I don't need you to come with me. I'll be fine," George retorted, grabbing her bag off the counter and reaching for the keys.

David held them above his head. "I know you don't need me, but I want to." His face was serious and determined.

There wasn't time to argue. "All right, but make yourself useful when you're there. I don't need a voyeur or a gunslinger once we're in the house."

"I can do whatever you need me to," said David.

George slung the bag over her shoulder and patted Pedro on the back as she moved past him. "I'll do what I can, Pedro." She headed out with David in tow and a sick feeling in her stomach.

Chapter Seven

GEORGE LISTENED TO THE old woman's chest and shook her head. She spoke a few words in Spanish to the older woman, who weakly replied between shallow gasps.

David could only understand a couple of words or phrases here and there as he watched from the doorway. George was efficient and kind as she moved from one form of assessment to another.

For all her exterior hardness, she was warm and gentle when it mattered with those who needed it the most. She tucked the old woman under more blankets, adjusted her pillow, and with a smile that quickly faded when her back was turned to the woman, she left the bedroom.

He followed and watched as she poured some water into a glass. She took a sip and tapped the counter with her fingers.

"I heard you say pneumonia," he said.

"I did," she replied. "We tried treating it with a Z-Pak, but it's getting worse."

"A Z-Pak?"

"An antibiotic for bacterial pneumonia. Probably has a re-sistant strain." George went rummaging through the cabinets until she found a bottle of Patron in one above the stove. She pulled it down with two single-malt glasses. "Tequila?"

He raised a brow at her and chuckled. "I'm driving."

George poured half a glass full. "If you take off, that's fine. Just come back in the morning..." She blew out a slow, un-steady breath. "If she lives that long."

If she was staying, so was he. David sat down at the kitchen table. "Go on and pour me a glass." He nodded toward the bottle.

George placed a glass in front of him and poured it like hers. The clear liquid looked deceptively like water. He drank the first sip, and it burned going down. "That is damn good. I'd forgotten what good tequila tastes like."

"She normally has whiskey and beer, too, but she'd been trading that for things Pedro needed." George downed the first glass quickly and poured herself another.

"So, what are you going to do about it? About her? What's next?"

She leaned forward with a heavy sigh, her eyes appearing weary. "This is the part I hate. I have to let nature take its course. The only reason I gave her the drugs in the first place was because someone needed to take care of the kid. His par-ents are gone. She's all he has. Margarita is a good person. People like her are hard to come by these days."

George was about to pour herself another drink when David put his hand over the glass. "Don't you think you ought to slow down?" he asked. The alcohol was already going to his head after one glass. He could only imagine what it was doing to her.

"It's going to be a long night. The woman is going to either die tonight or tomorrow. There's no way around it. And when I go home, I have to tell a boy that the only family he has left is dead. I think I can get a little drunk tonight." She snatched the glass away and poured another.

"If you know that she's going to die, then why are we here?"

George took another drink and slammed the glass down. "Because she's going to die. Who wants to die alone?" she challenged.

He looked at her. *Who wants to be alone,* she'd said while he was still in his coma. She stayed with him because he had no one to claim him. There was no one to come. No one else bothered to sit with him... at least that he could remember.

Georgianna Harris was constantly adapting. She'd molded herself into a harsh, calculating human being because that's who she had to be. Underneath it all, she was still the same gentle soul she'd been before. Her survival instinct was just turned on now, and she adjusted to the world they lived in, not the world that was.

David finished his second glass and stood. He walked around the table to where she was sitting and held his hand out.

She smiled. "What are you doing, David?"

They both needed something lighter. Something silly that meant nothing at all. A distraction from the misery of the long night ahead.

"I want you to dance with me."

George giggled, clearly a little buzzed. It was light and melodic, a new sound for him to capture and commit to memory. "There's no music."

"I'll sing. I don't sing as well as you, but I can hold a tune."

She took his hand and got to her feet. David held her close and with one hand firmly wrapped around her waist. He began to sing what few lyrics he knew of *I'll be Seeing You,* then switched to a soft *da, da, da* in the melody of the music.

George sang softly. "*I'll be Seeing You.* What made you pick that?"

"That seems to be our song," he said.

"Our song," she repeated as if she'd never thought of it before.

Maybe it was the moment, or perhaps it was the alcohol, but George stopped dancing, her breath hitching as she locked eyes with him. Silence permeated the air, leaving only the sounds of their breathing as they watched one another. Then she rose onto her tiptoes, her lips brushing his— soft, hesitant at first, as if testing the waters.

David stiffened, caught off guard, but it took only a moment for his brain to catch up with his body. He opened his mouth just enough to invite her in, a silent plea for more.

Seemingly encouraged, her kiss deepened, hungry and urgent. His arms tightened around her waist, pulling her flush against him as their bodies pressed together. They moved in sync, stumbling blindly through the kitchen, lips and tongues tangling in a frantic, breath-stealing dance.

The kiss was a wildfire, igniting everything in its path. His hands roamed down the curve of her back, gripping her as if letting go would shatter everything. The edge of the counter dug into his spine, but he barely noticed— too lost in the way her fingers teased the hem of his shirt, slipping beneath to explore the heat of his skin.

Off came David's shirt, tossed carelessly onto the floor, followed by hers. The flimsy sports bra she wore barely contained her full, heaving breasts, her nipples stiff and straining against the thin fabric. His breath hitched at the sight, his pulse hammering in his throat.

She fumbled with his belt, fingers clumsy with urgency, while he toed off his shoes, never breaking contact. They stumbled out of the kitchen and into the living room, colliding with the couch in a tangle of limbs before tumbling onto the cushions. The impact knocked a breathless laugh from her, but David barely noticed; his body was burning, aching, desperate.

Then he pulled back, panting, his forehead pressed against hers. "Are you sure you want this?" His voice was rough, hoarse with need, but his gaze was steady, searching. If she said no, this would all end.

Please, don't let her say no, he thought, his body taut with restraint. His cock throbbed painfully, trapped behind the fabric of his jeans, but still, he waited.

George swallowed hard, her eyes dark with heat. Her fingers curled into the waistband of his pants as she whispered, "Yes."

That was what he wanted.

"I want to do this," George said, her voice steady.

David searched her face, but there was no hesitation, no flicker of doubt. Just certainty.

She made quick work of the button on his trousers, her fingers brushing against the growing heat beneath the fabric. But something about the moment nagged at him. A plastic-covered couch. The crackling sound of vinyl beneath their skin. It felt... wrong.

"I saw a spare bedroom upstairs," David offered, his voice thick with restraint. "Let's go up there. More private."

"All right."

She rose, leaving behind a trail of undergarments and clothes like breadcrumbs, leading to something inevitable. David chuckled, stepping out of his pants as he followed her, heat licking at his spine as he watched her curves disappear up the stairs.

By the time he reached the bedroom, George was already under the sheets, the flickering light of an oil lamp casting golden shadows across her bare skin.

David let out a slow breath. She was breathtaking. Not in the manufactured way of airbrushed magazine covers, but in the way that spoke of resilience, of a body shaped by survival. A small scar adorned her hip, and the faint silver lines of rapid weight loss marked her stomach.

She was real. Beautiful.

The most beautiful woman he'd ever seen.

He climbed onto the bed, pressing a reverent kiss against the scar on her hip. "You're gorgeous."

George snorted. "Mr. Andrews, if you wanted to get me into bed, you didn't have to butter me up with pretty words. I'm already here."

He lifted his head, eyes locking with hers. "I mean it. You're stunning."

She blushed, then shifted as if to cover herself, arms crossing over her chest.

David caught her wrists, his lips grazing the shell of her ear. "Don't." His voice was a whisper, a plea. "I want to see you."

George stilled, then exhaled, letting him guide her back onto the mattress.

He took his time, savoring her, pressing open-mouthed kisses along her collarbone, her ribs, her stomach. His hands followed, mapping the warmth of her skin, learning the way she shivered under his touch.

He kissed the inside of her thigh, gently nudging her legs apart—

"Wait."

David froze. Every muscle in his body went tight. Damn. She was going to call the whole thing off. He just knew it.

She cleared her throat. "Before we get too into this... there's some lambskins in my bag. Downstairs."

Relief crashed over him. That was all? Condoms.

David exhaled a quiet laugh. "You're a lifesaver."

He slid off the bed, pulled on his pants, and headed down-stairs. George's bag was near the old woman's door, and just as he reached for it, a weak, raspy moan stopped him cold.

He hesitated. His body was still thrumming with need, his mind lingering on George upstairs, waiting for him. But...

"Shit," he muttered under his breath, stepping into the dimly lit room.

The old woman was sweating, her breathing shallow. Fevered.

David moved instinctively. He ran the bathroom sink until the water was ice-cold, then soaked several rags before plac-ing them on her forehead, neck, and chest. Her eyes fluttered open, dark and glassy.

"Agua," she whispered, voice barely above a breath.

David grabbed the glass by her bedside and gently lifted her head, helping her sip.

"Gracias," she murmured.

"You're welcome."

He adjusted the blankets, pulling the heavy comforter down so only the sheets covered her fragile frame. Her breathing slowed, body relaxing. Satisfied, he turned back to George's bag and pulled out the condoms. A question burned at the back of his mind: why did she have them in the first place? But that was a thought for later.

Right now, there was only one thing he cared about.

David reached the bedroom door and grinned. "I hope you didn't start without me, gorgeous."

He stripped back down and slipped under the sheets, reaching for her.

But as soon as he touched her, she let out a soft, sleep-heavy groan.

His heart sank. "Sweetheart?"

No response.

David sighed, his body still wound taut with lingering desire. He pressed a kiss to her temple, resigning himself to the only option left.

Spooning.

David woke to the first pale strands of dawn creeping through the window. He reached for George only to find an empty space where she'd been.

Frowning, he dressed quickly and made his way downstairs.

George was at the old woman's bedside, carefully wiping her face and hands. Her movements were precise, practiced. Gentle.

"Go get Pedro," she said softly. "It's almost time. He's going to want to say goodbye."

David nodded. The keys to the truck were in his pocket, the morning air biting as he stepped outside.

By the time he reached the house, frost was beginning to collect on the windows. Inside, it was eerily quiet. He found the boy curled up in one of the patient beds, shoes and socks neatly placed on a chair beside him.

David knelt, giving him a gentle shake.

Pedro stirred, blinking groggily. "Is it Ya-ya?"

David nodded.

The boy didn't hesitate. He pulled on his shoes, grabbed his coat, and followed without another word.

They were silent as David drove them both to Pedro's house. Before he'd even turned off the ignition, Pedro had gone inside without a backward glance, but David lingered.

The air inside the house was thick with grief, pressing down like a tangible thing. He needed space.

Behind the garage, a small garden lay dormant, tucked beneath the weight of winter. Something about it called to him.

David knelt beside a barren apple tree, hands sinking into the frozen earth. He worked without thinking, pulling stubborn weeds and turning the soil.

Back home, he'd paid people to care for his plants— avoided yard work like the plague. Now, as his fingers traced rough bark and cold dirt, something in him settled.

He didn't know how long he stayed there, lost in the rhythm of his task, but eventually, George's voice cut through the silence, "Nice tune."

David glanced up. He hadn't even realized he'd been humming.

Exhaustion clung to her features as if she hadn't slept at all.

He smirked. "It was the *Simpsons* theme."

A soft chuckle escaped her. "I used to love that show."

She shifted, revealing a shovel in her grip. "I figured we should dig the hole over there. By the rose bushes. Mrs. Ramirez loved her roses."

David followed her gaze. The bushes were bare now, stripped of their beauty by the cold. He swallowed hard. "Is she...?"

"Not yet." George exhaled. "She's close, though."

"I'll do it," he said. "You stay inside with the boy."

She hesitated. "Are you sure?"

"Yeah."

After a moment, she handed him the shovel. Then she turned and went inside.

David took a deep breath and started digging.

Of all the ways he'd disposed of a body, he'd never dug an actual grave before.

This was different. Heavier.

By noon, Pedro emerged from the house, tear tracks cutting through the dirt on his cheeks. He carried a shovel.

Without a word, the boy stepped into the grave and started digging beside him.

David didn't speak. He had nothing to offer— no words of wisdom, no comfort that would ease the weight of grief.

So he did what his father had once done for him.

He worked in silence. And let the boy do the same.

Chapter Eight

PEDRO RAN AHEAD, DRAGGING his suitcases into the living room before letting them drop near the door with a heavy thud. Without a word, he made a beeline for the kitchen, the quiet shuffle of his worn shoes the only sound in the house.

Ana emerged from one of the spare rooms, peeling off a pair of gloves. A faint scent of antiseptic clung to her as she wiped her hands on her apron, her gaze settling on the boy. Pedro was already pouring himself a cup of coffee, his small hands steady despite the weight of the day.

"That's not good for his heart," Ana remarked disapprovingly.

"Let him," George said. "He's earned it. Kid dug the grave and helped us bury his grandma himself." Her voice was flat, but there was something deeper beneath it: an understanding, a quiet acknowledgment of the toll it had taken on him.

David entered behind them, Pedro's remaining belongings stacked in his arms. "Where do you want me to put these?" he asked.

"Upstairs. Your room," George replied.

Silence fell. Ana's head snapped toward her. David blinked.

"My room?" he echoed, clearly unsure if he'd heard her correctly.

"It'll save on heating during the winter," George explained. "I'd like to keep as few rooms occupied as possible."

Ana folded her arms. "And where, pray tell, will David sleep?"

George barely hesitated. "In my room. There's a couch that folds out in the sitting area. I'll sleep there. He can have the bed. It's the least I can do for displacing him." She spoke matter-of-factly, as though she was discussing firewood or rationing instead of where a man would be sleeping in relation to her.

She turned, heading up the stairs.

Ana wasn't done. "I finished that dress for you," she called after her. "I want you to try it on."

George stopped mid-step, her hand gripping the banister. She turned slightly. "What for?"

"Because tonight, we're going to a party."

George fully turned now, her brows drawn. "Ana, we don't have time—"

Ana gave her a look that quelled any argument before it could begin. "The kid could use a distraction, and so could you. Now, go on upstairs and try it on. I'll see what Pedro wants for dinner."

George said nothing, only turned and continued up the stairs, leaving David in the hallway and Ana with Pedro.

When she got to her room, she shut the door firmly behind her, needing a moment to breathe. There was too much happening... too much change. She needed time to unpack it.

The dress was draped over the chair, a seafoam-colored thing made of soft fabric that shimmered in the dim light. It was beautiful. That was the problem.

George had never thought of herself as someone who should wear something beautiful. Dresses like this belonged on women with smooth, unblemished skin, on women with delicate wrists and effortless grace. Not on her. Not on a body marked by scars and hardship.

David had called her beautiful, but men said a lot of things in the heat of the moment.

Still, when he kissed her, she had felt something. Something warm, something dangerous. His touch had set her skin alight, had made her want more... made her forget.

She needed to forget now.

Turning away from the dress, she stepped into the adjoining bathroom and turned on the shower. She didn't wait for the water to warm. The icy shock jolted her, cutting through the dull throb of the headache forming behind her temples.

One more mouth to feed.

The thought clung to her like the cold water sliding down her skin.

They were turning into a damn halfway house for strays.

A soft heart wouldn't keep them alive through the winter. A soft heart wouldn't put food on the table or wood in the fireplace.

Pedro was old enough to work. He'd have to pull his weight, just like David was. Of course, there would be a mourning period, but winter didn't care about grief. Food was already scarce in the colder months unless you'd stored enough.

And now they had two unknowns to account for.

The food they'd stocked during the summer had been meant for her, Ana, and maybe the occasional patient. But now? Now, there were four of them. Two women, one man, and a growing teenager who would eat as much as an adult before long.

Ana had already started canning more aggressively since David arrived, but even with the extra effort, would it be enough?

George shut the water off and stood there, dripping, watching as steam curled against the cracked mirror.

The first winter had been hard. Each one after had gotten easier because she and Ana had turned survival into a science. They knew exactly how much to ration. How much they needed.

Now?

Now, it was back to the unknown.

They'd manage. They had to.

Because no matter how much she tried to pretend otherwise, she wasn't going to let Pedro or David starve on the streets.

The mental to-do list kept growing, causing the first stirrings of a headache to form. She was tired and stressed. George frowned at the dress draped over the chair. She didn't have time for pretty and frivolous things.

But Ana had made an effort. They'd settled into a rhythm that had been unchanged for so long that the gift was something George knew she shouldn't reject outright.

She stepped out of the shower and toweled off, wringing the excess water from her thick, unruly curls. She reached for the comb and began braiding her hair, her fingers moving with practiced ease. She hadn't yet decided if she was going to follow Ana's decree, but if there was any chance of looking respectable, she needed to get her hair under control.

Every time she resolved to say no, her gaze would drift to the dress draped over the chair. And every time, she could practically hear Ana's inevitable fury if she refused. Ana didn't often crave social outings, but when she did, resistance was futile. George knew better than to be the one to ruin her plans.

She was still debating when David stepped into the room, closing the door quickly behind him when he realized she was wrapped in nothing but a towel. He averted his eyes, his jaw tensing slightly.

"You've already seen me naked," George teased, smirking as she smoothed lotion over her arms. "Might as well see me in a towel."

David cleared his throat and looked at the floor with a crooked smile. "I'm trying to be respectful."

She chuckled, but the way his ears tinged pink made something flicker in her chest.

"Where do you want me to put my stuff?" he asked, shifting the bundle of clothes in his arms.

She glanced at the backpack and the worn clothing they'd given him when he first arrived. The ones he'd come in wearing had been too torn and bloodied to salvage.

"The bottom two drawers in the dresser are empty. You can also make some space in the closet."

He nodded, setting his pack on the closet floor. As he straightened, his gaze settled on her again, more serious now. "You don't have to sleep on the couch, you know."

"I know," George replied evenly, fastening the towel tighter around her chest. "But I didn't want Ana getting any ideas."

His lips quirked. "I can behave myself."

"I'm sure you can."

He gestured toward the bathroom. "Mind if I shower and get ready? Ana says I'm going too."

George arched a brow. "By all means, Mr. Andrews. Be my guest."

David grabbed a change of clothes and disappeared into the bathroom, leaving behind the faint scent of worn leather and musk.

George turned back to the dress, sighing and pulling on the undergarments Ana had made to match it, then slipping the gown over her head. The seafoam fabric settled over her curves, fitting far too well for her comfort. She had no business wearing something this elegant, but she couldn't deny that Ana had skill.

Hastily, she made her way down the hall to Ana's room.

Her friend sat before the vanity, pinning her hair back, her dressing robe loosely tied at the waist. The moment she spotted George in the doorway, her face lit up.

"You actually put it on!" Ana beamed, immediately standing to inspect her work. She circled George like an artist admiring their finished masterpiece. "That looks terrific on you." She zipped up the back, then rummaged through the vanity drawer. "I have a little mascara and some red lipstick. You're going to look amazing."

George frowned. "Why does it matter what I look like? And do you really think we should take Pedro along?"

Ana met her gaze in the mirror. "I think he's adjusting well. Seeing his friends will help. We can't understand what he's going through the way his peers can. He has to learn to move forward. It's survival."

She turned George by the shoulders and carefully unbraided her hair, pinning it into an elegant updo with a few loose tendrils framing her face. Then, she brushed a light coat of mascara over her lashes and painted her lips with a deep red hue.

"There," Ana murmured, stepping back to admire her. "You look fantastic."

George stared at her reflection. The girl in the mirror was a stranger. Softer. Almost... hopeful. For a brief moment, she caught a glimpse of the person she used to be, a version of herself that seemed like a lifetime ago.

A knock sounded at the door, pulling her from her thoughts.

"Ladies, we'd better get a move on," David called.

"Just a moment!" Ana yelled back.

George helped Ana into her dress, and as she adjusted the bodice, Ana handed her a pair of black heels.

"I kept them because they were niceshoes," Ana grinned. "You never know when you'll have to look your best."

"Ladies," David's voice came again, this time more impatient. "Pedro is getting antsy."

Ana smirked. "Go on ahead without us. You and Pedro walk. We'll take the truck."

There was a long pause before a muffled sigh came through the door. "Fine. There's still a few minutes of daylight left. We'll meet you there."

George turned to Ana with a suspicious look. "Why did you do that?"

Ana's grin grew wide like a chesire cat. "Because I want to see the look on his face when you walk into that room."

George rolled her eyes, but Ana pressed on.

"I mean, the way he looks at you now, you can tell he's already on the hook. Now, it's time to reel him in." Her voice softened slightly, her expression wistful. "John looked at me like that once. I'll never forget it."

George stiffened. John's name had been practically forbidden in this house since his death. Ana never spoke of him.

Her friend met her eyes. "All I'm saying is you deserve to have someone look at you like that."

George swallowed. "Ana, I—"

"Don't you dare," Ana interrupted. "You're going. You're going to dance with that man, and maybe, just maybe, you two will finally say what you've been wanting to say."

George folded her arms. "And what's that?"

Ana smirked. "I like you. I want to be with you. At least for now."

George didn't argue. Because the truth was, she *did* like him. And if she let herself admit it, she did want to be with him.

Ana slipped on her earrings. "You ready?"

George took one last look in the mirror, then grabbed a sweater from the bed. "Yeah. I'm ready."

Music spilled from the open doors, the lively melody of a fiddle weaving through the hum of conversation. George parked the truck, and both women, dressed in their finest, made their way to the door.

Ana linked arms with her at the entrance. "Wait here," she whispered before slipping inside.

George frowned but stayed put. From her vantage point, she could see Pedro near the bar, likely trying to sneak a sip of something strong. But it wasn't Pedro her gaze locked onto.

David stood in the middle of the room, caught mid-conversation. Then his eyes found hers.

The noise around them faded.

For a moment, it was just them.

Time slowed as they stared at one another, a silent exchange passing between them. Then, as if pulled by invisible strings, she descended the three steps to the dance floor.

So this is what Cinderella must've felt like.

David was already moving, hand out stretched. She took it, letting him lead her to a small table near the stage.

"You look fantastic," he murmured, settling into the chair beside her.

She smoothed the fabric of her dress, cheeks flushing. "Ana made it."

"It looks great on you." His hand found her knee, his touch warm and grounding. "Perfect for a first date."

She arched a brow. "Is that what this is?"

"Only if you want it to be."

George glanced down at his hand, then slowly covered it with her own.

When she looked back up, he was smiling.

He had his answer.

Elliot approached them, swinging a bottle of cider in his hand, a smirk tugging at his lips.

"Georgie girl," he drawled.

George stiffened. She hated that nickname.

"Lelliot," she replied, her voice flat.

His smirk faltered for just a second. He stopped short of them, then casually slid into the empty chair across from

George, making himself comfortable. "Aren't you going to introduce me to your friend?"

George sighed. "Elliot, this is David. David, Elliot."

"Her brother," Elliot added smoothly, extending his hand.

"*Step*brother," George corrected under her breath.

David shook his hand once, firm but brief, then let go. His focus was already shifting away. "I'm going to grab a beer. You want one?" he asked George.

"She doesn't drink beer," Elliot answered before she could.

George arched a brow. "I do, actually. Beer sounds good."

David gave her a knowing smile before heading toward one of the microbrew tables.

Elliot watched him go, then turned back to George. "Since when do you like beer?"

"Since I had time to learn." She met his gaze head on. "I take it you didn't come over here just to meet David."

He took a slow sip of his cider. "No. I came to see if you've read my proposal."

She stiffened. "I have."

Elliot leaned forward, eyes gleaming. "And?"

George exhaled, already bracing for his reaction. "I think it needs some work before you start showing it around the city."

The excitement in his face vanished. His hands curled into fists, knuckles whitening.

"Damn it, Georgianna," he snapped, slamming his fist against the table.

A few nearby patrons glanced over at the sound, but Elliot quickly recovered, forcing a placid smile and waving them off like nothing had happened. When he turned back to George, the smile remained, but his voice dropped into something too smooth, too rehearsed.

"I need your backing, George. The factions respect you."

George crossed her arms, unimpressed. "And if I say no?"

Elliot tilted his head, feigning amusement. "Then I'll find other ways to bring them in line."

A chill crawled up her spine.

"You and Ana have a... comfortable setup here," he continued, voice light but calculated. "I'd hate to see it disrupted."

George clenched her jaw.

"Not a threat," Elliot added, raising his hands innocently. "Just reality. We need order. And you can either be part of the solution— or just another problem to solve."

George forced a smirk. "Is that what Kate sees in you? A problem solver?"

His jaw twitched.

Good, she thought. *He doesn't like being challenged.*

"Don't you see what I'm trying to accomplish?" he pressed.

"I do," she said evenly. "It's admirable. I just think your plan needs work first, that's all. Nothing personal."

David returned, setting a beer in front of George before sliding into the seat beside her. His eyes flicked between them, his instincts sharp. "Everything okay?"

"Fine. Just a sibling squabble," George said smoothly.

Elliot, however, was visibly seething, his face tinged red with anger.

She decided to shift the subject. "How's Kate?"

His expression darkened further. "Fine," he bit out. Then, without warning, he pushed back his chair and stood. As he turned to leave, he glanced at David and sneered.

"Whatever you do, wear protection when you bang this one. Don't get her knocked up." Elliot spat the words like venom. Then he was gone.

George kept her expression neutral, refusing to let his parting shot get a rise out of her. But inside, her nerves buzzed. She had only seen Elliot this angry a handful of times, and it never boded well.

David, however, wasn't as composed. His eyes followed Elliot's retreating figure, jaw tight.

George exhaled and turned to him. "His wife may not survive her pregnancy," she said, keeping her tone cool. "I guess he's mad at me for being the bearer of bad news."

David frowned, his grip tightening around his beer. "There's something wrong with that guy."

George scoffed. "Elliot? He's just used to getting his way. He's been like that since we were kids. His mother coddled him."

David shook his head, still watching the doorway. "I don't know, George. He's just... off."

She waved a dismissive hand. "Elliot is harmless. He's probably had too much to drink."

David didn't look convinced.

George leaned in, placing a hand on his arm, redirecting his attention back to her. Her lips curled into a small, knowing smile.

"Now," she murmured, "would you rather talk about my brother... or us?"

The tension in David's shoulders eased slightly, and the corner of his mouth lifted.

"Us," he said without hesitation. "I didn't realize there was an *us*."

"There isn't— yet. That's what we're going to talk about."

He chuckled. "Miss Harris, you are ever so calculating."

"Mr. Andrews, my calculations have served me well."

David leaned in, so close their foreheads brushed. His fingers skimmed over the back of her hand, tracing absentminded circles. "Well, I'm glad for that," he murmured. "I thought of you often, even after I woke up. It was like you were some kind of distant dream." His voice was soft, intimate. "I'm glad you're not, though."

George tilted her head, watching him. "Do I live up to the dream?"

David kissed her cheek, his lips lingering near her ear as he whispered, "Better. You are far better."

Heat curled in her belly, a warmth she hadn't felt in far too long.

She turned and kissed him, testing, tasting, savoring the way he responded instantly. His lips were warm and inviting, a contrast to the cold that had settled in her bones.

When she pulled away, her eyes flicked toward the bar.

Ana was watching with a smug expression, standing next to Melody Savage, Aces' daughter.

George smirked and took David's hand. "I feel like dancing. Don't you?"

"I most certainly do."

David stood without letting go, pulling her with him.

Before they could step onto the dance floor, a familiar voice interrupted. "Well, well, well, look who's on his feet again."

Trixie sauntered toward them, hips swaying, a mischievous smirk curving her lips. The client she'd been entertaining moments ago had already slunk back into the crowd, forgotten.

"David," she purred, eyes dragging over him slowly like she was assessing him.

David gave her a warm smile. "Trix. Good to see you."

Trixie reached out, running a hand down his arm in an intimate touch that George immediately clocked. "You're looking damn fine for a man who was half-dead a few weeks ago," she mused. "Glad to see you've still got some fight left in you."

"I had a good nurse," he said, glancing at George.

Trixie's lips thinned for a fraction of a second before she recovered, plastering on another coy smile.

"I'm real happy to see you're doing better," she continued, eyes gleaming.

"Yeah, I owe you one," David said sincerely.

Trixie waved it off, but took a step closer, her body almost brushing his. "Don't mention it. Think of it as payback for all the times you helped me with a dangerous customer."

George leaned back in her seat, watching the exchange with mild amusement. She'd dealt with plenty of women who didn't like her, but Trixie was an interesting case. She wasn't outright hostile, just possessive.

The bruising on Trixie's neck was faint but noticeable under the dim bar lights. George noted the marks along her throat, the shadow of a bruise near her lip. Someone had put their hands on her recently. And not in a sexual way.

"I haven't seen you around much," Trixie continued, tilting her head toward David.

"I've been working around the clinic, paying back my debts."

Trixie narrowed her eyes at George. "I *said* I'd pay it."

George shrugged. "He insisted. Far be it from me to stop him."

David's voice was smooth, like he was soothing a child. "Trixie, I pay my own debts. But thank you."

Trixie frowned, then plastered on a grin that didn't quite reach her eyes.

"Well then, since you're all healed up," she said, grabbing David's hand and tugging him toward her, "why don't you dance with me? I want to see what my quick thinking has done."

David hesitated, glancing at George.

She arched a brow, sipping her beer. "Go ahead," she said dryly. "I'll finish my drink."

Trixie shot her a triumphant look before dragging David onto the dance floor.

George leaned back, watching with a smirk as Trixie wasted no time pressing herself against him.

David, to his credit, did his best to maintain some distance. He was polite, but his hands stayed firmly at her waist instead of anywhere lower. However, that didn't stop Trixie from attempting to slink closer every chance she got.

George took a shot of vodka, bemused as David emphatically gestured while prying Trixie's hands off his ass.

It was *hilarious*.

Still, she'd seen enough. She got up from the table and headed outside.

The first snow had arrived.

At first, it was just a light dusting, but soon, the flakes thickened, falling in lazy spirals.

George held out her hand, catching them, watching them melt against her palm.

The cold was quiet and still, starkly contrasting the noise inside.

"There you are." David's voice was warm as he draped his coat over her shoulders. "It's cold enough that you need something more substantial than a sweater."

She wrapped it around herself, inhaling his scent— pine, soap, something distinctly *him*. "You'll freeze," she protested.

He shrugged, standing casually with his hands in his pockets. "I'll be fine. I'm from colder climates."

She turned to face him fully. "You never talk about where you're from."

"And neither do you." He smiled. "I think we can agree that the past is the past."

She considered that. It wasn't that the past was behind them, but more so that it felt like another life entirely.

George exhaled, shaking off the thought. "Trixie seemed awfully *friendly* back there."

David sighed, rubbing the back of his neck. "She's... persistent."

George smirked. "You didn't enjoy dancing with her?"

Instead of answering, David stepped forward, his hands sliding around her waist, pulling her in.

His cologne was subtle, but she caught it now, the scent sending a delicious warmth through her body.

"You," he murmured, "are the only woman I want to dance with." His breath was hot against her skin, his voice low and husky.

Desire coiled in her belly, sharp and consuming.

He kissed the delicate skin beneath her ear, and George's fingers curled into his shirt. She ached for him.

His touch, his warmth—it sent something molten through her veins, something dangerous and undeniable.

She wanted him. Badly.

David's lips brushed along her jaw, his hands firm on her hips, and George swallowed hard.

Last night, exhaustion had won.

Tonight?

Tonight, she wouldn't let it.

"Shall we go back in?" David murmured.

George barely heard him. "I don't think Ana will be looking for me," she said, voice breathy. "She was flirting."

"With who?"

"Melody Savage."

David blinked. "I thought you said she liked boys."

George chuckled. "I thought she did."

She glanced toward the entrance just as Ana and Melody burst out of the bar, giggling together. Pedro stumbled behind them, swearing up a storm.

Melody twirled her keys, and Ana grinned. "Melody is taking me and Pedro home," she announced. "He's already puked behind the bar from sneaking alcohol."

David whistled. "He'll learn a lesson from the hangover in the morning. You two have fun. That's an order." He gave them a pointed look.

Ana cackled as Melody helped her into the car.

And then, just like that, they were alone again.

David took George's hand, his fingers rough and calloused from hard labor.

She liked it.

She liked him.

He squeezed her hand gently, tilting his head. "So... back inside?"

George shook her head. "No. Let's go home."

She saw the flicker of understanding in his eyes.

Home.

And this time, they both knew exactly what that meant.

David sighed. George reached into the pocket sewn into the dress. The truck keys weren't there. She frowned. Not only did she not have her truck keys, she didn't have anything she could use to help hotwire the truck.

"You're scowling. That's not good," said David.

"Ana has the keys, and I don't have a screwdriver."

"Shit." He looked around. "I'm going inside to see if I can borrow a lantern. Looks like we're going to have to walk."

"It's too cold. I'll see if Elliot can give us a lift."

"It'll be fine," David said. "Besides, it'll be a cold day in hell before I ask that guy for anything. He creeps me out." He ran inside. When David came back a few minutes later, he had a lantern. "If we hurry, I won't get frostbite."

"It's four blocks. It takes longer than that to get frostbite in this weather," retorted George.

He chuckled. "It was a joke, Miss Harris."

"I know." She smiled. "I just thought it was imperative that you know frostbite takes much longer to get when it's warm enough to snow."

"George..."

"Yeah?"

"You're killing me. Let's go." He took her hand once more, and they began to walk.

She'd forgotten how hard it was to walk in heels when the pavement was slick with snow melt. George slipped and would've ended up on her butt had it not been for David's quick grasp. He held her in his arms and looked at her. Both of their breaths were labored.

"You okay?" he asked, brows creased in concern.

"Fine." Physically. Inside, however, she ached.

"I've got you. I won't let you fall." Something about the way he said it let her know he wasn't just talking about the snow.

They eventually made it home in one piece, amidst small talk and innuendo. George led the way to their bedroom. It was strange to think of it as theirs.

The large room had always been hers. Her study... her respite. Now, she shared the space. David went into the room first while George stopped to check on Pedro. He was sound asleep on his stomach, his head partially off the bed, and a bucket beneath him. There'd be no choking on his own vomit in her house.

George steadied her nerves and went into the room. She knew what she wanted, and provided he didn't say no, she'd get it tonight. David was shirtless, brushing his teeth in the bathroom. George joined him at the sink, brushing her teeth before removing the pins from her hair.

She turned so her back was to him. "Can you help me with the zipper?"

David unzipped the dress and stepped back. George slinked out of it and let the satin fabric pool at her feet. David stood there and watched her with unsure eyes. She smiled and reached for his face.

"Are you just going to stand there," she reached down and cupped his hard cock through his pants, "or are you going to do something?"

He kissed her ferociously while his hands undid the clasp on her bra. The article of clothing hung precariously between them as they moved toward the bed. David walked backward and held George. They were in a tango of desire, each moving with precision to the mattress. Her most intimate muscles clenched with excitement as she undid his pants.

David stumbled backward onto the bed, falling into the sheets as he laughed. "I guess we can forget about separate sleeping arrangements," he said.

George yanked his boxers off and tossed them onto the ground. David sat up and hooked his fingers in the delicate fabric of her panties. In one quick motion, they were down over her hips, and she took them off.

The fire was dying, and, under normal circumstances, she'd be worried about putting another log in the fireplace. She'd be warm enough in a minute. George climbed onto David's lap. His erection brushed her thighs as she positioned herself near it, but not near enough for accidental penetration.

David grabbed a fistful of her hair and gently tugged it, pulling her head back. He kissed her chin and moved down her neck, planting tiny kisses on her skin. She shivered with delight as her body responded to his touch. Without a doubt, she was wet for him.

A low moan filled the hush in the room as David lowered his head to kiss her nipples.

It took a moment, but George realized it was her. She positioned her body to give him a better angle and enjoyed the sensation of his mouth on her breasts.

The hand not tangled in her hair found her clitoris. David rubbed it, first back and forth, then gently circling it. Her moaning grew more frequent as pleasure clouded her every sense, and she allowed herself not to think of anything but him and the sensations he was giving her body.

David's finger entered her, teasing at first. He inserted a second one, this time plunging it into the depths of her body fast and hard. George gasped at the intrusion as she ground against his fingers, helping him to get her closer to an orgasm.

It wasn't enough.

George whimpered and put her head in the crook of his neck. "Please, David." Her voice was breathy.

"Please, what, Miss Harris?" He managed to sound controlled.

"It's not enough. I want you."

He removed his fingers from inside of her. "Condom?"

"In the nightstand." George climbed off him and positioned herself among the pillows. David raised an eyebrow. She smiled. "Don't look at me that way. I knew that with you and I sharing a room, it was bound to come up sometime."

"You sound like you were sure."

"I didn't know about you but knew I wanted to get laid. Now, hurry up and fuck me."

David reached into the nightstand drawer and pulled out a condom. He tore the wrapper and rolled the lambskin sheath over his erect penis. "There's one problem with your conclusion."

George looked at him, confused about what part of her conclusion was wrong.

"I'm not going to fuck you, George."

"Why not?"

David's eyes held hers, steady and certain.

"Because I'm in love with you," he said, his voice rough, unshaken. "I'm going to make love to you."

The words hit her like a hammer to the chest.

No. No, he wasn't supposed to say that.

George had been expecting something else, something simple. Lust, need, pleasure— but not *this*.

Love was dangerous. Love made people weak... made them dependent. She had spent too long making herself strong... too long ensuring she could survive without anyone.

She swallowed hard, forcing out a sharp laugh. "Mr. Andrews, need I remind you that I'm already naked and with my legs thoroughly spread beneath you? There's no need for pretty words."

He didn't flinch. "They're not pretty words. I mean it."

A knot twisted in her stomach.

She couldn't let this be something deeper. Wouldn't.

So she did the only thing she knew how to do— she moved.

George pushed him onto his back, straddling him before he could say another damn word.

If she kissed him, he wouldn't speak. If she touched him, he wouldn't have the chance to tell her things that made her chest ache and made her want things she shouldn't.

David let her take control, his hands skimming up her thighs as she sank onto him. She exhaled a shuddering breath, closing her eyes, losing herself in the feel of it.

This? This was simple.

The way his hands gripped her hips, guiding her movements. The way their bodies connected, skin against skin, heat against heat. The rhythm they found together was primal and intoxicating.

This wasn't love. This was just need. Just the physical.

But then David sat up, wrapping his arms around her, holding her so close their foreheads nearly touched.

Too close.

He wasn't supposed to hold her like this.

He wasn't supposed to look at her like this, like she was something precious. Like she mattered more than just the moment.

She squeezed her eyes shut and tilted her head, kissing him hard, trying to silence whatever tenderness was brewing between them.

But he didn't let her escape.

His lips were soft, coaxing, dragging her deeper instead of allowing her to keep this as something shallow.

Her hands curled against his shoulders, nails pressing into his skin— not to pull him closer, but to hold on, because for the first time in a long time, she felt like she was slipping.

She wanted to be in control.

But David wouldn't let her keep her walls up.

She wanted this to be just physical.

He whispered her name against her lips like it *meant* something.

And she hated that her body reacted to that just as much as it did to the way he moved inside her. She hated that she could feel herself breaking apart, unraveling, losing the part of herself that had kept her safe for so damn long.

Her climax crashed over her before she was ready, pulling a desperate sound from her throat.

David swallowed the noise with his mouth, kissing her deeply, murmuring her name again, and she thought, *Damn him. Damn him for making me feel this.*

Before the trembling in her body had fully subsided, David shifted their positions, pressing her into the mattress beneath him.

His thrusts grew deeper, harder, his forehead against hers, breaths mingling.

George squeezed her eyes shut, trying to ignore how much she *liked* this.

She clung to him, but only because she needed an anchor.

She moaned his name, but only because she needed release.

She pulled him deeper, but only because it felt good, not because she wanted *him*. At least, that's what she told herself.

The moment built again, her body tightening, the pleasure surging through her veins like fire.

She came hard, back arching, nails digging into his skin. David followed seconds later, letting out a low, guttural groan as he collapsed onto his forearms above her.

Their bodies were still tangled together, their breaths still erratic.

George knew she should move.

She should roll away, say something flippant, get up, and put distance between them before he could look at her like that again.

But her body felt heavy, exhausted, and satisfied in a way she hadn't been in... well, she couldn't even remember how long.

One last kiss and David finally pulled away, disposing of the condom before settling beside her.

George tugged the blanket over herself, staring at the ceiling, willing her heart to steady.

David turned to her, voice still rough with pleasure. "Well, Miss Harris, how was that?"

It had been spectacular. It had been too much.

She shrugged. "It was okay."

David huffed a laugh. "Just okay?"

She looked up at him, keeping her face neutral. "Uh-huh."

He gave her a slow, knowing smile. "Give me a minute to catch my breath. I'll show you just okay."

Before she could respond, he tickled her side, making her jump and let out a startled laugh.

George scowled, but the warmth in his expression made her stomach twist again. Damn him.

They spent the rest of the night alternating between pleasure and teasing, between hard breaths and laughter.

By the time the first hints of dawn filtered through the window, she was tangled against him, exhausted, unable to fight off sleep. Before she let herself drift, before she let the night fully end, one last thought slipped into her mind.

I think I'm falling for him, too.

And that scared her more than anything.

Chapter Nine

GEORGE THREW ANOTHER LOG on the fire, watching as the flames licked hungrily at the fresh wood, sending waves of warmth through the room. Winter was tightening its grip, and though she'd slept later than usual, there was still work to be done.

She padded downstairs to the sunroom, the cold biting at her bare arms, before she pulled on her coat, gloves, and snow boots. The house was eerily quiet, with only the soft creak of settling wood and the distant whistle of wind filling the silence.

Outside, snow blanketed the yard in a soft, pristine layer, fresh flakes dusting the ground as she made her way toward the annex. It wasn't too deep yet, but it would be soon. The annex was noticeably warmer, the heat from the thick stone walls and the animals themselves helping to stave off the worst of the cold. Inside, the animals were bundled in wool blankets, their breaths visible in soft puffs of steam.

Ana emerged from one of the horse pens, shovel in hand, pushing a wheelbarrow full of manure. She smirked as soon as she saw George.

"You slept in." The knowing grin on her face made it clear she knew exactly why.

George rolled her eyes, trying to fight the blush creeping up her neck. "I did. Sorry. Did you already feed up?"

Ana nodded. "And mucked."

George glanced into one of the pig stalls. The animal was happily buried in fresh straw, snorting contentedly.

"Did Melody stay over?" she asked casually, leaning against the wooden stall.

Ana pursed her lips. "Maybe."

George snorted. "Must not have been very good if you got up early enough to do *my* chores."

Ana huffed out a laugh, shaking her head. "We talked."

George arched a brow. "Just talked?"

Ana ignored the question and instead turned the tables. "What about David? I thought I heard that metal bed creaking."

George definitely blushed then, turning away toward the door. "I guess I'll go make breakfast since everything else is done."

Ana chuckled as George hurried back toward the house.

Inside, the kitchen was still cool, the scent of last night's fire lingering faintly in the air. George stopped by the locked cabinet in the pantry, grabbing a pair of aspirin tablets for Pedro. The kid was going to have a hell of a hangover after all the liquor he'd snuck. *Let this be a lesson to him*, she thought.

She prepared a simple but hearty breakfast: scrambled eggs, toast, smoked trout, and fresh-pressed coffee. It was enough to fill five stomachs— three grown women, one man, and one idiot teenager who'd likely need more food than he deserved this morning.

As she worked, George pulled out the small notepad from her pocket, carefully noting the exact amount of each ingredient used. Every meal was a calculation now, with every bit of food accounted for.

This winter was going to be leaner than the last. More mouths to feed meant tighter rations.

And if Melody was going to keep staying over, George and Ana might need to leverage her relationship with her father. Ace had resources. Men to hunt for him, and a network of pharmacists producing synthetics.

Synthetics could mean trade.

Trade meant survival.

Maybe even deals with merchants from St. Paul, Apple Valley, or Stillwater when they passed through.

George exhaled, staring at the rising steam from the coffee. It was too early in the morning to be thinking about potential trading partners. But winter was only just beginning. And she had a feeling it was going to be a long one. Sooner or later, she'd need to address it.

Pedro groaned as he stumbled into the kitchen, his voice thick with regret. "My head hurts."

George smirked as she slammed the cabinet shut after pulling down a cup. The sharp *clack* made Pedro flinch, his whole body tensing. He let out a miserable sound, and she chuckled.

Good.

She filled the glass with water and set it in front of him, dropping two aspirins beside it. "Take these and stay hydrated. The hangover will pass," she said. "And get some food in you. Breakfast is on the stove."

Pedro muttered something unintelligible under his breath before croaking out, "Thank you, Miss George."

The sound of whistling floated through the doorway.

David entered the kitchen, humming the melody to *Paint It Black*, his easy swagger making it impossible to ignore him. He strolled over to the stove, where George's half-empty coffee mug sat, and topped it off without asking.

Then, to her surprise, he took a sip.

George blinked. "That's mine."

David's lips curled into a smirk as he swallowed. "Sugar, right?"

She eyed him, her heart doing something it had no business doing. "Yeah," she said, hesitating only a moment before nodding.

That damn smile of his widened, and it should have been illegal how handsome he was when he grinned like that.

George turned back to her plate, trying to focus on literally anything else, but her body had other plans. Every nerve in her skin was suddenly too aware of his presence, the way the air shifted whenever he was near.

It wasn't fair.

David grabbed the sugar tin and added two spoonfuls, along with a splash of milk. He stirred, then handed the mug back to her.

"I prefer mine black," he said.

George snorted. "I remember reading an article once that linked drinking black coffee to sociopaths."

David shrugged. "I've been called worse." He grabbed a plate and began helping himself to the food on the stove. Then he slid into the chair beside Pedro, acting like it was the most natural thing in the world, and started eating. "Plans for today?"

George cleared her throat, refocusing. "I have to make the rounds in Downtown and Midtown," she said. "I'll probably be late. Might have to find a place to bunk."

She took another sip of coffee, then turned to Pedro. "You're staying here today, working with Ana. If you're going to live here, you need to be useful."

Pedro groaned. "But my head—"

"A hangover is punishment enough for drinking," she cut in. "Now you'll learn what the rest of us have: how to recover and still get things done. No sympathy. And when you're done eating, clean up the kitchen."

Pedro muttered something in Spanish that she was pretty sure translated to some kind of creative swearing, but he still mumbled, "Yes, ma'am."

Having a teenager around was going to be so much fun.

George soon finished her plate and pushed back from the table. Without another word, she made her way upstairs to her room, where she showered and pulled her damp hair into a practical braid. By the time she finished dressing in layers, she had mentally gone over her route for the day twice.

She was fastening her pack when she heard the door shut behind her.

David stood there watching her, his expression unreadable.

"You're staring," she said without looking up.

"I can't help it," he replied simply. "I can't get over how beautiful you are."

George forced a scoff, shouldering her bag. "Beauty fades. Don't praise me for it."

David leaned against the doorframe, arms crossed. "Inner beauty doesn't." His voice was quieter now, softer. "I don't know what I did to deserve finding someone like you."

Her stomach twisted.

She hated that he said things like that.

She hated that it made her feel warm and fuzzy.

She tried to wave it off, forcing a smirk. "You damn near died, and Trixie had enough sense to drag you here. That's what you did." She gave him a pointed look. "Don't do it again."

David chuckled, his accent slipping into something lazy and southern. "Why, Georgianna Harris, was that a note of concern?"

"It was common sense advice," she said, adjusting the strap of her bag.

She turned toward the door, but his hand caught hers before she could brush past him.

The touch was light. Barely there. But it stopped her like an iron lock.

Her breath hitched as he traced his thumb over the rough skin of her palm, as though memorizing the shape of her hand... the callouses... the lines.

Her whole body went taut.

She could handle a lot of things.

Pain.

Hunger.

She could even handle the brutality of this world and everything it took to survive.

But this?

This was different.

Because this made her want things.

This made her dream. And she couldn't.

Not now.

Not ever.

David's fingers skimmed hers, and for a split second, she thought he was going to kiss her.

She should have pulled away.

She should have laughed it off, tossed out some sarcastic remark, done anything to shatter the moment.

But instead, she stood there, frozen, like a deer caught in the glow of something too warm, too bright.

David licked his lips, then cleared his throat, as though shaking himself free of whatever had settled between them.

"I can come with you," he offered.

George blinked, suddenly remembering how to breathe. She pulled her hand from his grip, flexing her fingers.

"I'm fine," she said, too quickly. "I make this trip all the time."

"I didn't mean to imply you wouldn't be," David replied, hesitating. "I just—" He stopped, shaking his head.

George knew what he wanted to say.

She wasn't ready to hear it.

She busied herself adjusting the strap on her bag again. "You can come," she finally said, forcing her voice back to normal. "I could use the extra set of hands."

She strode past him before he could look at her like *that* again.

"Hurry up," she called over her shoulder. "We're burning daylight, and I've got things to do."

David didn't say anything.

But as she walked away, she swore she could still feel the ghost of his touch lingering in her palm.

And damn it, she hated how much she liked it.

George pulled open the supply closet, efficiently stocking up on the essentials she'd need for her rounds. Syringes, disinfectants, medical tape, bandages. Some antibiotics she'd managed to hoard. A few vials of painkillers— rare, precious things, better than currency in this world.

In the living room, Ana was sitting cross-legged on the floor with Pedro, sorting through a pile of books. Thick textbooks on anatomy, microbiology, and chemistry were spread out around them. Pedro was already flipping through one, lips pursed in concentration.

They were college-level texts, advanced for a kid his age. But Pedro was sharp, and he had nothing but time. He'd get it soon enough.

"Anything special I should get?" George called from the back door as she shrugged into her coat and pulled on her snow boots.

Ana barely looked up. "Nope. Just the usual. Take the gun and extra bullets."

"And be safe," Pedro added, mimicking Ana's tone with a smirk.

"Yes, *dear*," George teased. She laughed when Ana rolled her eyes.

David appeared a moment later, jogging out of the house with a backpack slung over one shoulder and a thick blanket tucked under his arm. He'd dressed for the cold— heavy coat, wool pants— but his boots were wrong. Just regular everyday ones.

They'd need to find him something with better traction before the real ice set in.

David loaded his gear into the truck and climbed into the passenger seat. He was grinning, the kind of full, unguarded smile that made the corners of his eyes crinkle.

George was tempted to ask what had him so damn cheerful, but she resisted. She wasn't in the mood for small talk, especially if it meant getting some corny answer about adventure or fresh air.

Instead, she started the truck and drove in silence.

Some roads had been cleared overtime, with vehicles pushed aside to make narrow, usable paths. Others remained impassable, blocked by sheer bad luck, a car stalling at just the wrong moment when the world went dark.

They drove as far as they could, stopping at the corner of Dayton Avenue and Western.

David glanced out the window. "Have you been to St. Paul since everything happened?"

She nodded. "It's quieter than downtown Minneapolis. But that doesn't mean you shouldn't be on your toes."

They both grabbed their supplies and set off on foot. Their tracks left crisp impressions in the fresh snow as they moved through the streets.

Their first stop was a veterinary clinic. Most people raided human hospitals and pharmacies first, leaving places like these overlooked.

Which was stupid.

Vet clinics had supplies that were just as valuable— suture kits, painkillers, IV solutions. Most of the medicines used on dogs and humans weren't all that different.

David watched as George filled her bag, grabbing surgical tools still wrapped and sterile, bottles of antibiotics, and enough sutures to last them through the season.

"Can I ask something?" he saidfinally.

George nodded, slipping a handfulof scalpels into her pack.

"Why are we grabbing vet meds?"

She glanced at him before setting a pile of gauze into her bag. "Because a lot of the drugs they use for animals are the same for humans, just different dosages. Everyone raids the human pharmacies first. The vet clinics are passed over."

David exhaled, shaking his head. "And the pharmacists?"

"They're more interested in other trades," she said, picking up a notebook and some pens from a desk tucked in the corner. "There's more money in helping people forget the world they live in now. Easier business model."

David frowned. "I wonder if anyone could've predicted the world would turn to shit like this."

George snorted, giving him a wry look. "People did. *Doomsday Preppers* was a show, remember? The whole thing was due for a reset. Overpopulation, destruction. Disease is the great equalizer."

She paused in front of an empty cage. George hadn't thought much about it before-- how many pets had been left behind when people panicked. Some had made it. Packs of dogs roamed the outskirts, scavengers now.

Others hadn't been so lucky.

Just like the people in hospitals. The babies in NICUs.

George forced the thought away. Thinking too much could get you killed.

She adjusted the strap of her bag. "Come on. We still have appointments."

Their next stop was Summit Avenue. The street had once been filled with sprawling mansions, old-world money built from timber and railroads.

Most were abandoned now; too expensive to heat, too large to defend. Some, however, had been repurposed.

George gestured toward a boarded-up house. "That was the Fitzgerald place. You know ,the author?"

David nodded, but they didn't stop.

Their destination was at the very end of the street— a house turned into a brothel and gambling den.

A tall, muscular woman with cropped red hair stood at the entrance, her stance casual but alert. Her fitted shirt did little to hide the way her body had been built for combat.

She smiled when she saw George. "Harris. Been a while."

"It has, Rachel," George replied politely. "Evan and Scott in?"

"Scott's out scouting. Evan's in the kitchen." Rachel's gaze flicked past George to David. "Who's this?"

"David." George smirked. "He's my bodyguard today."

Rachel snorted. "Lucky guy."

She led them through the house to a small back room. It was once a servant's quarters, now converted into an exam space.

George wasted no time setting up her instruments, laying them out in meticulous order.

"David, go with Rachel," she instructed, slipping into work mode. "I need extra linens, vodka, lots of boiled water, and access to the wood stove."

David gave a mock salute. "Yes, ma'am."

Rachel chuckled. "Come on, city boy. Let's see what you're made of."

George tended to her patients while Rachel kept David busy. By the time George had finished her third pap smear exam, the room was growing dark.

Evan entered, setting a lantern on the bedside table. "It's getting late," he said. "I had a room made up for you."

"Thanks." George peeled off her gloves and scrubbed her hands in the wash basin.

Evan was a bit older than George, maybe five years, give or take. But he already had salt and pepper hair. He'd once told her he had started greying in his twenties. Some people were just early greys. He never told her much about what he did prior to the world going to hell. Occasionally, hints would drop, and she suspected he'd been an engineer.

It didn't matter now. The infrastructure for that sort of work was gone. But the skills were valuable, and he'd successfully managed to make a prototype battery to store solar electricity. Once he figured out how to get it to store more than a few hours of power, they'd have something.

Evan leaned against the doorframe. "Elliot talked to me."

George exhaled through her nose. "And?"

Evan snorted. "That cockamamie plan of his? He doesn't have the temperament to pull it off."

"I agree. Elliot is smart, but he's selfish. He likes power."

"We all like power, George," Evan pointed out. "Even you."

George glanced at him, but he wasn't smiling.

"You don't think you have influence?" Evan pressed. "You've got no real competition. You go places others don't. You have what people *need*."

"I provide a service," she countered.

Evan laughed. "Yeah. And you made sure no one else provides it *better*."

George crossed her arms. "I don't like politics."

"But you play them." Evan studied her. "And that boyfriend of yours? He's got potential."

She stiffened. "David isn't—"

"Spare me," Evan interrupted. "You could build something with him."

George clenched her jaw. She wasn't naïve. She understood power.

And David? He was dangerously perfect for it. Charismatic. Intelligent. Steady.

If she shaped him right, he could be the face of something bigger.

But she didn't want to think about it. So, she shook her head. "I'm hungry. You cooking?"

"Fish stew."

"Then let's eat."

After dinner, when it was just the two of them in a comfortable room at the top of the stairs, George lay in bed thinking about Evan's words. David had been in the butler's pantry, but between moving back and forth between rooms for her tools, she didn't know what or how much he had heard. If he knew anything, he didn't say it.

"You deserve a house like this," David said after a while.

"A brothel?" George replied.

He turned on his side, propping himself up on one elbow. "A well-appointed mansion."

"And how would I heat it? The place we have now is hard enough to keep up."

David kissed her. "The world won't always be like this. And when it changes, I want to give you everything in life you deserve."

George cupped his face with her hand, lightly stroking his cheek. The way he talked made her think of tomorrow, even if it was uncertain. If she wasn't careful, he'd worm his way into her heart, past all her well-constructed defenses.

No, the world wouldn't always belike this. It could be worse, or it could be some semblance of what it had always been. People always found a way. Maybe she ought to get in while they were still at bottom.

George pushed the thought out of her mind. She didn't need the problems. The peace of mind she had now was well-fought. And if she wanted to keep it, she'd stay out of the game.

She ran a hand through David's thick head of hair. He was handsome, with movie-star good looks and the ability to charm a room when he wanted to. From what she'd seen, he was a hell of a lot more stable than Elliot. The intimacy between them could be used to influence things. Just another mechanism. He had everything it took to be the face of anew world order.

She bit her lip, and David kissed the inside of her wrist. The longer she thought about the idea, the less far-fetched it seemed. But what did Evan gain by her being the puppet? They were on good terms. Perhaps he wanted to subtly influence her using his network to sway things in his favor.

"A penny for your thoughts, Miss Harris," David said, trailing kisses up her arm.

George debated telling him for a moment. Then decided it was in her best interest to test the waters. "Evan seems to think I'm influential."

David sat up, lacing his fingers with hers. His eyes seemed to probe her face, studying it the way one would the Mona Lisa. "You are. You didn't realize it?"

She shrugged. "What little influence I have is only because I provide a service."

"George, Aces' guys told me somethings in the past—"

"I didn't know you knew Aces," replied George.

David shrugged. "I don't. I've done some odd jobs for people who work for him. We all have to find a way to get what we need." His lips brushed the back of her hand. "But I've seen the way people are with you. The deference. I don't know the whole story, but I see why Elliot wants you on board from what I've seen.

"You go everywhere, and no one messes with you. There are very few who can accomplish that. You and Ana. And I think Ana is only really afforded that privilege because of her connection to you."

David had been doing a lot of watching and a lot of piecing together.

He placed a light kiss on her shoulder. "None of it is shocking. It boils down to you understanding the rules of survival."

"And what about you?"

"What about me?"

"Have you done things that would shock me? Do you understand survival?"

David went rigid, and she knew there were things that he was keeping from her. He had the right, and though she'd always suspected, his expression confirmed it. He had the look of a soldier who'd seen too much and wouldn't share.

"I understand it better than most," he finally said.

George nodded. "Good." That was all she needed to know.

Chapter Ten

MELODY SAVAGE SITTING ACROSS from him at the breakfast table had become such a regular occurrence over the past few weeks that David half-suspected she lived here, too. Not that he minded. At least she was a better cook than Ana. That alone might justify letting her stay permanently.

George could cook exceptionally well, but she did it so rarely that David wondered if he'd ever have a decent meal again. At least with Melody around, his odds improved.

He took a slow sip of his coffee, eyeing Pedro sitting across from him, bits of toilet paper stuck to his face from yet another failed attempt at shaving.

Jesus, the kid's going to bleed out before he ever grows a proper beard.

Pedro groaned into his hands. "My face hurts."

Melody snorted. "That's what happens when you dry shave, like a dumbass."

Pedro scowled. "I was in a hurry."

"Looks like it," David muttered into his mug.

Ana came in, slipping her arms into her coat, then slung her backpack over her shoulder. "We're off," she announced, placing a soft kiss on the corner of Melody's lips. "That baby isn't going to deliver itself."

George followed behind, dressed in an old pair of scrubs underneath her thick coat, her loose braid slightly messy from her rush to get ready.

David put down his toast and stood, reaching for her before she could escape. He kissed her slowly and thoroughly, not caring about the audience.

Girlfriend felt like such a childish word for what she was to him, but *his,* she was. "You be careful," he murmured, reluctant to let her go.

"I always am." She kissed him again, soft and quick. "Besides, it's just Elliot. It's Ana you should be worried about. She can't stand the man. Might say something stupid to get under his skin."

"Oh, I am," Melody said, sidling up beside Ana and squeezing her ass.

Ana grinned and giggled like a love-struck schoolgirl.

"George, keep this one out of trouble," instructed Melody.

"She always does." Ana adjusted her pack. "Don't worry if we don't come back tonight. Babies take forever."

Pedro rose from the table and announced, "Come on, David! You promised I could cut down the tree!"

The kid had been obsessed with the damn Christmas tree for days now. Considering everything that had happened, it was good that he took joy in something so normal.

David sighed, grabbing his coat. "All right, all right."

George arched a brow at them. "Please be careful. I don't want to have to patch you up when I get back."

"It'll be fine," David said, sneaking a last peck when everyone else had busied themselves with other things. "I used to cut Christmas trees with my dad all the time."

That earned him a smile. God, he lived for her smiles.

Pedro was already out the door, shouting for David to hurry up.

David followed George and Ana outside, watching as they mounted their horses and rode off, leaving him with Melody on the porch.

Melody shivered, rubbing her arms. "This is weird." They'd never been at the house alone together before. George or Ana was always around as a buffer.

"Yep," he replied, aware of their awkwardness without their partners.

"You got her a gift yet for Christmas?"

David shook his head. "She's too practical for most things. I thought about getting her some jewelry, but I'm afraid she'd hate it. You got something for Ana?"

Melody gave a broad smile and stood a little taller. "Thinking about asking her to marry me."

David nearly choked. "Seriously?"

"Yeah. We've been screwing around for a year now, though we've only went public recently. I figure it's time."

"Seems fast," replied David. Though, how fast was too fast with the current state of things?

Melody shot him a look. "It's not. I've known Ana for years. The only reason she hesitated to be open was because of George."

David frowned. "Why?"

It wasn't like there was anything between the two women. George and Ana were old friends. That was it.

"She always felt guilty about moving on. Like it meant leaving George behind." Melody sighed. "It's stupid, but that's how enmeshed they are."

David didn't say anything. It made sense in a way. Trauma bonds.

The truck horn blared outside, shattering the moment. Pedro must've been growing impatient.

"Jesus," Melody groaned. "Go before I kill the kid myself."

David picked up the ax outside the shed and put it behind the seat in the truck.

"Can I drive?" Pedro asked, putting his seat belt on.

He didn't bother with the seatbelt. "Nope," David replied firmly.

"I should learn," Pedro insisted.

"You should, but not when the ice is on the ground. Pretty soon, we'll have to walk or take the horses anyway." He thought about the life of gasoline. Soon enough, it'd be too degraded to be useful. Then cars would be truly obsolete.

Pedro crossed his arms and pouted.

The roads leading into Hidden Falls Regional Park were blocked by overgrown flora and decaying vehicles. David reached behind the seat and got out the ax, handing it to

Pedro. He kept the rifle himself. They got out of the truck and trudged down the snow-laden path to the heart of the park, reclaimed by wilderness, to the smaller trees growing near the entrance.

"You want to cut it?" David asked. He hoped the kid said yes because he didn't trust him with the gun. Pedro moved the ax from hand to hand like he was evaluating the weight. Then he tightened his grip, lifted the shaft, and chose a seven-foot fir. David sighed. Of course, the kid wanted a big ass tree to have to haul up to the truck.

Pedro swung and began working on chopping through the thick tree trunk. David stood guard with the gun, ready to shoot any menacing wolf or human that may have been lurking. Across the field, there was a large buck, partially hidden by the trees. Fresh meat would be good. The hide could be used to make another blanket.

David raised his rifle and focused his aim.

"That buck is too far away," Pedro said. "No one can hit it."

For just about anyone else, Pedro would've been right. David had hit harder targets than the deer. David considered closely. If he hit the deer, Pedro would run back and tell everyone. George might question how he'd become such an expert marksman. He couldn't give up the peace he had with her. Too many years had been wasted. He had to preserve it.

David did the unthinkable. For the first time ever, he purposely missed a shot. The buck, alerted by the bullet hitting a nearby tree, ran off to safety. David shrugged. "You were right. Now, let's get the tree and get out of here."

A few more solid chops and the tree came crashing down. David lifted the more substantial base of the tree, and Pedro carried the top. They loaded the tree and drove back into the town. He pulled into an abandoned gas station. "I'm going to run across the street and see if I can't find something useful in the pawn shop. You fill up the cans and the truck, and I'll let you drive home," David said. He left the gun with Pedro. "You shoot anyone who gets too close."

Pedro nodded.

David ran across the street to the pawn shop. The door was already open, broken into from the days of looting after the blackout. Inside, the shop was a mess. Items were on the floor or left on shelves, dusty and forgotten. The jewelry case had been smashed in, and some were missing. There were still gold chains and a few gemstones left behind.

He went to the back office. A picture was on the ground, and the safe in the wall was exposed. He tried the latch. It was still locked. Apparently, no one knew how to crack a safe. David looked around the office a little more. The desk drawers were an unkempt mess of papers and garbage. He picked up the papers, curious about their contents. One by one, David scanned them and discarded them on the floor. Hidden at the bottom of the drawer was a small slip of paper with a set of numbers. David went to the safe and tried the numbers. It stuck for a moment, but he pulled it harder, and it gave.

Inside were several stacks of large bills, a handgun and extra magazine— which he pocketed— and a small black box. David opened the box. It was a diamond ring. Not just any diamond. A blue diamond surrounded by a plethora of white in a platinum band. The ring had to be worth millions. He wasn't ready to give it to George, but it wouldn't hurt to keep around for later.

There was still the small matter of a Christmas present.

David searched the pawn shop and settled on an antique rose gold locket for George and a pocket knife for Pedro. Gifts done, he decided to do what he was supposed to: find something useful. He rutted around among the tools left behind before deciding to check the yard outback. David slowly opened the door. Two male voices stopped him. He left the door cracked so that anyone glancing over couldn't tell it was opened unless they looked hard. Closing it all the way would catch their attention with the noise.

"I want you to watch her. You'll report back to me everything you see or hear. I want to know when she eats, sleeps, pisses...everything. Hell, I want to know if the bitch is a fucking cocksucker or takes it in the ass. Anything you find out, you tell me. Got it?" The first man said. David tried to place the voice. He knew it from somewhere.

"I'll watch her, but I won't hurt her," said the second man.

"I didn't ask you to hurt her. I just asked you to watch her. Do it, and you'll be rewarded."

"Okay."

"Good man," the first said.

David realized where he'd heard the first man's voice before. It was at the dance. The first man was Elliot, but he should've been home, waiting for his children to be delivered.

He got up and hurried from the shop. Pedro was sitting in the truck behind the wheel. "Did you find anything," asked Pedro.

"No. Nothing," David said, pushing him out of the way as he slid behind the wheel.

"You said I could drive," Pedro argued.

"I changed my mind. We'll try it another time."

Later that night, Pedro sat at the table with his textbooks, and David helped him with his Algebra. The front door opened, and George walked in, dropping her bag on the floor without saying a word.

Something was wrong.

Ana followed a moment later, looking exhausted but still managing a small smile for Melody, who greeted her with open arms.

But George?

She didn't even glance at him. Instead, she walked upstairs in silence.

David finished with Pedro and then followed George upstairs. When he reached the bedroom, she was pacing. The water in the tub was running, steam filling the air, curling in soft tendrils toward the ceiling.

Her lips moved, whispering something too quiet for him to hear at first. As he got closer, he realized she was muttering steps to some procedure, as though she was running through a checklist.

David leaned against the dresser near the door. "What happened?"

George stopped. For a long moment, she didn't look at him. Then, finally, she turned.

"Kate…"She hesitated, her voice small. Then she sat in the middle of the floor as if her legs couldn't hold her up anymore. "I told him to choose."

David took a step closer. "Told who to choose?"

She clenched her hands together so tightly her knuckles turned blanched. "Elliot. I told him to choose. We couldn't save them all. It was too complicated. There was so much blood, and we couldn't control it. Elliot…" her voice broke and became small, "he wasn't there until toward the end. I told him he had to pick fast or lose them all."

David's chest went tight.

"He took too long," she whispered. "He chose wrong. Too much blood. So much blood." A sharp sob tore out of her.

David moved instantly, kneeling beside her and gathering her into his arms.

She stiffened at first, like she couldn't bear to be touched. But then something inside her broke, and she collapsed against him, fingers digging into his shirt.

"I had to tell my niece her mother and siblings were gone," she choked out. Her tears wet the front of his shirt where she'd buried his face. "I killed Kate. We had to have missed something." George let go of him, pulling back before grabbing a fistful of her own hair. "More bodies to be buried. Three more. Everything I touch turns to shit. I take everyone's happiness and destroy it."

David gently tugged her back toward him, pressing a kiss to her hair.

She didn't realize what she'd done for him. She had plucked him out of his own darkness and *saved* him from a version of himself he no longer wanted to be.

George was the one thing in this world that made sense to him.

The one person worth fighting for.

He reached into his pocket and pulled out a small locket he'd found at the pawn shop.

"That's not true," he murmured, fastening it around her neck.

George sniffled, her fingers closing around the locket. "What is this?"

David swallowed. "You make me incredibly happy. You're the only thing that does. You saved me, George. You don't destroy people's happiness. This fucked-up world does. You just have to be the one to deliver the bad news."

Her breath shuddered. She looked at him then, her brown eyes full of something fragile, something raw.

He cupped her face, brushing his thumb over her cheek. "I love you."

The words had been sitting on his tongue for so long, heavy, aching to be let free. Saying them felt like releasing a breath he hadn't realized he'd been holding.

George stared at him.

She pulled back just enough to see his face. "You love me?"

David smiled softly. "I thought it was obvious."

She was quiet for a long moment. Then she went to turn off the bathwater.

David watched as she pulled off her clothes, dropping them carelessly to the floor before stepping into the tub.

She glanced over her shoulder. "Mr. Andrews, I believe we both need a bath."

David huffed a laugh and stood, stripping down.

He caught her off guard, scooping her into his arms before they tumbled into the water, sending a wave over the edges of the tub.

She gasped but allowed him to hold her close, unbothered by the mess.

David kissed her... her lips... her face... her neck... her shoulders. It wasn't sexual.

It was relief.

It was gratitude.

It was love.

She saw him for who he wanted to be, not who he had been.

As George leaned against him, her back pressed to his chest, the heat of her skin mixing with the warmth of the water, David knew one thing with absolute certainty.

No one would touch her.

If there was breath in his body, no one would ever hurt her again.

It was well past midnight when David woke. The room's chill slipped under the thick blankets as the fire in the hearth burned low to embers. George was sleeping soundly beside him, her dark hair fanned out against the pillow, her breathing slow and even.

For a moment, he didn't move.

She was beautiful like this— soft, unguarded, and bathed in silver moonlight. She looked like some kind of winter goddess, all bare skin and tangled sheets, glowing where the light kissed her.

David leaned over, kissing her cheek, careful not to wake her. Then, silently, he slid out of bed.

He pulled on his clothes, heavy snow boots, and a thick coat before making his way through the quiet house. Room by room, he checked every door, every window, ensuring that everything was exactly as they'd left it.

He'd learned early in life that complacency got people killed.

Outside, the cold bit through the fabric of his coat, sharp and unforgiving. The air smelled like frost, crisp and clean, and the world was silent except for the occasional creak of ice forming along the edges of the barn.

Icicles clung to the roof, long and heavy, some sharp enough to impale a man if they fell. Snow glittered under the moon, undisturbed except for the tracks left behind by animals searching for food.

Then movement.

A shadow darted near the barn.

David stilled, watching.

The figure moved fast, circling between the barn and the house like a rat sniffing out an opportunity.

David ducked into the butcher shed, grabbing a knife from the hanging rack. It was sharp and familiar, the weight settling into his hand like an old friend.

His pulse steadied.

Time to work.

He slipped into the barn, moving through the darkness like he was born of it. The figure stepped out again, pausing at the barn door.

David struck fast, grabbing the intruder from behind, twisting the smaller man into a chokehold, and pressing the knife against his throat.

"Who the fuck are you," David hissed, his voice ice and steel, "and why the fuck shouldn't I kill you?"

The man stiffened, breath hitching. He reeked of sweat and filth, the sour tang of someone who hadn't washed in days.

"M-my name is Ralph," the junkie stammered, his body trembling against David. "I come around sometimes. George knows me. She gives me food and clothes."

David's grip tightened.

That voice-- he knew it. The pawnshop.

Elliot's errand boy.

David pressed the knife harder, just enough to nick the skin. A thin line of blood beaded at the blade's edge. "What the fuck are you doing here so late?" David growled. "George is in bed."

Ralph trembled. "I... I thought she might be up. Sometimes, she works late."

Bullshit.

George worked late if there were patients or something to be done. Otherwise, she slept.

David leaned in close, letting his voice drop into something lethal. "You're lying. That's not why you're here." He exhaled sharply against the man's ear. "Three seconds to tell me the truth before I end this. Three... two—"

"I'm supposed to watch her!" Ralph blurted out, his body jerking as if he might collapse under the weight of his own terror.

David didn't loosen his grip. "Why?"

"I don't know." Ralph's voice cracked. "Elliot just wants me to keep an eye on her."

David held him for a long moment, considering. Then, with a flick of his wrist, he released the junkie.

Ralph stumbled backward, clutching his throat, coughing like he'd been drowning. He backed into the barn wall, eyes darting around like a rabbit caught in a snare.

David straightened, tilting his head slightly. "What's he paying you?"

Ralph hesitated.

David's voice sharpened. "What's.He. Paying. You." Every word sounded strangled as he tried to remain quiet.

The junkie swallowed. "Three months of methgen and a place to stay."

David nodded slowly. "I'll give you better."

Ralph's eyes flicked up, wary but interested.

"Three months of methgen," David said, voice casual, almost bored. "A place. *And* some Dilaudid."

The offer barely left his lips before Ralph jumped on it. "Deal."

The desperation was almost pathetic. Junkies had no loyalty. They followed whoever gave them their next hit.

David smiled, slipping the knife onto a bale of hay. "Good man," he murmured. He stepped closer, stretching his hands out. "Let's seal it with a good old-fashioned handshake."

Ralph visibly relaxed, exhaling in relief.

David moved swiftly, grabbing the man's head in both hands.

One sharp yank—

A sickening *pop*.

Ralph's body went limp instantly, dead before he hit the floor.

He never saw it coming.

David exhaled slowly, rolling his shoulders as he slung the body over one shoulder. The Mississippi would do the rest.

He carried Ralph's corpse through the snow, down to the riverbank. The moon cast a glowing reflection over the dark, slow churn of the water, turning it into a silver ribbon cutting through the city. It hadn't frozen over yet. That was luck. David didn't hesitate to toss the body in.

The current grabbed hold, pulling Ralph downstream and carrying him toward the unknown. David watched until the corpse disappeared.

No remorse. No hesitation.

Ralph had been a problem. A loose end.

David had neutralized him.

Another body added to the tally. Another name lost to the river. But it had been for a good cause: protecting George and the fledgling life they were carving out.

Now, David knew the truth.

Elliot wasn't just a problem. He was a threat.

George's stepbrother or not, he needed to be put down.

Chapter Eleven

THE HOUSE SMELLED LIKE pine, roasted goose, and the buttery warmth of mashed potatoes.

A hand-cranked record player crackled softly in the background, filling the room with the familiar notes of an old Christmas song. But the original lyrics had been abandoned— Pedro and Melody had taken it upon themselves to 'improve' upon the classics, belting out off-key, ridiculous renditions while they decorated the table with sprigs of holly and candles.

George checked the goose, leaning over the oven, the heat warming her face as she basted it in its own golden juices. It had to be perfect. This was the first Christmas she and Ana had truly celebrated in four years. Not just endured and passed in silence but actually celebrated.

Ana was near the counter, glaring at her green bean casserole like it had personally offended her, muttering profanities under her breath.

David— who had somehow been convinced to wear an argyle sweater Ana had scavenged from God knows where— set the table with a level of precision that suggested he took the task as seriously as battlefield strategy.

It was domestic bliss.

The kind of warmth and normalcy that had once been taken for granted.

The kind that felt like it belonged in an old Norman Rockwell painting, except messier and louder. Real.

They weren't just surviving. They were *living*.

For all the suffering and cruelty that still gnawed at the world outside, they had kept each other from being swallowed by it.

They were a family. An awkward, ungainly, patchwork family.

And as much as George tried not to dwell on it, some part of her ached at the realization. She'd spent so long making herself hard. Keeping people at arm's length, believing that attachment only made it hurt more when you inevitably lost them.

And yet, here she was.

Here they all were.

David came up behind her, wrapping his arms around her waist, the heat of his body warm against her back.

Since the night she'd broken down after losing Kate, since the moment she'd *let* herself unravel in his arms, she had slowly allowed herself to *soften*. To accept that maybe, *just maybe*, it was okay to let someone in.

To allow herself to be *loved*.

And worse, far worse, she had begun to accept the thing she'd been avoiding the most.

She had fallen for him.

She hadn't said the words yet. But they were there.

David kissed the side of her neck, his lips warm against her chilled skin. "That goose smells good, Miss Harris. And so do you."

George smirked. "Can't tell if you're thinking with your stomach or your head."

"A little of both," he mused, his voice dropping into something low and teasing. "If by head, you're referring to—"

"Enough, you two," Ana interrupted, pulling the goose from the oven with exaggerated exasperation. "Some of us still have an appetite and would like to keep it that way."

David chuckled, giving George's ass a playful pat before stepping back with a mock salute. "As the lady commands."

Ana arched a brow. "Make yourself useful and carve the *roast beast*."

David obeyed, rolling up his sleeves with a theatrical flourish before grabbing a knife and carving fork. "Yes, ma'am."

They all gathered around the table, plates piled high with food. George and Ana sat at opposite ends— unspoken tradition placing them there— while Pedro sat to George's left, Melody to Ana's right, and David on George's other side.

It was warm, *too* warm, the fire crackling in the hearth, candlelight flickering across their plates.

And under the table, something unexpected happened.

David's foot nudged against hers.

At first, George thought it was an accident, but then he did it again. A slow, teasing brush of his ankle against hers, sending a ripple of something unsteady through her chest.

She froze for half a second, thrown off by how utterly silly it was. She'd never played footsie with anyone before.

It was ridiculous.

Childish.

And yet...

She nudged him back, a smirk tugging at the corner of her mouth as she met his gaze.

David's eyes gleamed with something playful, something warm.

And just like that, George found herself smiling— truly, genuinely smiling— as laughter and conversation swirled around them, wrapping around the table like the final ribbon on a well-worn gift.

For the first time in a long, *long* time, Christmas felt like Christmas again.

Melody cleared her throat and rose from her seat, digging into her pocket with an uncharacteristic seriousness. "I think now's a good time to do this, since we're all... friends."

Conversation halted.

Even Ana, usually quick with a quip, glanced up in mild amusement. The only one who didn't seem to care was Pedro, who continued shoveling food into his mouth with the kind of reckless abandon only a teenage boy could manage.

Then Melody pulled her hand from her pocket, revealing a small black ring box.

The amusement on Ana's face vanished.

The room held its breath as Melody dropped to one knee.

"Anabelle Hilk," Melody said, voice steady, sure, "I love you. I've loved you from the first time you told me to shut my mouth, and I think you're the most beautiful woman in the world. Will you marry me?"

A stunned silence followed.

Pedro finally stopped eating, his fork frozen halfway to his mouth, eyes wide as a deer caught in headlights.

Ana's expression had shifted from shock to something close to horror. Before anyone could process what was happening, she shot up from her seat and bolted from the room, disappearing out the front door into the freezing night.

The joyful warmth of the evening cracked apart like thin ice in early spring.

Melody's smile faltered as she rose to her feet, looking around the room in confusion. "What... what just happened?"

George knew.

God, she knew.

Melody had done nothing wrong. It should have been a happy moment. But it wasn't.

The past had its claws in them all, no matter how often they tried to forget it. Some nights, it was easy to pretend the world before hadn't existed. That this was all there ever had been: this house, this family they'd built, this *life*.

But it had existed.

And for Ana, it had ended in blood and grief.

George swallowed hard, placed her napkin on the table, and followed Ana outside.

The cold hit her instantly.

She'd rushed out without a coat, without thinking, her breath curling in thick white clouds around her face. The snow-covered porch groaned under her weight as she stepped outside.

Ana was there, standing at the edge of the railing, staring out at the ruins of the distant city skyline beyond the river. Her arms were wrapped around herself, her breath coming in slow, heavy exhales.

George didn't speak at first. She just stood beside her, rubbing her arms for warmth, waiting.

"I'm not a lesbian," Ana finally said, her voice barely above a whisper.

George glanced at her, unsure of what to say. "I know."

"I'm not bisexual either."

"I know."

What else *could* she say? Ana had spent years being one thing and then everything changed and maybe she was struggling to define something that didn't need to be defined. It was inconsequential, but in the moment, maybe that was what she was grasping at.

Maybe it was guilt.

And yet, there was Melody. Melody Savage, who burned bright and loud, who filled a room with energy and life and color in a way none of them could anymore.

Ana turned, her blue eyes piercing in the moonlight. "It's just her."

George nodded. "And you love her?"

Ana hesitated. Then, slowly, she nodded.

But there was fear there.

Fear and something else. Something haunted.

She turned her gaze back toward the house, watching through the window as Melody twisted the ring in her fingers, lips pressed together in a tight line, waiting for Ana to come back inside.

"I loved John once," Ana whispered.

And there it was.

The *ghost*.

The one neither of them ever spoke of, but both lived with every single day. It was the thing that bound them together— tighter than friendship, tighter than sisterhood.

The thing George could *never* make up for, no matter how much time passed.

Because Ana had lost more than George could ever fathom, and it was her fault.

She could never leave Ana. Not for David, not for anyone. She would never abandon her, not after what she had done.

And Ana knew it.

Ana would *always* know it.

"How could I possibly know if this isn't just a phase?" Ana asked, voice barely above the wind. "How do I know that I won't miss the touch of a man?"

George sighed. "Do you love her?"

"Of course I love her, but is it enough?" Ana stepped back toward the railing. "What if I wake up one day and regret it?"

George exhaled, frustration curling at the edges of her words. "What do you want more?"

Ana closed her eyes. Then, as if she had already made up her mind, she spoke. "I know how I can be sure." She turned to face George, her expression unreadable. And then, without hesitation... without shame... she said it. "You could let me have David."

George's stomach twisted. She blinked, sure she had misheard.

But Ana continued, her voice calm, almost practical. "Don't look at me like that, George. It makes sense, doesn't it? I only want him for an hour or two. Just to see."

George's hands clenched into fists.

Ana kept talking. "I know he's clean. I know he's gentle. He'd understand." Ana stepped closer. "Please, George. You owe me this."

Something inside George broke.

The pity, the sorrow, the guilt— it shattered, sharp and jagged as ice. This was the one thing she'd managed to carve out for herself. Her own bit of happiness in an otherwise mirthless existence. "He's *mine*," George said, her voice low and dangerous.

Ana didn't flinch.

"I'm not keeping him," she said smoothly. "He'll return to you. I promise."

"No."

"George, if it weren't for you, we wouldn't be having this conversation. I'd be married. Ella would be here, making macaroni art for me instead of—"

"Don't." George's voice cracked.

But Ana didn't stop.

"You made the choice for me." Ana's voice wavered. "You talked me into staying. If I had left, I could have saved her."

"You think she would have survived this world?" George snapped. "You think Ella would have lived to see five? Or ten? The infant mortality—"

"Stop it!" Ana's voice rose, sharp as a blade. "Stop with the facts. Stop justifying it. If I marry Melody, then I will never be a mother again. You don't understand."

George took a step forward, her body trembling. "You know I wanted to be a mom." Her voice was hoarse. "It just never happened for me. And now? Now, I wouldn't risk it."

"Then I don't see the problem." Ana's voice softened. "Let me have one night with him. Then I'll marry Melody. And in nine months, I might have a child again."

"If you ever valued our friendship, don't ask this of me."

Ana's eyes gleamed with something cold, calculating. "It's not like I'm asking you to give him up forever."

It was hard to breathe.

George's chest ached with the weight of it all.

Every single day since the world ended, she had lived for Ana. She had kept her safe, fed, alive.

And now—

Ana wanted *this*.

George looked through the window again. Pedro unwrapped his gift, a textbook. His future. David handed him another box. A gun. A promise to teach him how to use it.

There were more people to consider than just herself.

Ana knew it. And that was why Ana knew she had already won.

George swallowed the bile rising in her throat, her entire body numb as she whispered the word. "Fine."

Ana smiled.

She didn't gloat. She didn't celebrate. Ana simply nodded and walked inside.

And as George watched David, *her* David, laugh with Pedro, her heart crumbled.

She should have let Ana die.

"Absolutely not."

David's voice thundered through their bedroom, his boots scuffing the floor as he paced in sharp, angry strides. He moved so much in the same spot, she half expected the wood to wear thin beneath him.

George sat on the edge of the bed, hands clenched together in her lap, spine rigid as she tried to push through the suffocating weight pressing down on her chest. "Keep your voice down," she said, though there was no force behind it. Defeat coated her words like oil—thick and suffocating. "It's what she wants."

David let out a sharp, humorless laugh. "I don't give a shit what she wants." He spun to face her, eyes blazing. "The only woman I plan on fucking is you. The only woman I'd ever want to have a child with is you. If we ever even got to that point."

George flinched.

Her throat tightened as she forced herself to say the words. "I can't have kids."

David stilled.

"I mean—" she exhaled sharply, pressing a hand against her stomach. The memory of Kate was still a fresh wound. "Physically, I can. But I won't risk it. Not in this world. If Ana wants to, she can."

David moved to her, kneeling so he could take her hands in his. "I don't care about kids, George. I care about you. I was just making a point."

She nodded, but her gaze was distant, fixed on something past him, past this moment, past this life.

"I told her I'd talk to you," she admitted, voice barely above a whisper. "I—"

David's fingers tightened around hers. "Please tell me she didn't just snap her fingers and you gave in."

George swallowed. "No." *Not exactly.*

David released her hands and stood, running both palms through his hair in frustration.

"What does it matter?" she asked, voice hollow. "There's more than just you and me to consider here."

He let out a slow, measured breath before sitting beside her, his fingers gentle as they brushed against her cheek. The warmth of his touch should have comforted her. Should have made her feel safe.

Instead, it only made her feel cold.

"We'll find another way," he murmured, pressing his forehead to hers. "You've gotten by this long. Together, we'll get by even further."

Did he even realize how much she feared that every house call, every trip into town, could be the last? That one day, she'd take a step too far, trust the wrong person, and never come back?

Did he see that? Or was her mask, her carefully crafted armor, so impenetrable that *even he* believed she was unshakable?

"Georgianna." His voice was soft, coaxing. "I promise I won't let anything happen to you or Pedro."

Her throat ached. "I'm worried about you too."

David smiled, though it didn't quite reach his eyes. "I'm an old shit-kicker, sweetheart. You can't keep us down. As long as you're okay, I'll be just fine."

George turned away, staring at the floor. At the scuffs his boots had left behind.

"I can't tell her no," she whispered.

David stilled. Then, with slow deliberation, he stood. "Fuck her," he said.

George's head snapped up.

David's expression was cold, unreadable. "Fuck her and your fucking guilt." His voice was razor-sharp now, laced with a fury she hadn't seen before. "There's nothing she could have done. Nothing. She would have wound up buried next to that girl, and you know it. You two are too goddamn co-dependent, anyway."

He turned, pacing again. "Maybe we ought to move on. When spring comes, you and I can leave. Find somewhere new. Somewhere away from her."

George had dreaded this moment.

"I can't," she said. The words came out sharper than she intended. "Everything I have is here. Everything I've worked for."

David stopped, studying her for along, quiet moment. Then, he nodded. "It's not just her, then?"

George shook her head.

David exhaled, the fight draining from his shoulders. "I didn't think so."

He turned and strode toward the door.

"Where are you going?" she asked, a thread of panic curling around her ribs.

David didn't look back. "To have a talk with Ana." He opened the door and shut it behind him.

The sound was final. Curt. Distant.

George sat frozen, staring at the space he'd left behind.

She should've felt relief. Instead, her heart clenched, breaking— just a little— as she realized the damage was already done.

There was a time before him. A time when she didn't know his warmth, his voice, the way he looked at her like she was the only thing keeping him anchored to this world.

She had gotten by.

She had survived.

But God, she was so tired of just getting by.

She wanted more... a life. A future

But instead, she had this.

Ana had demanded a sacrifice, and for the greater good, George had given her David.

He was an offering to the angry gods of loyalty and guilt; a penance for debts that could never be repaid.

Ana would get what she wanted.

And George...

George would be left with the ashes.

She would never forgive Ana for this.

Never.

Far worse was the realization that she would never forgive herself.

As much as she wanted to cast blame, to pin the weight of this on someone else, the truth was bitter and clear.

It had been *her choice*.

It had *always* been her choice.

Ana had only asked what she already knew George would give. And now, she had. The guilt— the suffocating, all-consuming guilt— was gone. This was the price of her *freedom*.

She had taken Ana's happiness, and now, she had given Ana hers.

It was an *even trade*.

And yet...

As she sat there, staring at the closed door, waiting for David to come back— if he ever did— she had never felt so completely and utterly alone.

Chapter Twelve

DAVID STEPPED OUTSIDE, INHALING the crisp night air as if it could cleanse his mind of the conversation that had unraveled everything. The cold bit through his coat, but he welcomed it— it was grounding. He pulled on his gloves and headed toward the carriage house he'd converted into a workshop, its low-burning heater barely keeping the space tolerable. He stripped off a glove, turned the dial to raise the heat, and fed more wood into the furnace. Then, shoving both gloves into his pocket, he returned to the workbench, gripping a length of wood and sanding it with a force that betrayed his inner turmoil.

Work would be his escape. He needed to forget, to bury the sickening weight in his chest. How could Ana even ask such a thing? And worse, what had she said to George to make her agree?

The faintest hint of perfume curled through the air, cutting through the scent of sawdust and woodsmoke. He stiffened.

Ana stood in the doorway, her bulky coat swallowing her frame, boots laced over bare legs. The only other thing she wore was a nightgown— delicate and thin— entirely useless against the cold. In her hands, she held two glasses of whiskey, nearly brimming.

"I thought you might need warming up," she said, offering one to him.

David took the glass but set it down untouched. He picked up the sandpaper again, resuming his work.

"George must've spoken to you," Ana mused, leaning against the wall. "It can't be that distasteful."

"It's disgusting." He didn't look up. "You don't want to know what I think of you right now."

She sighed, a half-laugh in her breath. "It's not like I even want you that much. You're not really my type."

He stopped sanding, the wood trembling beneath his grip. "Then why ask her? Not that it was hers to give."

Ana pushed off the wall, stepping closer. The workbench between them was the only barrier left. In the dim light, he could make out the sad, twisted smile curving her lips. "I want to start over."

"This isn't a game, Ana. You don't just start over."

"She's never going to give you a baby."

David shrugged. "There are more important things in life. Plenty of orphans out there if *we* decide."

Ana pouted, but he remained unmoved. "She gave her permission." There was something calculated in her tone, something off. David studied her, trying to peel away the layers of deceit. Ana was beautiful, cunning, and plenty of men would have jumped at the chance to be with her. So why him?

"I'm not doing it," he said, voice steady. "I don't care what you said to her to make her agree. I'm not doing it."

Ana shook her head slowly. "I knew she loved you, but I didn't realize how in love with her you were."

It hit him then. This wasn't about longing or even desperation. It was revenge. Ana wanted to punish George, and George, shackled by guilt, would allow it. Their relationship had been splintered for years. What remained was a fragile, bitter alliance, held together by necessity.

He had been blind not to see it.

"I wanted to call you heinous," David murmured. "I wanted to tear you apart for your audacity, but now I get it."

Ana downed the whiskey in a single gulp. "Get what?"

"You hate her."

"Don't be absurd."

"I'm not." He leaned in, voice quiet but cutting. "You must have loved her once, because only love can turn into something this venomous."

Her hands curled into fists. "I don't hate her," she bit out.

"Then why do this? Why me?"

"Because you're available."

"There are other men. You chose me to make her suffer." David leaned across the table, their faces inches apart. "You want her to doubt what we have. To wake up every morning wondering if I see you when I look at her. You want to rip away whatever security she has left."

Ana flinched, unshed tears glistening in her blue eyes. The mask cracked. People could endure being hated, but being seen for who they truly were? That was unbearable.

Her hand struck him hard across the face. He barely moved.

"If you don't want to fuck me, all you have to do is say so." Her voice wavered.

"I don't want to fuck you."

For a moment, she lingered, her expression searching his, as if looking for a sliver of weakness. Then, her shoulders slumped. "Fine. Tell George we're even."

"I'm not telling her shit. That's on you."

She wiped her tears with her sleeve. "Goodnight, David."

"Ana." His voice was ice.

He watched her go, exhaling when she finally disappeared. Relief coursed through him, but it was fleeting. He stepped outside, glancing toward the house. George stood in the window, watching.

David turned away and extinguished the lamps. There was only one thing left to do.

He found George in their bedroom, the tension in the air coiling tight around them. He shut the door. "I didn't do it."

She looked startled, as if the answer had never been guaranteed.

"What'd she say?"

"She wasn't pleased. But I don't care. I love you, George. You're the only one I want."

He crossed the room, sweeping her into his arms, his lips crashing onto hers. His hands tangled in her thick curls, desperation bleeding into every touch. "We need to leave," he murmured. "This house.... it's not a home. It's a casket, and we're suffocating in it."

George trembled in his hold, and for the first time in a long time, he felt hope. Maybe, just maybe, they still had a chance.

"What about Pedro?" she whispered.

"Of course, the kid comes." His lips crashed into hers, raw and urgent. Every muscle in his body strained against the primal instinct to take her right then and there.

Her hands slipped from his hair and roamed down his chest, fingers grazing the fabric of his sweater before tugging at it. He was more than willing to shed the barrier between them. Clothes disappeared in hurried, feverish movements, their bodies pressing together as they tumbled onto the bed. David pinned her beneath him, his mouth trailing over every inch of exposed skin, branding her with his kisses.

She reached for him, her fingers curling around his length, stroking with just enough pressure to send pleasure crackling through him like wildfire. If she was trying to get him hard, she needn't have bothered. Just seeing her like this—eager, willing, waiting—made him rigid with need.

Sex between them had always been easy, a perfect balance of playfulness and intensity. David ran a hand along her slick folds, teasing her, feeling how ready she was. He brought his fingers to his lips, tasting her, savoring the intoxicating essence of her desire. His restraint crumbled. With a single thrust, he buried himself inside her.

George gasped, her fingers digging into his back. She parted her legs wider, inviting him to sink even deeper.

She was warmth and velvet, gripping him, pulling him in with every movement. He withdrew slowly, almost entirely, before slamming back into her with deliberate force. Her moans filled the room, each sound stoking the fire burning in his veins. He gritted his teeth, fighting for control, but she felt too good, too perfect.

He needed release.

With a final, shuddering thrust, he let go, groaning her name as pleasure shattered through him. He collapsed against her, his breath ragged, pressing kisses along her jaw, her lips, anywhere he could reach.

"You're the only woman I want. The only one I need," he murmured against her skin. "I love you, George."

"Good," she whispered, a sleepy smile curving her lips. "Because I'm pretty sure I love you too."

David wrapped his arms around her, pulling her close, inhaling the scent of her. He pressed a kiss to the top of her head, his voice soft yet certain. "I'm going to call you my wife someday."

She hummed against him, pressing a kiss to his wrist. "We'll see."

Within moments, her breathing deepened, the steady rise and fall of her chest signaling sleep. He held her tighter, willing the world outside to disappear, if only for tonight.

Chapter Thirteen

THE FORMER LUXURY HOTEL had once been a haven for elite business travelers visiting the Twin Cities. Now, it was a den of vice, a sanctuary for lust and excess. The wealthy still came, but now they sought the premium methgen and coracanne that Aces Wild produced— or the women who called the place both home and work. The exterior was grimy, its former grandeur eroded by time and neglect, but inside, it was a different world: pristine and well-maintained, a deceptive illusion of civility amidst depravity.

"If you want to get a drink at the bar, you can," George said, her voice calm as she began setting up shop in one of the empty rooms on the tenth floor. The space had been repurposed into something clinical—a stark exam table with stirrups and fresh sheets, a sturdy dresser now serving as a workstation for her tools, and a garbage can tucked in the corner.

David took in the surroundings, his gaze drifting to the bathroom. There was a double sink, a Jacuzzi tub, and a view that had probably been breathtaking once. Now, it was just a bleak glimpse into a ruined world. "This looks like a posh hospital room."

"Aces wanted a private place where he could be examined without an audience," she said. "Eventually, I convinced him to let the girls have monthly health checks too."

David picked up a speculum, turning it over in his hand, frowning. The cold steel gleamed under the dim light, looking more like an archaic torture device than a medical tool.

George gently took it from him, replacing it with another instrument before setting out a bottle of isopropyl alcohol. "Go up to the terrace bar on twelve. Tell them I sent you."

He nodded, glancing at her before stepping toward the door. "I'll see you later. Love you."

"Love you, too."

He never got tired of hearing her say it.

As he made his way to the stairwell, a line of women had already begun forming outside the room. Some looked older than Trixie, others impossibly young. He swore one of them was pregnant. His stomach clenched. He turned away and kept walking, but the weight of the place settled deep in his bones, pressing down like something he couldn't shake.

David climbed the two flights of stairs and followed the hall until he reached a set of double doors with frosted glass inlays. With a push, he stepped into another world. Potted plants sat in the corners, their lush green leaves basking under warm lamplight. Water features designed to resemble flowing rivers flanked the narrow walkway, koi fish lazily gliding beneath the surface. From a record player in the background, Mendelssohn played at a controlled volume, lending an air of cultivated elegance to the space.

A bartender greeted him with a polite smile. "I'm sorry, sir, but this is a private lounge. The bar for guests is on the fifth floor."

"George said to tell you she sent me," David said.

"You must be Mr. Andrews." A deep voice cut through the atmosphere and large man stepped from behind a dividing wall. "Pat, get our guest a drink."

The bartender nodded. "What'll you have, sir? We have a nice two-thousand twelve merlot."

"I'll take a beer, if you have any," David replied.

"Porter, stout, or lager?"

"Porter sounds good."

The bartender poured a dark liquid into a glass and handed it over. David took a sip. It was smooth. But even as the beer settled in his stomach, he couldn't shake the feeling of being watched. Aces Wild studied him with quiet intensity, swirling his wine before taking a measured sip.

"Thanks. You must be Aces Wild," he remarked.

"I am." Aces was more than just a large man. He was broad and built like a statue carved for intimidation. Yet, despite his reputation as one of the most feared men in the city, he exuded an unsettling air of refinement. George had mentioned that Aces had once been a pharmacist and chemist, a man of science before the world crumbled. Now, he manufactured synthetic drugs and ran a tightly controlled empire of vice.

David once asked why Aces hadn't tried to produce lifesaving medications instead. George's answer had been simple: the resources weren't there. Most pharmaceuticals required components that were no longer accessible. But synthetics—dangerous, highly addictive, and very lucrative— were easy to make. People paid well for them.

Aces took another sip of wine, his gaze never leaving David. "*Song of the Gondolier*. One of my favorites." He gestured at the record player.

"I recognized it. I've always been more partial to his violin concertos."

"They have their merits, but this piece..." Aces exhaled, eyes distant. "This song evokes something else. Memories of simpler times. Dancers, ballerinas."

David hadn't expected a man like Aces to appreciate classical music, much less to speak of it with nostalgia. It struck him as an odd contradiction. Then again, so did his daughter, Melody— a girl utterly uninterested in the arts or literature, the opposite of her cultured father.

The record reached its end with a scratch. Aces moved to reset the needle. The room filled with the haunting strains of a Piano Trio in D minor.

"You've been around a lot lately." Aces' voice was casual, but the weight behind it was not. "You live with George, don't you?"

David had the distinct feeling that the man already knew the answer. Still, he replied, "We're sort of a thing."

"Good." Aces took another sip of wine, his expression unreadable. "How much do you know about what she does?"

There was something in his tone that sent a chill through David's spine, a suggestion that her work wasn't as simple as she made it seem. He set his beer down on the granite bar. "She's a nurse. What's there to know?"

Aces smirked, a slow, knowing curve of his lips. "If only that were all."

He walked to a pair of chairs and sat down, setting his wine on the glass table in front of him. He gestured for David to join him.

Reluctantly, David picked up his beer and sat.

Aces continued, "One doesn't get to the top by simply being nice. I knew Georgianna before the world fell apart. We worked together at the U. People liked her. She never seemed like a threat. But Georgianna had a talent. One I always admired. She could get people to talk. To tell her things they should have taken to the grave."

David tensed, gripping his glass a little tighter.

Aces leaned forward slightly, his voice almost amused. "She collects secrets, Mr. Andrews. Not just favors. And if you think you know everything about her, I'd reconsider. Because I can assure you— she knows something about every faction leader in this city."

"Even you?" asked David.

"Except for me. Like I said, I know George." Aces took a sip of his drink but never took his eyes off David. It was almost as if the older man was sizing him up, trying to calculate what his use could be or how much of a threat he was.

David nodded slowly. He understood the value of a well-placed secret. Sometimes, they were worth more than gold. "So, she knows things. Who cares?"

Aces smirked, swirling the wine in his glass. "It's not what she knows, it's what she does with it. There's a reason why George is at the top."

He shrugged. "There are other healers in town."

"And have you ever wondered why people don't go to the others? Why they'd trade their last candle or scrap of bread for her services?"

David hadn't. He'd been too caught up in George, in *them*, to think about anything else. "Why?"

Aces turned slightly in his chair, his gaze shifting to the koi pond beside them. "In the first year, there was a doctor trying to make a name for himself. He wanted to be top dog. George knew him. And she knew something his wife didn't. One day, the good doctor stepped on her toes, so she let it slip. Soon after, he got his hands on peanut butter. His throat closed up. His people called for her because she had the epinephrine. She went. She looked him over, watched him struggle. And then she walked away. The doctor died, and the message was clear— work with her, or don't work at all. After that, everyone fell in line. There isn't a faction leader in this town whose ear she hasn't whispered into. Including me."

David's fingers tightened around his glass. "And you all just listen to her?"

Aces smiled, slow and deliberate. "We give her words very careful consideration."

David swallowed, but his mouth was dry. He took another sip of beer, but it did little to help. "So there's a war coming?"

"Inevitable," Aces said, his voice smooth. "They'll all come for her. Even if she won't admit she's the king, or queen, however you want to see it. That idiot brother of hers is only stoking the flames of resentment to form an alliance, however temporary."

David frowned. The woman he thought he knew— the healer, the survivor— was something else entirely. He'd seen her as strong, but fragile in her own way. Capable, but compassionate. But if Aces was telling the truth, George wasn't just capable. She was dangerous. Just as dangerous as those coming for her.

"And if they succeed?" he asked.

Aces chuckled. "They won't all be in charge. They'll turn on each other the moment she's gone."

David exhaled sharply. "And you?"

"I'll do what I always do. I'll wait. Let them burn each other out. Then, whoever's left standing is either an ally— or someone I need to remove." Aces lifted his empty wine glass, and within moments, someone refilled it. "Would you like another beer, David?"

A woman changed the music. Mozart's Requiem in D Minor filled the room, an ominous backdrop to the conversation. Aces took a sip, his head tilting slightly. "Absolutely beautiful, don't you think?"

David glanced at the fresh beer that had appeared in front of him. He hadn't even noticed the bartender return. His thoughts were elsewhere. George. He had put her on a pedestal, seen her as an angel, but the truth was something else. Maybe before the world ended, she had been that person. But now? Now, she thrived. Now, she survived. And maybe she'd been manipulating him all along.

He pushed the thought away. No. He knew her. He knew her in ways no one else did. George would only do what was necessary.

Still, a terrible thought took root in his mind.

They were the same.

The ride back to the house was unbearable. The wind was sharp, biting at his skin, but it wasn't the cold that unsettled him— it was the woman holding onto him, her arms wrapped around his waist as they rode. Even with her body against his, he couldn't get warm. Not when he wasn't sure who she really was.

When they arrived, George went inside while he lingered to tend the horse. Ana stepped out of the chicken pen, a basket of eggs in her hands. They hadn't spoken much since that night. Since her offer. She didn't look at him as she passed.

Now or never.

"Ana, wait." He put the bucket of feed down.

She hesitated at the door. "What?"

"I need to ask you something."

She turned, leaning against the frame. "What? You want to accuse me of hating my best friend again?"

He shook his head. "Aces told me something. I need to know if it's true."

"What?"

"Did George kill someone?"

Ana studied him for a long moment. "You mean the doctor?"

His stomach clenched. "Yes."

A slow, knowing smile spread across her lips. "She didn't kill him. She just let him die. He was screwing around on his wife. His mistress wanted revenge. He was a threat... to George... to us. He wanted control of the clinic and the house. He wasn't even a good doctor, just a guy who relied on fancy equipment that doesn't exist anymore." She exhaled, watching him closely. "I'll say this about George— she always does what needs to be done."

David said nothing. His angel of mercy was a sinner, just like him.

Ana left him standing there. He had questions, but none of them mattered now. He only had one that did: could he live with the truth?

George came out to the barn. She smiled and hugged him, but he was too lost in thought to relax.

"What's wrong?" she asked.

He shook his head. He had admired her strength. So why did it unnerve him now?

David brushed a hand against her cheek. "Nothing. Just thinking about the supplies. We'll need to plant wheat in the spring."

Another lie. But if he asked about her past, she might ask about his. And that door was one he would never open.

He could live with her secrets. Because she could never live with his.

"Let's go inside before you freeze, darling." He kissed her forehead and took her hand. "I'm thinking I'd like a hot bath."

"I'll run you one," she offered.

"Only if you promise to join me."

She smiled. "Mr. Andrews, I believe I can oblige."

He had to believe it was real. Because if it wasn't, then neither was he.

Chapter Fourteen

IT WAS THE WEE hours of the morning when George rose. Her stomach lurched violently, and she barely made it to the bathroom before she heaved into the toilet, emptying her gut of dinner, lunch, and seemingly every meal she'd ingested over the last twenty-four hours. She gripped the cold porcelain, her fingers trembling.

Oh no.

Kneeling on the chilled tile, she willed herself to breathe, but it wasn't just sickness making her lightheaded. For nearly two and a half months, she had convinced herself it was stress. That was why she'd skipped her cycle. That was why she was exhausted, why her body felt off-kilter. But stress didn't make you sick at midnight.

No...no...no.

The thing that should have once filled her with joy now pressed down on her like a crushing weight. A baby wasn't a gift. It was a death sentence. She did the math in her head, calculating her odds of surviving childbirth, and like her foremothers before medical advances, they were low. Sickeningly low.

David had made her careless.

He had made her feel safe, invincible, like the world outside their little cocoon couldn't touch them. He made her giddy enough to forget herself, to forget this was something she could never, ever afford to let happen.

A soft knock startled her.

She looked up, swallowing hard as David filled the doorway, his bare chest illuminated by the dim light of the fire.

"Are you okay?" he asked, his voice thick with sleep.

She forced a weak smile. "Just something I ate."

His brows knitted together. "You look pale."

"Do I?" She touched her face, as if pressing her palm to her skin could somehow erase the evidence.

"Yeah." He crouched beside her, brushing his fingers through her hair, his touch unbearably gentle. He pressed his forehead to hers, testing her temperature. "You don't feel warm. In fact, you're ice cold."

George hesitated, the words hovering on the tip of her tongue. She could tell him now. Say it plainly, rip the bandage off. And then what? Watch his face light up before she crushed it all with, By the way, I'm not having it, because I don't want to die like Kate.

No.

She swallowed back the truth. "I'll be okay. Did I wake you?"

David shook his head. "I was just coming to bed. The sled is nearly done."

A lie.

George stilled.

He hadn't been working on the sled. She had checked. It sat untouched in the garden shed. He hadn't been in the carriage house either. She'd assumed he had gone for a walk, as he sometimes did when his thoughts got too heavy. Her intuition told her he hadn't been walking.

And now he was lying.

"Come on," he said, sliding an arm around her. "Let's get you back to bed. I'll bring you some water."

She nodded and moved to the sink, forcing herself to go through the motions. She made a paste out of baking soda, scrubbing the taste of sickness from her mouth with the foul, gritty mixture. She didn't want to think about David's lie. She didn't want to think about anything at all.

David returned, setting a glass of water on the nightstand. "Still okay?"

She nodded.

"I'll throw another log on the fire," he said, his voice casual. "I'll be happy when the thaw finishes. Winter's been here long enough."

George sipped the water, letting it settle heavy in her stomach. She wanted to ask him where he'd been. Wanted to press him, demand the truth. But what good would it do? She had her own secrets.

In the morning, she would find Ana. They weren't on good terms, but that didn't matter now. She needed her. There was no way George could conduct her own pelvic exam, and if Ana confirmed the pregnancy, they would discuss options.

She already knew what she would do.

When she crawled back into bed, the fire burned brightly, and her side of the bed had been remade, the sheets neatly turned down. David, ever attentive, tucked another blanket over her, ensuring she was warm enough.

He was always so sweet... so considerate.

Maybe he really had just been out walking. Maybe he hadn't wanted to worry her, knowing she'd nag him about frostbite. Maybe she was overthinking everything.

Maybe.

"I love you," she murmured, voice barely above a breath.

David smiled, stroking her hair in that slow, careful way that always made her chest ache. "I love you too, Sweetheart. Now let's try and get some sleep."

George curled against him, his warmth seeping into her skin. He spooned her, his presence steady, familiar. For just a fragile, wavering second, she reconsidered.

Ana covered George up once more and went to the bathroom to wash her hands. When she returned, her voice was soft, almost reluctant. "You're pregnant, all right," she said. "I'm sorry."

George sat up slowly, the blanket pulled tight around her shoulders like armor. "It's not your fault."

"Not this, though it isn't ideal. I'm sorry about the whole David thing." Ana's hands fidgeted at her sides, a rare show of unease. "I've been thinking about it, and it was wrong of me to ask you. I'm so sorry, George."

George curled into herself, pressing her knees against her chest. She didn't want to rehash that. "Let's not talk about it anymore." It was done. Over with. As far as she was concerned, they were even. Maybe they could still be friends.

Ana hesitated, then sat next to her on the bed. "So, what do you want to do?"

"You know what I have to do."

Ana exhaled through her nose, then wrapped her arms around George and held her close. "You're still early in the first trimester. It'll be easy to induce a miscarriage. You might have to take two rounds of Misoprostol, but it should clear without dilation and curettage."

George nodded, numb, even as her heart thudded against her ribs. "Do we have any left?"

"Last two doses," Ana murmured, pulling away. "We're going to have to start giving the working girls herbal remedies instead."

Her stomach clenched, and for a moment, she thought she'd be sick again. She knew the side effects. The cramps. The blood. The pain. It didn't matter. Her life was worth more than this. People needed her. At least, she had to believe that.

Ana got up and went to the locked cabinet just outside the door. The soft rustle of pill cards and bottles filled the silence until she returned with a blister pack of eight small pills. "Do you know when you'll do it?"

George took the package, turning it over in her hands. "Probably when David and Pedro go on the ice fishing trip."

Ana frowned. "Melody and I are going to her father's to get married that weekend. I can stay if you want."

George shook her head. "I want you to go."

"You'll be alone."

"I need to be alone." Her fingers curled around the package like a lifeline. "I have to do this alone."

Ana studied her, her jaw tight. She didn't argue. Didn't push... just quietly handed George two Tylenols. "You'll need these for the pain. I don't want to give you anything stronger if you're going to be here by yourself."

George gave a bitter smirk. "It's not like I don't know where to find the stronger stuff. But I'd rather not pass out on painkillers."

Ana snorted. "Yeah, well, you get all the side effects anyway. Right down to not being able to shit."

"Or hold down food," George added dryly.

The laughter was short-lived, but it softened the edges of the moment. They held hands.

"You sure you don't want me to stay?" Ana asked again, quieter this time.

George squeezed her fingers once before letting go. "No. I want you to go and be happy with your fiancée. I'm sorry I'll have to miss your wedding."

Ana smiled, but her eyes were glassy. "It's okay. Besides, you'd just be bored and worried about who's watching the clinic." She stood and stretched. "I'm making dinner. Thinking stew."

"It's getting closer to spring," George muttered. "How about something lighter?"

"I'm making stew. If you don't want to eat it, don't." Ana disappeared into the kitchen.

George exhaled sharply and went upstairs. She tucked the pills into the nightstand, pressed between the pages of *The Complete Works of Edgar Allan Poe*. Fitting.

A creak of the door interrupted her.

She snapped the drawer shut just as Pedro peeked inside. "David says to ask if it's okay to use the wagon when we go hunting. Might also hunt while we're out."

"Yeah. You're gonna need something to haul back the spoils," she said.

Pedro rolled his eyes. "If we shoot anything at all. I don't know what I can kill with a handgun besides a person."

"We're not shooting people," she said sternly, feeling every bit the matron. "Not unless we have to."

Pedro snorted. "Right."

"I once killed a wolf with a pistol," she added.

He blinked. "You killed a wolf? With a pistol?"

"It was a Ruger, but yes. The trick is good aim."

His eyes widened like a kid hearing a campfire story. George smirked. He wouldn't be so eager when he realized most of his upcoming medical training would involve diagnosing syphilis and pubic lice. Nothing like reality to curb a boy's excitement.

"Go on," she urged. "David's waiting."

Pedro bolted downstairs.

Alone again, George leaned against the door, her hands gripping the frame. She could hear the water running in the kitchen, the occasional clatter of pots as Ana cooked. She could tell David. He deserved to know. He would be gentle. He would try to support her.

But she didn't want support.

At dinner, she forced herself to be present. David's little touches, normally grounding, felt suffocating. He kept glancing at her, sensing something was off but saying nothing. He didn't know. He couldn't know.

After the obligatory cleanup, George went straight to bed. David wasn't far behind, slipping beneath the covers, his warmth pressing against her back. His hand drifted under her shirt, fingers skimming her breast.

Nausea rolled through her. "Not right now, baby," she murmured, prying his hand away.

David kissed her neck, unfazed. "Okay, sweetheart. I guess we'll just play when I get back."

She clenched her jaw and stared at the ceiling.

When the morning of her planned solitude arrived, George felt a sense of hesitation. The house bustled with morning activity. Ana and Melody bickered as they packed last-minute things. Two of Aces men sat in the kitchen, sipping coffee like they had all the time in the world.

George sat on the stairs, coffee in hand, watching it all unfold. This was a good morning. The last good one before she turned it all to shit.

David sat next to her, rubbing his hands together for warmth. "You gonna be all right by yourself?"

She smirked. "I'll be fine. I do know how to take care of myself."

"I left you plenty of bullets," he said, rubbing the back of his neck. "A few I made. Use the other ones first."

She sighed. "I'll be fine, David. You and Pedro go have fun. Do guy things. Kill something. Bring us food." She kissed his cheek.

David grinned, standing. "Can do. Love you."

She smiled back, but it felt hollow. "Love you too."

After everyone left, the silence was unbearable.

She locked the doors. Moved logs into her room. Made the space as warm and comfortable as possible.

Then, she retrieved the pills. Small, insignificant looking.

She turned them over in her palm, staring.

What was she doing? Wasn't this what she wanted?

She closed her eyes.

In another life, she was married to David, working as a nurse practitioner, reading in a sunlit room. Their son— because in her dreams, it was always a son— was giggling as David played with him on the floor.

A life that could never be.

She shoved the pills in her mouth, swallowing them with a gulp of water.

And then panic.

George gagged herself, retching into the toilet.

The pills were gone, out of her body before absorption could even start.

She pressed a hand to her stomach, trembling. The gravity of her actions hit her. Childbirth was a death sentence.

What have I done?

She was going to have to tell David. But how?

Curling into bed, cold and shaking, she stared at the ceiling. For the first time in a long time, she let herself hope.

Chapter Fifteen

PEDRO HEAVED THE LAST deer off the wagon, dragging the carcass into the slaughterhouse. The early spring air was thick with the metallic scent of blood, sharp against the crispness of snow and pine. He wiped his hands on his already-stained apron and turned to David. "Can I start on them?" he asked, slipping the leather strap over his head.

David nodded. "Yeah, go ahead and start skinning the buck. I'm going to let George know we're back."

Normally, she would've been out on the porch to greet them, arms crossed, eyes squinting against the morning sun, murmuring some half-serious complaint about the smell of fresh kill. Unless she was with a patient.

But the porch was empty and the house was quiet, lacking the usual hum that had become the rhythm of their lives.

A nagging feeling started in David's gut.

Something was *off*.

He stepped inside, kicking the slush off his boots as he crossed the threshold. "George?"

No answer.

David took the stairs two at a time.

Their bedroom was dim, the heavy curtains drawn against the daylight. He saw her instantly, still curled beneath the blankets, unmoving. The unease twisted into something darker.

David moved to her side of the bed, resisting the urge to climb in with her, to wrap himself around George and feel the steady rise and fall of her breath against his chest. He was still in his hunting clothes, smelling of sweat and fresh kill. She'd have a fit if he got in bed like this.

He reached out, brushing damp strands of hair from her forehead.

"Baby..." His voice softened. He bent closer.

She didn't stir. A drop of sweat trailed down her temple.

David pressed his palm to her cheek, then to her forehead. *Shit. She's burning up.* "Georgianna, Baby, wake up."

Her lashes fluttered, just barely. Her gaze flickered open, glassy and unfocused. She looked at him, recognition slow to dawn, then shut her eyes again.

His stomach sank.

Something was *wrong*.

He shot into the bathroom, yanking open the cabinets with a force that rattled the hinges. Tylenol. Aspirin. *Something.*

Nothing.

Then his eyes caught on a small, empty pill card, carelessly sitting atop the counter. David grabbed it, turning it over in his fingers.

Misoprostol.

His brain stalled.

George never took anything. Never even kept painkillers unless it was for patient care.

His grip tightened around the empty packet. He slipped it into his pocket, already knowing he'd be looking this up later in one of the drug guides in the house.

Finally he found a travel packet of two ibuprofen tucked in a vanity drawer. David returned to the bed, gently coaxing George up against his chest. Her body was damp with sweat, her breathing shallow. He pressed the pills he'd managed to scavenge against her lips. "Take these, baby," he murmured. "Come on, just a little."

She swallowed sluggishly, barely able to hold up her own weight. He tipped the water glass to her mouth, making her drink.

When she sagged against him, he moved quickly running a cold bath. David wet washcloths in cold water, wringing them out before draping them over her burning skin. He pulled the covers back, letting the chill of the room combat the fever wracking her body.

His mind raced.

Had Elliot done this? Had one of the faction leaders poisoned her?

Had she been targeted... just like she'd arranged for that doctor to be poisoned?

His blood ran cold.

David shoved open the window. "Pedro!"

Pedro emerged from the slaughterhouse, apron splattered in blood and tufts of deer fur. "You okay?" Pedro called, squinting up at him.

"George is sick," David shouted. "I need you to manage on your own for a while."

Pedro's expression changed instantly. "Is she—"

"She'll be fine," David lied. "Just a fever. But I don't want her left alone."

Pedro nodded, wiping his hands against his apron. "Got it."

David shut the window and went back to her.

She needed to cool down. Fast.

Stripping the sweat-soaked fabric from her overheated body, he lifted her into his arms and carried her into the bathroom. Her skin was clammy against his, her breathing still shallow.

David lowered her into the cold bath, wincing as she shivered violently in response. "I know, baby. I know," he whispered, holding her hand above the water. "Just for a little while, okay?"

She didn't respond.

For all his years of casual flings, of moving from one woman to the next in places he barely remembered, it was strange to find himself so wholly devoted to just one.

But he was.

And it wasn't just devotion. It wasn't just some infatuation born of necessity.

He loved her.

And the thought of losing her made something unhinged claw at the edges of his mind.

He forced himself to breathe.

While she soaked, he moved to the bookshelf in their room, pulling out her drug guide. He flipped through the pages, his heart hammering as he found the listing for Misoprostol.

And then he saw it.

Misoprostol. Used for ulcers. *Or pregnancy termination when combined with mifepristone.*

The book slipped from his hands, landing on the floor with a hollow *thud*.

His world tilted.

George had been pregnant.

Not only that. He had been the father.

He counted back. Their nights together. The times they'd been too drunk, too careless to use protection.

It hit him then.

The cold sweat. The way she had trembled against him in bed the other night, ice-cold despite the blankets.

The nausea. The exhaustion.

She had been terrified. And now she was sick because of it.

David clenched his jaw. He forced himself to move, to get her out of the bath, to dry her shivering body and dress her in clean clothes.

Her fever had begun to break. That was good.

It was something.

He tucked her back into bed, brushing damp hair from her face.

Then he heard the front door open.

"We're home!" Ana's voice carried from downstairs.

David was out of the room in an instant. "Ana, get up here *now*," he called down the hall. The urgency in his voice startled even *him*.

Ana rushed up the stairs, eyes scanning his face before shifting to George. Without hesitation, she pressed a hand to her forehead, frowning. Seconds later, she was gone, returning with an IV bag and a line.

David barely registered anything as she set the IV in place.

"How long has she been like this?" Ana asked.

"I don't know. Pedro and I got back from hunting and found her like this."

Ana exhaled through her nose, watching the fluid drip steadily into George's vein. "She's dehydrated, but she'll be fine."

David hesitated.

Should he tell Ana? Should he *ask*?

Or was this something George didn't want *anyone* knowing?

He clenched his fists.

"Thank you," he said finally.

Ana gave him a quiet look. "Don't mention it." She straightened. "Now, you should probably go outside and help Pedro. When Melody and I came in, it looked like he was *mangling* that deer carcass."

David hesitated at the door. "You come get me if anything changes."

"I will." Her hand touched his briefly. Reassuring. Familiar. Like old times.

David nodded, but as he stepped into the hall, his mind was a storm.

He had never cared for anyone like this.

And now, for the first time in his life...

He was afraid.

David didn't go back to help Pedro. He wandered instead, hands shoved deep in his pockets, boots crunching over ice and slush as he let the streets pull him in whatever direction they wanted. The world was quieter now, the air sharp with the kind of cold that threatened to crack skin if you stayed out too long. His feet found their way downtown, past abandoned storefronts and gutted office buildings, past the carcasses of a world that had collapsed in on itself.

And then, like some unspoken gravity had drawn him there, he was standing in front of *The Wild Club*, the former luxury hotel that made up Aces' domain.

David exhaled slowly, watching the fog of his breath dissipate. He didn't know what brought him here. Not really. But he knew it was the right place.

With a deep breath, he stepped inside.

A woman met him in the lobby. A tall blonde, wrapped in a silk robe that did little to hide the sheer lingerie beneath it. She smiled, slow and knowing, her red-painted lips curving into something predatory. "How can I help you?" she purred, her voice a syrupy invitation.

David cleared his throat. "I'd like to see Mr. Wild."

The woman cocked her head, considering him, then slinked closer, draping herself onto his arm. The scent of vanilla and cheap perfume clung to her, thick enough to choke.

"Mr. Wild doesn't see anyone," she murmured, fingers trailing along his forearm, nails just sharp enough to tease. "Not unless he summons them first."

David stiffened. He was not in the mood for whatever game she was playing.

"I... uh..." He hesitated. He had no appointment. No real reason to be here. He was nobody important enough to demand time from Aces.

And yet...

"George Harris sent me."

The woman stilled.

Something in her face changed, just for a second. Then she sighed, stepping away, arms crossing over her chest as she regarded him with something close to disappointment. "You're her man, aren't you?"

He nodded.

"Well, then you're off-limits." She pouted. "I'd hate to have to explain to her why you were in my bed."

David fought the urge to roll his eyes.

The blonde gestured for him to follow, leading him toward a stairwell. He expected it to be like every other stairwell in the city— filthy, rotted, filled with the remnants of overdoses and forgotten bodies. But it was clean. Spotless. Not a junkie or corpse in sight. Almost like Aces had a full janitorial staff, keeping even the hidden corners of his empire pristine.

She stopped on the ninth floor, leading him down a hallway to a door without a number. Knocking once, she announced, "I have George's man here to see you. Are you available?"

Aces' voice rumbled through the door. "Let him in."

The blonde stepped aside, and David entered.

Aces sat in a large leather chair by the fire, a book resting open in his lap. A naked redhead was on her knees before him, his cock in her mouth.

David didn't react.

It was a power play. A test.

Aces was watching him, measuring his response. If David looked away, it would show weakness. If he lingered, it would mark him as a man with appetites... a man Aces could leverage, manipulate.

Instead, David walked to the chair opposite Aces, took a seat, and met his eyes. "Thank you for seeing me."

Aces smirked, lazily running his fingers through the redhead's hair. "My pleasure. Would you like a girl? On the house."

"No thanks."

Aces pushed the woman's head down, making her gag. He groaned as he finished, then zipped his pants. "Leave us," he ordered, voice cool.

The redhead and the blonde left, shutting the door behind them.

Aces leaned back, adjusting himself in his chair. "You ever read *Interview with a Vampire*?" He held up the book.

David shook his head. "Saw the movie."

Aces chuckled. "Even though Anne Rice wrote the screenplay, it doesn't do the book justice."

"Movie adaptations rarely do."

"*Did*," Aces corrected. "There's no movie industry anymore. Remember?" He laughed, a low, amused sound. "Ah, the things we miss. So..." he set the book aside, "To what do I owe the pleasure of your company?"

David sighed. He hadn't meant to. It just sort of... came out. The weight of everything pressing down on his chest, curling around his ribs like a vice.

In another life, he would've married George. The child she had just gotten rid of— it never would have been a question. He would've given up the intelligence game, settled into a normal life. A house. Family vacations. Kids' soccer games on Saturday mornings. Dinners at the table, where they would talk about their days like normal people.

But that world was gone.

And the brutal, gut-wrenching truth was that if the world hadn't ended, he never would've met George at all.

He shouldn't regret it.

And yet, the thought of her, alone, making that choice— it fucking gutted him. He didn't blame her, but she shouldn't have been alone. He should've been with her.

He turned away from the fire, looking Aces in the eye. "I've done something terrible."

Aces tilted his head, watching him closely. "What did you do?"

"I killed someone."

Aces snorted. "Look around, David. There's a whole lot of that going around."

"I killed a man who didn't stand a chance." David's voice was hoarse. "I killed him because I saw him as a threat to my family."

It hit him then like a punch to the ribs.

He had a family.

Pedro was like a son to him. George... George was his wife in every way that mattered. He would kill for them. Die for them. There wasn't a single part of his soul he wouldn't burn to ash if it meant keeping them safe.

"Who was it?" Aces asked.

David exhaled. "Ralph."

Aces lifted a brow. "Ralph Briggs?" He leaned forward. "He was harmless. Why kill him?"

"He was working for Elliot."

Silence.

Aces pressed his fingertips together, expression unreadable. "So he's making moves now."

David's stomach twisted. "You knew?" His voice dropped to something dark, something dangerous.

Aces shrugged. "I know everything. Thought he was all talk though, riling other people up."

David's jaw clenched. "Why?"

Aces shrugged. "What does it matter? He'd probably say because she let his wife die. But that's not it. That man has been laying the groundwork against her for years. He's just finally found willing ears." Aces gave him an infuriatingly calm look.

David stood abruptly, hands bracing against the desk, trying to ground himself, trying to keep the fury from boiling over.

Aces just watched him, smug. "There's a reason people in this city fear her, David. They don't respect her because she's kind. They respect her because she's dangerous. Because she knows where the bodies are buried. Because she's a necessary evil and is just as calculating as the rest of us. She just makes it seem a whole lot nicer."

David's hands curled into fists.

Aces smirked, pulling out a flask and drinking from it before tossing a folded piece of paper onto the desk. "That's everyone I know who's working with Elliott."

David took it.

He didn't read it. Didn't need to.

He already knew exactly what he was going to do.

Aces grinned, pouring another drink. "So what now?"

David's voice was quiet. Steady. "I'm going to kill every single son of a bitch on this list."

Aces laughed and clapped like a delighted child. "There he is," he crowed. "The real David Andrews."

David crumpled the paper in his hand.

The Mississippi would be full of bodies.

Minneapolis would run red. And he would be the storm that washed it all away.

Chapter Sixteen

GEORGE'S EYES FLUTTERED OPEN. The room was dark, the weight of the fever still clinging to her body like a second skin. The IV line in her arm fed her cool liquid, sending a shiver through her overheated veins. She blinked a few times, her mind trying to piece together where she was— home, safe, in her bed.

The door creaked open, and Ana entered the room, a soft glow from the hallway illuminating her face. Her usual sharp edges were absent, replaced with something softer, almost relieved.

Ana smiled, not the tight-lipped, barely contained tolerance they had been exchanging over the past few weeks, but a genuine, warm smile. "Welcome back, sleepyhead," she said, voice light.

George swallowed, her throat scratchy and raw. "Thanks," she murmured, shifting slightly beneath the blankets. The movement was sluggish, her limbs aching from disuse. "Did I see David earlier, or was that just a fever-induced fantasy?"

Ana moved to the foot of the bed, tugging on a pair of gloves. "You saw him."

Panic snapped George fully awake. "You didn't—"

"No," Ana interrupted, shaking her head. "I didn't tell him."

Relief flooded through her, but it was short-lived. "Where is he now?"

Ana shrugged, checking the IV line before grabbing the solar-powered lamp they reserved for special cases. "He was supposed to help Pedro, but he went for a walk instead. No idea where."

The news made her uneasy. David wasn't the type to disappear when there was work to do.

Ana lit the oil lamp, the dim glow casting soft shadows against the walls. Her tone shifted, turning clinical. "Open your legs. We need to make sure it cleared. You saw the embryonic sac, didn't you?"

George stilled.

She hesitated, her heartbeat drumming painfully against her ribs. The words clotted in her throat, thick and heavy.

Ana glanced up, confused by her silence.

"I didn't do it," George finally admitted, voice barely above a whisper.

Ana's hands froze mid-motion. Her lips parted slightly, but no words came. A rare thing, Ana speechless. Her brows drew together in confusion before her expression shifted, realization dawning like the slow rise of the sun.

"You didn't take the pills?" she asked carefully.

"I took them," George said. "I threw them up."

The admission rang in the silence between them, unspoken truths filling the space like thick smoke.

Ana's eyes widened. "You couldn't go through with it."

George clenched her jaw, looking away. She didn't need Ana's pity or understanding. She didn't need to be told she had made a mistake.

Ana's shock melted into something softer, something George wasn't ready to face.

"You want this baby," Ana said, voice gentle but sure.

"What I want is irrelevant," George snapped, a weak attempt at deflection. "Wanting something doesn't make it any more likely to survive in this world."

But that was a lie. A bold-faced, flimsy lie.

She *did* want this baby. Wanted it with a fierceness that scared her more than the thought of bringing a child into a world that was crumbling at the edges.

Ana watched her closely, letting the words settle before speaking again. "I know you, George. If you truly wanted it gone, you would have done it. No hesitation. You let your heart win out." She paused, then asked the question that had been hanging unspoken in the air. "So, you're going to tell David now, right?"

George swallowed hard, fingers curling into the blanket.

"I will," she said finally. "Eventually."

Ana scoffed. "Eventually?"

"I'm still trying to figure things out," she admitted, voice tight. "He said kids weren't important. That was before he knew I was pregnant. If I tell him now, when I'm already scared out of my damn mind, what if..."

Ana sighed, rubbing a hand down her face. "If you wait too long, he's going to be pissed that you didn't tell him sooner."

George didn't respond.

Ana exhaled, pulling off her gloves and switching off the lamp. "Fine. Your secret, your timeline. But if you have even an ounce of love left for me as a friend, you'll keep my secret too."

"You didn't tell Melody?"

Ana shook her head. "No."

"Good."

They sat in silence for a moment before Ana straightened, regaining her usual no-nonsense demeanor. "You're on bed rest for the next couple of days. Pedro will bring your dinner up."

George gave a lazy salute, exhaustion already pulling her under again. "Aye, aye."

She let her eyes drift shut, listening as Ana's footsteps retreated down the hall.

The weight of a body pressing into the mattress woke her.

The scent of whiskey filled her nose before the warmth of arms wrapped around her.

David.

He was drunk.

His breath was hot against her neck, the scent of liquor clinging to his skin. He buried his face in her shoulder, his grip on her tightening.

"I'm sorry, baby," he slurred, voice thick with something heavier than alcohol. "I love you."

George's throat constricted, tears burning the edges of her vision.

He sounded broken.

What did he have to be sorry for?

Was it just the drinking? Or was it something deeper?

The thought of him carrying some unseen weight, something he wasn't telling her, made her ache in a way she wasn't ready to confront.

She bit her lip, trying to hold back the sob that threatened to escape.

This man, this soldier, this killer—he was supposed to be unshakable. Unbreakable. And yet, here he was, pressing himself against her as if anchoring himself to the only thing that kept him from slipping into the abyss.

She cried silently, desperate not to wake him.

David pulled her closer, his body molding against hers, his quiet breathing lulling her back into the safety of sleep.

Chapter Seventeen

THE BAR WAS LITTLE more than a brothel, soaked in the stench of sweat, booze, and desperation. Sex clung to the air like old smoke, curling around the dim lights and making the room feel smaller, heavier. Cheap liquor kept the joint lively, but David saw it for what it was: a graveyard of the living. The men and women who filled the space were barely people anymore, just shells of flesh looking to forget, to disappear into the haze of indulgence before reality came crashing back in the morning.

David moved through the disease-laden prostitutes and glassy-eyed drunks, stepping over puddles of spilled beer and God-knew-what-else. The whole place reeked of bodies pressed together in ways no one would remember when the sun rose. A woman with needle scars on her arms brushed against him, her too-wide smile revealing the telltale rot of a methgen habit. He ignored her as he pressed further into the den, searching for the reason he was here tonight.

He spotted Roberta Klacker before she saw him. The madam of Drop Dead Sally's was exactly as he remembered;

corpulent, draped in gaudy lace, her peroxide-blonde hair a wiry mess around her round, sweaty face. The years had thickened her, but she still teetered around in heels like a woman half her size, the wobbling of her steps the only thing betraying her age. She flitted from table to table, laughing, collecting debts, making sure her girls and boys kept the customers happy.

She dealt only in gold, silver, and jewels. No bartering, no goods, no bullshit. You had to pay up front for whatever sin you wanted indulged in, and Roberta always got her cut.

When her gaze finally landed on him, she grinned— a slow, syrupy thing that might have fooled weaker men into thinking she was sweet. But David knew better. He had seen the kind of women who built empires out of suffering. The kind who sold flesh with a smile and knew exactly when to press a knife to someone's ribs to collect a debt.

And she was on the list of Elliot's co-conspirators.

She swayed over to his table, pressing her thick hands onto the scarred wood. "Well, well. Ain't you a pretty thing," she purred. "You don't have a drink in front of you. What can I get you, darling?"

David smiled back. He could be charming when he wanted to be. And tonight, charm was a weapon as sharp as any blade. He reached into his pocket and pulled out the small, velvet ring box. He flipped it open, the soft glow of the oil lamps catching the rare blue diamond nestled inside.

Roberta's eyes flickered with greed.

"How about you for the night?" he asked, his gaze sliding over her body like he was genuinely appraising her.

Roberta let out a husky chuckle. The kind that sounded heavy as if she smoke several packs of cigarettes a day for most of her adult life. "That's a mighty fine ring, sweetheart." She reached between her breasts and pulled out a jeweler's loupe, pressing it to her eye as she inspected the diamond. After a long moment, she set it back in the box with a satisfied hum. "That's real nice. But you sure you wouldn't rather spend the night with one of my younger girls? Ain't no need to waste your time on an old woman like me."

David chuckled. "Why would I want a silly girl? My tastes run toward experience. A woman who knows what she's doing." He let his fingers trace the hem of her negligee, pretending not to feel the bile rising in his throat.

Roberta grinned, flattered. She picked up the ring and slipped it between her cleavage. "Follow me, then. We'll oblige."

She led him up a narrow, creaking staircase. The scent of sweat and cheap perfume thickened in the air, mingling with the underlying stink of decay. Curtains lined the attic space, sectioning off crypts where the prostitutes entertained their guests. David expected her to pull him into one, which would have complicated things. Too many witnesses. Too many risks.

Instead, she led him to a second door, pushing it open to reveal a private bedroom. It was small, but luxurious compared to the rest of the establishment. Silken drapes covered the walls, casting the room in warm, muted light. A four-poster bed took up most of the space, the sheets rumpled from earlier business.

Roberta shut the door behind him and lit an oil lamp, turning back with a slow, knowing smile. "I thought this would be more to your liking."

David unbuttoned the top of his shirt, letting his hands brush against the wire in his pocket. It was still there, right where he needed it.

He sat on the edge of the bed, casual. "I heard you were a hell of a dancer back in the day," he said, his voice smooth as honey. "I'd like to see that for myself."

Roberta preened at the compliment. "You really do like 'em with experience," she teased, swaying her hips.

"Give me a slow strip," he said, stretching back against the pillows.

She chuckled and moved to the record player, dropping the needle on an old burlesque album. The music warbled to life, sultry and slow.

As she started to move— rolling her hips, running her hands over her body, peeling the lace from her arms— David kept his expression neutral. He watched, but not with lust. His mind was elsewhere, already playing out the next steps. He had seen men like Elliott build power before, and they were all the same. They relied on others to be strong for them. They whispered in the dark, sent others to do their dirty work. Taking away his allies, one by one, would leave him exposed. And then David would cut the bastard down.

Roberta let her negligee fall to the floor, stepping out of it with a slow, deliberate sway. "Why don't you show me what you're working with, sweetie?" she purred.

David undid his belt. "Why don't you get on your knees?"

She licked her lips and obeyed, settling between his legs with practiced ease.

He stood, stepping behind her.

"Did you always do this?" he asked, pulling the guide wire from his pocket.

"I used to be an investment banker," she said with a smirk.

David placed a firm hand on her head. "Stay just as you are," he murmured. "I'm appraising my investment."

Before she could react, he wrapped the wire around her thick neck and pulled.

The shock barely had time to register before the fight began. She thrashed, clawing at his gloved hands, her breath coming in desperate, choking gasps. Her heavy body jerked, trying to buck him off, but David knew how to kill. He used her weight against her, pulling the noose tighter, cutting off her air supply. Her heels scraped against the wooden floor, her fingers clutching at nothing, until finally stillness.

Just to be sure, he pulled out the knife strapped to his back and slit her throat. Blood gushed from the wound, spilling onto the floor in thick, hot rivulets.

David grabbed the ring from her lifeless chest.

He couldn't leave the way he came. That'd be too obvious. He dragged her body to a closet and stuffed her inside. It would be morning before anyone noticed she hadn't finished with her John. For all they knew, he had bought her for the night.

Then, without hesitation, he climbed out the window onto the icy rooftop.

The rain had started, making the shingles slick beneath his boots. He moved carefully, gripping onto the bricks for balance, but the ice was too thin, too treacherous. His foot slipped.

He tumbled.

At the last second, his fingers caught the gutter, jerking his body to a sudden halt. Pain lanced through his shoulders, but he held on, swinging himself toward the shed roof below. He landed hard, rolling onto his side. He took a deep breath.

Then he climbed down, boots crunching against the wet pavement.

David looked back up at the window, at the dark space where she lay cooling in the closet.

Elliot would know soon enough.

And when he did, he'd realize something far worse than a mere warning.

Someone was coming for him.

And he wouldn't see it coming.

Unfamiliar masculine laughter carried down the hall as David made his way up the stairs. It was a deep unsettling sound that made his hair stand on end.

David quickened his pace, his instincts tightening like a vice around his ribs. He reached their bedroom door and shoved it open.

Standing over George was *him*.

Elliot.

David recognized the man's broad shoulders, the sharp lines of his face half-obscured by the dim glow of the oil lamp. For a split second, raw fury gripped him, burning hot and fast through his veins. His fingers twitched toward the iron stoker by the fireplace. It would be easy to swing— to hear the crunch of bone, to watch Elliot drop in a lifeless heap at his feet.

It wasn't time.

Not yet.

David forced himself to ease his grip, letting his hand fall away from the stoker as both George and Elliot turned to face him.

"David," George greeted him, her voice laced with something soft, almost amused.

The anger didn't leave him. He didn't smile. "What's he doing here?"

"I heard my sister was sick." Elliot's voice was calm, even pleasant. A fucking lie wrapped in silk. "I came to check on her."

David didn't move from the doorway. His body was taut, ready, waiting for an excuse to strike.

"I've already lost my wife," Elliot continued. "I can't bear the thought of burying my sister too."

Bullshit.

David said nothing.

"He's been telling me about a school opening," George said, filling the silence. "An honest-to-goodness school."

David exhaled, slow and measured. "It'd be good for the kids. They should have some time to just be kids."

"That's exactly what I was saying," Elliot agreed smoothly.

David still didn't look at him. He stepped forward, pressing a kiss to George's forehead, his lips lingering against her warm skin as his fingers found hers.

Elliot watched them.

David didn't fucking care.

Elliot cleared his throat and shifted back toward the door. "Anyway, I better get going. Abigail will be home soon."

George reached for his hand, giving it a gentle squeeze. "Elliott, you never told me how you were holding up. I'm so sorry about—"

"I'll be all right," Elliott cut in. "You warned me. You did your best." He patted her hand. A gesture meant to seem warm, but to David, it looked rehearsed. A move played for the audience.

George gave a small nod. "You get some rest, okay?"

Elliot's eyes flicked toward David. "Take care of my sister."

Then he was gone.

David let out a breath through his nose, waiting until the sound of footsteps faded down the hall before turning back to George. The firelight bathed her in soft gold and deep shadows, making her look almost ethereal, too beautiful for this ruined world. He reached for her hair, stroking the loose strands away from her face.

She wasn't just his anymore. She never really had been. The weight of his sins had transferred to her, pulling her down to his level. He'd dirtied her, tainted her with the same ruthless pragmatism that had once belonged solely to him. But she wasn't afraid of it. She carried it like armor.

He would not forsake her.

When he really thought about it, he *couldn't*.

She was air and light, music and melody. She was everything he had left to live for.

"I missed you today," she murmured.

He smiled. "I missed you too. Do you really think it's a good idea having company here while you're supposed to be on bed rest?"

"Oh, Elliot is hardly company." Her tone was dry. "Besides, you really think I'd let Pedro take care of my patients downstairs alone?"

"No, but—"

"I'm awful at staying in bed," she admitted. "Ana says I can resume normal activities tomorrow."

David leaned forward and kissed her lips. They were soft, warm, still slightly fevered. "Do you want me to read to you?"

She shook her head. "I just want to lie with you and listen to some music."

David got up and went to the Victrola. He ran his fingers over the collection of albums she had salvaged, picking out the one that had always stood out to him.

As *I'll Be Seeing You* began to play, he stretched out beside her, resting his head on her stomach. "Our song," he murmured.

George's fingers threaded through his hair. "And when did you decide this was ours?"

"When I was in a coma," he said simply. "You used to sing this. I thought I was dreaming. Hell, I thought *you* were a dream. And then some asshole decided to rob me blind and beat the hell out of me. Trixie dragged me here, and I met you. The love of my life."

George let out a soft laugh, though there was something wistful beneath it. "And what if I didn't like you at all? What if I'd listened to Ana and sent you on your way?"

"Then I'd be fucked, because I was already infatuated with you."

She was quiet for a moment. Then, softer she said, "I thought you were fairly attractive. It made me nervous because I'd spent so much time avoiding relationships since the blackout."

"What made you change your mind?"

She shrugged slightly. "I just did."

"I'm glad you did." He hesitated, then asked, "Do you regret it?"

A sad smile crossed her lips. She turned her face toward the window. "I regret a lot of things," she admitted. "But not you."

Something about her tone made his chest tighten. He studied her, the way the firelight flickered over her skin, the way her fingers had stilled against his scalp.

"George," he said carefully, "if I ever make you unhappy, if you ever want to leave, promise me you'll tell me."

She turned her gaze back to him, and for the first time in a long time, he saw the gloss of tears in her eyes. "Do you want to leave?"

He sat up, gathering her into his arms. "I don't want to leave. I *never* want to leave." He cupped her face. "I just... I want you to be happy."

"I *am*," she whispered. "Oh, Christ, I am."

But there was something there. A fracture, a hairline crack that even she might not fully see yet.

"It's just you seem off," he said.

"I'm not off."

"You are."

"I've been sick."

David exhaled sharply through his nose. She was lying. And *fuck*, he was so tired of pretending he didn't know it.

He had spent his whole life deciphering people, breaking them down into truths they didn't even know about themselves. But with George? He didn't *want* to break her down. He wanted her to trust him. To *give* him the truth, not make him dig for it.

But he wouldn't push. Not yet.

So instead, he climbed out of bed. "You, mademoiselle, need to get some food in your belly. I'm going to see what Ana whipped up for dinner."

"I'll save you the trouble. It's venison steaks and potatoes."

"I hope you can stomach tough venison."

She smirked. "I'll have to. I'm starving. Vomiting really makes you hungry."

David stopped in his tracks.

She said it so casually. So *offhandedly*.

As if it were just a passing symptom, and not something that confirmed every single suspicion clawing at the back of his skull.

But he didn't say anything.

Not yet.

"Dinner for two, coming right up."

As he turned and headed downstairs, the weight of an unspoken truth settled heavy on his shoulders.

She was lying to him.

Chapter Eighteen

THE WARM SPRING SUN was divine on her face as George worked in the garden, a welcome contrast to the cool mud clinging to her fingers. The last remnants of winter had finally surrendered, the snow melting into the softened earth beneath her nails.

The sound of hurried footsteps yanked her from the peaceful moment. Pedro burst through the back gate, his breath coming in sharp gasps. "You have to come... they found a body down on the river shore."

George froze, trowel halfway buried in the soil. "What? Where?"

"A block from here. Some guy was fishing." He didn't wait for her response. Pedro turned and ran, expecting her to follow.

George plunged her hands into a nearby bucket, wincing at the shock of icy water as she rinsed the dirt away. Then she was moving, her boots pounding against the thawing ground.

By the time she reached the riverbank, a crowd had already gathered. People parted as she pushed through, coming to a stop beside Pedro. Martin, the mortician, knelt next to the body, his blue dungarees darkened with moisture from the mud. He examined the corpse with a detached precision that came from years of handling the dead.

George swallowed against the sickly-sweet stench of decay. Her stomach turned—this pregnancy was making her soft.

"Who is it?" she asked, forcing herself to breathe through her mouth.

Martin didn't look up. "Don't know. But whoever he was, he didn't die easy."

She crouched beside him, her gaze following the tip of his pen as he pointed. "See the elongation in the neck?" Martin pointed to the unnatural way the neck stretched. "It's broken. And there's no rope nearby. Someone dumped him here. Snow must've covered him through the winter. He's been dead for months."

George shifted, angling for a better look. Then she saw the face— or what was left of it— and gasped. "Ralph."

Martin pulled a notepad from his pocket, clicking a pen open. "You got a last name and and age?"

"Briggs. He was forty-two, maybe forty-three. Used to be a cop before the blackout. Then..." She hesitated. "Then he got hooked on methgen."

Martin jotted it down with a disapproving shake of his head. "That stuff's worse than crack. Back in the day, people were smart enough to avoid shit like this. Now they test their limits until it kills them." He sighed and gestured to a couple of teenage boys lingering nearby who must've been his assistants. "He got family?"

"Had a wife, but..." George shrugged. "He never talked about her."

"Cremation, then."

George stepped away, needing space. Who would want to kill Ralph? He was harmless—just another soul lost to the world's collapse.

A horse approached, hooves squelching in the mud. Elliot dismounted, lifting Abigail down before she wriggled free and ran for the crowd. George caught her niece before she got too close, steering her away from the gruesome sight.

"Hey, Abby. How's it going?" She knelt, pulling the girl into a hug.

"It's fine. Daddy was taking me to school, but someone said there was a body. Can I see?"

That was the last thing she needed. Even though the world was harsher now, some part of George wanted to shield Abigail as long as possible, even if it was an inevitability she'd have to learn all the ugliness soon enough. "No, sweetheart. You don't need to see that."

Elliot frowned. "How bad is it?"

George shook her head.

He exhaled. "Abby, why don't you go find some worms for fishing later?"

"Okay," she huffed, trudging away to dig in the dirt.

"Who is it?" Elliot asked once she was out of earshot.

"Ralph."

Elliot's eyes widened with surprise. She wasn't aware he knew the man like that, but with the world being that much smaller, it was nearly impossible to not know those still around.

"Jesus. Was it an accident?" He asked.

"No. Martin says it was clean. Neck snapped. Someone knew what they were doing."

Elliot studied the crowd for a moment, something unreadable passing over his face. "That's... interesting."

George narrowed her eyes. "What's interesting?"

He hesitated. "I was out walking on Christmas Eve. Trying to clear my head. I thought I saw David down by the river. Looked like he was dumping something."

Her stomach twisted. "What are you saying, Elliot?"

"Nothing. Just that maybe he saw something. David wouldn't hurt Ralph. What reason would he have?"

George forced herself to stay neutral, but inside, her thoughts raced.

David had the time. He'd been leaving at night, slipping out when he thought she was asleep. She never questioned it. Maybe she should have.

She took a steadying breath. "I'll ask him."

Elliot's lips pressed into a thin line. "Not like it matters. We don't have a homicide unit. One sheriff and two deputies aren't gonna crack this case."

The conversation ended as Martin's assistants loaded Ralph's body onto a wagon, covering him with a white sheet. Elliot helped Abigail onto his horse and mounted behind her. "Keep me posted."

"I will." She barely heard herself say it.

As Elliot rode off, she turned to Pedro. "Come on. Ana's gonna have a fit if you're late."

They started the trek home, but her mind was elsewhere. How well did she really know David? He never talked about his past. For months, she'd shared her bed with a man she barely understood.

That night, she waited in the workshop, her hands restless over unfinished projects. She was still there when David returned, pulling open the doors with a smile.

"Didn't expect to find you here," he said, unloading scrap metal from the wagon.

"It was mine first," she retorted, her tone lacking any of its usual warmth when she was talking to him.

He stilled, seeming to sense her agitation. Then he continued to work. "What's wrong?"

She watched him for a long moment before speaking. "They found Ralph's body today. Down by the river."

David didn't stop moving. "What happened?"

"Murder. Someone killed him over the winter. Dumped him."

"That's a shame. I know you were fond of him."

She swallowed, then forced the words out. "Someone saw you down by the river around that time. Dumping something."

David turned slowly, arms crossing over his chest. "Yeah?"

"We don't dump our garbage. We burn it."

Silence thickened between them.

"Did you kill Ralph?" Asked George, her voice was steady. Her pulse was not.

He sighed. "Leave it be, George."

"Did you?" She wasn't letting this go.

"Yes," he said, his tone flat as if he were answering a question about the weather.

Her breath left her in a rush. If he had lied, she might have believed him. But he hadn't.

"Why?" Her voice cracked.

David held her gaze. "To protect you. Elliot was using him to spy on you. He's dangerous."

Her heart pounded as he took a step closer. Of course, Elliot was dangerous. He wasn't calculating though. He was more like a firecracker that went off aimlessly and created damage when he exploded. But he also needed George. He wouldn't hurt her, not really.

Her jaw clinched as she grit out, "You don't get to make that choice for me. I want you out of this house."

His face crumpled. "George—"

This had gone on for too long. David clouded her judgement and upset her stability. Sure, her life wasn't perfect and everyday since he'd been around had seemed that much easier, but if he was making moves on her behalf, without consulting her... it was a disruption to her carefully constructed ecosystem.

She held her hand up, gesturing to him to stop. "No. No more lies. I want you gone."

His brow furrowed and there was something akin to pain in his gaze. "You need space. We'll talk about it—"

"No," George said, her voice cold and unnatural. "You're gone."

David nodded, voice hollow. "I'll be gone by morning."

It gutted her that he didn't even fight her edict. That he wasn't fighting to stay with her. But she would never tell him that. Maybe it had all been an illusion.

Rather than ask, George turned and walked away.

George didn't stop until she reached the kitchen. Ana and Pedro barely looked up. She grabbed her equipment bag before heading for the door.

She needed to clear her head before she saw Trixie.

And she needed to shove it all down... like she did everything else.

Chapter Nineteen

WHAT COULD'VE BEEN?

That was the question that haunted David as he packed his meager belongings. The weight of it settled in his chest, gnawing at the edges of his resolve. He picked up the ring, the cold metal pressing into his palm. There would never be another woman he'd want to give it to. It had always been her. Only her.

He set the ring down with deliberate care, as if leaving it behind would hurt less if he was gentle about it. Grabbing his backpack, he took it downstairs to one of the patient rooms, trying to ignore the hollowness stretching inside him.

Ana knocked on the open door, stepping inside without waiting for permission. "I take it you'll be eating in here tonight."

"Yeah." He sat heavily on the bed.

She kept her distance— something she usually did with him. Yet there was no sharpness in her tone, no resentment. Just something softer. "I made you a picnic basket with some basics. There's an abandoned house two streets over. You could set up there instead of heading back to Downtown."

"Thanks," he said, though he barely heard himself. "But that'd be too close for George."

"But not for Pedro. He adores you." Her voice dipped, steady but insistent. "After losing his grandma, he can't afford to lose anyone else."

David blinked at her. Since when did Ana care if he left? She'd made it clear from the start that she didn't want him around, barely tolerated him at best. Now she almost seemed... sad.

He glanced out the window. Once upon a time, streetlights would have bathed Mississippi River Boulevard in their artificial glow. Cars would have sliced through the night, headlights carving paths through the dark. Now, nothing. Just a black void stretching out before him.

"Did George get back yet?" he asked.

Ana shook her head. "I thought she was staying Downtown."

He shot to his feet. No, she wouldn't. George hated Downtown... hated the unpredictability, the risk. She never put herself in harm's way. If she did, it was calculated, necessary. But this? This wasn't her.

"No." His mind raced. "Even if she was staying, she would've told someone."

Ana frowned. "Didn't she tell you? Before your fight?"

"No." He pressed his fingers to his temples, sifting through the conversations they'd had in the past few days. He should know this. He did know this. "She had something planned—something she mentioned— but where?" His pulse quickened. "It's after dark. She didn't take the truck. And she's not back."

"Didn't she take a horse?"

"No. She walked, I'm guessing." His stomach churned. "Ana, something's wrong."

The thought clawed at him, sinking in deep. Someone had finally gotten to her. Killed her.

Ana took a hesitant step forward. "She went to Trixie's."

David's breath came sharp and shallow. He met Ana's eyes, searching for a shred of reassurance and finding none. "You don't think—"

"I don't know," he cut in, voice raw. "I don't know what to think. Maybe she decided to stay somewhere safe, maybe she lost track of time, maybe..."

Maybe she was lying in the street, bleeding out, alone.

"I'm going to find her." He grabbed his coat, pulling it on in one swift motion. "I'm taking the truck. This is worth using the last of our gas."

Ana hesitated. "What if she's still mad at you?"

He didn't give a damn if she was. She could hate him, scream at him, throw whatever she wanted at his head. As long as she was alive to do it.

David bolted downstairs, snatched the truck keys off the counter, and burst outside. The truck groaned as he forced it to start, the gasoline breaking down from age, but by some miracle, it roared to life. He didn't waste a second, slamming his foot down on the gas and barreling toward the seedy remains of Downtown Minneapolis.

He parked near the entrance to the skywalk. A heavy rain turned the streets into a filthy river, garbage swirling at the edges. A dead junkie lay slumped against the door, pale and bloated from decay.

David kicked him once, just to be sure, then pushed the body aside.

He pulled the door open and stepped inside.

The corridors were dark, the stench of piss and rot thick in the air. He flicked the safety off Pedro's gun, his finger firm on the trigger. Anything moved, he'd shoot first, ask later.

A cough.

His head snapped to the right. At the top of the stairs, huddled together, was a woman and a small boy. The kid's tiny shoulders shook, his mother's arms wrapped around him in a futile attempt to keep warm.

David clenched his jaw. He could do nothing for them. There were too many. Too many starving, freezing, barely alive. Social services didn't exist anymore. Hell, civilization barely did.

But he hadn't come here to mourn the broken pieces of the world.

He had come for George.

If she wasn't at Trixie's, he'd check Ace's. If she wasn't there, he'd search the streets. He'd fight off wild dogs, gangs, whatever the hell he had to. He wasn't stopping until he found her.

It was hard to believe this place had once been his home. Back then, he hadn't noticed the despair, hadn't let himself. His world had been survival—finding food, shelter, water. Nothing else mattered.

Then he met George.

She changed him. Showed him another way. The house on River Terrace, the garden, the livestock.... they were more than just survival. They were stability. A future.

George had craved that future, even when she fought against hope. And she had loved him. That was the risk she had taken.

And he would not let that love be the thing that cost her life.

David's grip tightened on the gun. He moved forward, each step a promise.

He would find her.

Or he would die trying.

Lily's Candy

The neon light flickered in Trixie's window, casting warped shadows against the colored curtains. Two figures moved inside, their silhouettes shifting in an intimate dance. One was Trixie. The other? Male. Bigger. Not George.

David exhaled slowly, tucking his gun into the waistband of his jeans. No need to go in shooting—not yet. He was here for answers, not bodies. He pulled open the door.

The scent of sweat, candles, and sex clung to the air like a thick haze. Trixie was perched on the table, naked, legs wrapped tight around a broad-shouldered man's head. She moaned, lips forming a small, delighted *o* as she caught sight of him.

With a languid stretch, she shoved the man away. "Rain check, sugar," she purred. "A very important man just walked in."

The man— brawny, pissed-off, and still hard— grunted. "Come on, Trix. My cock—"

Trixie lobbed a shirt at his face. "Handle it yourself, babe. Come back tomorrow, and I'll make it worth your while. On the house."

David barely glanced at the man as he yanked his shirt back on and shouldered past him, throwing a glare that bounced off David like a pebble against steel. He had no interest in him.

The moment they were alone, Trixie peeled herself off the table, unbothered by her nudity. She moved deliberately, a slow, rolling sway of her hips, the arch of her back purposeful. Once, she had been just a kid to him. Now, she was making damn sure he saw her as something else.

"Where is she, Trixie?" His voice was tight, forced through clenched teeth.

Trixie pouted. "George? She left hours ago," she hummed. "Told me you two weren't together anymore. That right?"

"That's beside the point." His patience was thin, razor-edged. "Where did she go?"

"How should I know?" Trixie stepped closer, dragging her nails lightly down his chest. "You and I should be talking about us, David. I've never been shy about what I want. We could make a real go of it." She tilted her head up, lips brushing his cheek as her fingers tangled in his hair.

He grabbed her wrists, pulling her hands away. "No."

Trixie's face darkened. "She's out of the picture. I don't understand."

A flash of red.

David slammed her against the wall, his forearm pressing into her throat, his other hand punching the wood beside her head. "Where the fuck is she, Trixie?"

Trixie gasped, eyes flickering with real fear. He wasn't cutting off her air, yet. But, the pressure was there... a violent promise.

She darted a glance toward the back room. "He took her out back."

His heart stopped. Then pounded back to life with brutal force.

His blood turned cold. "Who?"

"I don't know," she rasped. "Never seen him before."

David released her, and she gasped, rubbing at her throat. He didn't care.

Gun drawn, he stormed toward the back room.

Trixie's voice followed him. "There are so many things I would've done for you. I could've made you happy."

He stopped at the threshold. Looked back, eyes hollow. "No, you couldn't have."

Then he was gone.

The door was barricaded with furniture. David didn't stop to assess it. He ripped it apart, tossing wood and broken chairs aside with reckless urgency. The stairwell to the alley was slick from rain, but his boots didn't falter.

A shape hunched over a motionless body.

A big man.

David raised the gun. "Get away from her."

The man turned. The glint of a knife in the moonlight drew his attention before he could register anything else. It didn't matter if there were witnesses, it didn't matter if he had people with him. If that body was George's...

He couldn't think that way.

The man moved.

David fired.

The man staggered, but didn't go down. David fired again. Head shot. The body hit the ground with a wet thud.

Then David was kneeling, hands trembling as he turned the woman over.

Blood soaked through the remnants of her clothing, pooling beneath her, too dark, too much. He refused to believe it. Refused to see. Refused to acknowledge.

But his hands moved on their own, brushing damp hair from her face.

"No." The word broke out of him, strangled and desperate. "No, no, no, no."

His cry echoed through the alley, raw and keening like a wounded beast.

David forced himself to focus. She had a pulse. Faint. Almost gone. But there. His vision blurred with fury. This shouldn't have happened.

He scanned her injuries. A deep, slashing wound just above her pubic bone. Blood trickled down her thighs. Her medical bag lay scattered, its contents useless in the filth. Any medicine she may have had ransacked and stolen.

David's stomach twisted. This was his fault. If he had come sooner... if he hadn't wasted time... if he had been the man George needed before tonight...

He shoved the guilt aside. It wouldn't help her now.

David tore off his coat, then his shirt, wrapping it tightly around her pelvis. His bare skin burned as cold rain pelted him, but he didn't feel it. All he felt was the terror of losing her.

He lifted her carefully. She was so small. So fragile.

George whimpered. Or maybe that was in his head, too.

David didn't stop moving.

He crashed into the house, nearly taking the porch stairs with him. Pedro was outside, eyes widening as David emerged from the truck, George bleeding out in his arms.

"Get Ana!" David screamed.

Pedro ran. David carried her inside.

Ana met him at the stairs, her face draining of color. "Oh, God."

"Help her," he rasped, pleaded.

Pedro returned, arms full of medical supplies. Ana was already in motion, checking George's vitals, listening to her chest. David couldn't breathe.

"She's alive," Ana said. Judging from her tone, there was a but. An unmistakable hint of bad news.

David set George down gently. Ana pushed him back.

"Step out," she ordered.

No... no.

He didn't want to leave her. Couldn't. "I'm—"

"David, NOW."

Ana's face brooked no argument.

David broke.

He turned as Pedro found a vein, clear liquid trickling into George's arm as soon as released a small white dial on the tubing.

Ana shut the door.

David stood outside it. He could hear murmurs. It was not enough. He needed to know what was going on. But in that room, he was useless.

His hands curled into fists, blood-streaked and shaking.

He walked, numb, to the bathroom. The sight that greeted him in the bedroom was shocking. It wasn't the first time he'd been covered in grime and blood. Those times had been different though. It hadn't been *her* blood.

He stripped down, the fabric of his shirt sticky with George's cooling blood. David turned on the shower and stepped in, not bothering to wait for the water to warm.

The water ran pink.

David braced against the wall, pounded it. Over and over until his knuckles split, until pain was the only thing keeping him upright.

Then he sank to the floor.

Curled in on himself.

And wept. Each tear stung his eyes, reminding him of his failure.

First the pregnancy. Now this.

He had failed George.

He refused to accept this.

David quickly dressed and went to the offices, tearing through their bookshelves, desperately flipping through old medical textbooks. There had to be something. This couldn't be it.

Pedro appeared in the doorway. "You should sit with her."

David didn't look up. "Leave me alone."

Pedro grabbed a book. Slammed it down. "If you're looking for what I think you are, start here." Then he was gone.

David read. Found a solution.

He ran to the room where Ana was still monitoring George. "I've got it," he said, breathless, clutching the yellowed pages.

Ana looked at him.

"We can transfuse her." His pulse raced. "Kimpton-Brown tube." He pointed to the instructions of the archaic transfusion device next to an old engraving in the textbook.

Ana considered. "It's risky. We don't even have a donor."

"She's dead anyway," Melody murmured.

Ana stared at the pages. Weighing. Calculating.

"I'm O-negative," David added. "The government tested us. Universal donor."

Ana's eyes sharpened. "What did you do?"

"I worked for the CIA."

Ana's lips parted. "Does George know?"

"No."

Too many secrets. Too many regrets.

Ana wiped her face. "We'll need old medical equipment. The medical school has some in display cases."

"I'll go."

Ana hesitated for a moment, then gave a curt nod in ascent.

David met her gaze, steel and desperation in his voice. "If she wakes up, tell her I love her."

Chapter Twenty

THE UNIVERSITY OF MINNESOTA Medical School stood in eerie silence, a monument to the past. A relic of knowledge swallowed by time. Ivy and moss climbed its concrete and steel walls, reclaiming what had once been pristine. The once-manicured lawns were wild now, thick with neglect.

David forced the front doors open with a crowbar, the rusted hinges groaning in protest. He reached into his waistband and pulled out Pedro's handgun, holding it low but ready. The silence inside was oppressive, the kind that made your breath feel too loud. His footfalls echoed across the cracked tile floor, filling the abandoned corridors with hollow sound.

The first lecture hall was a graveyard of decayed backpacks and peeling paint. A projector, still clinging to the ceiling mount by sheer stubbornness, threatened to drop at any moment. The next room was worse. The practice dummies, laid out on rusted gurneys, looked more like cadavers in a horror film than medical teaching tools. Their hollow plastic eyes seemed to watch him as he passed.

David headed upstairs. The halls were even darker, silver moonlight cutting through the grime-streaked windows in broken, pale orbs. He stopped, digging into his messenger bag and pulling out the camp lantern. He lit it, keeping the glow dim. He couldn't afford to lose his night vision— not in a place like this.

Then he heard it.

A whisper. Soft, fleeting, like wind slipping between walls.

For a moment he thought he'd imagined it. But it came again.

David stilled. His pulse hammered in his ears. It wasn't mice. Mice didn't whisper.

He set the lantern down, gun raised, safety off.

He listened.

The sound drifted from behind a lecture hall door.

David wrapped his fingers around the doorknob, tighter than necessary. A deep breath. Then he pushed it open.

Two men looked up from their desks. Their hands, stained with ink, froze over the textbooks they were painstakingly copying by hand, like monks from a forgotten era.

One of them, a bird-faced man with a beak-like nose, adjusted his lantern. His sharp eyes narrowed. "Can I help you?"

David grabbed his lantern and holstered the gun. If these men meant him harm, they wouldn't be staring at him like he had a star stamped on his belly.

"I'm looking for something," he said, stepping down the stairs. "Maybe you've seen it."

The bird-faced man, with wiry gray-haired poking from under his knit cap, snorted. "Well, what is it, boy?"

"You'll have to excuse Dr. Repesh," the other man interjected. He was shorter, thin, his voice mild but measured. "We're not used to visitors anymore. I'm Dr. Fitzpatrick."

David shook his outstretched hand. "David. I thought this place was abandoned."

"Oh, it was," Fitzpatrick said with a knowing smile. "But Dr. Repesh and I stayed behind. When civilization returns, it would be foolish to lose so much valuable knowledge. Now, what is it you're looking for?"

David pulled the folded illustration from his pocket and handed it over. Fitzpatrick held it up to the lantern's glow, examining it through a magnifying glass.

"Ah. Kimpton-Brown device. What do you need it for?"

David hesitated. If George had pissed these men off too, revealing too much could be a mistake. It seemed like half the city was gunning for her already.

"I have a friend who wants to figure out how to use it," he said carefully. "Just in case of an emergency."

Dr. Repesh scoffed, setting his pen down with a loud clatter. "It's far too important a piece of history to be handed over to some idiot who might break it."

David exhaled, forcing down his frustration. Shooting was easier than talking. He didn't want to beg, but if that's what it took, he would.

"It's for my wife," he admitted. "Something bad happened to her. A blood transfusion might be her only hope."

Repesh's face shifted. Something softened behind his stern gaze.

"I would've given anything to save my wife," he murmured.

Fitzpatrick cast him a glance. "Mrs. Repesh died of ovarian cancer," he explained quietly.

"A colleague told us surgery was too risky," Repesh continued, his voice hollow. "So Lillian made her peace."

"She died beautifully," Fitzpatrick said.

David frowned. How could death be beautiful? "Did she suffer?"

Repesh shook his head. "When her time came, I injected her with two vials of morphine. She fell asleep in my arms."

He spoke as if he were there again, lost in memory. David never wanted to look that way.

Fitzpatrick took his arm, leading him through a side door into a smaller room. Repesh followed, lantern held high, illuminating the macabre collection of preserved medical tools and dusty specimen jars.

Fitzpatrick reached into a glass case, withdrawing a flask and tube set. "This is what you need," he said, handing it carefully to David.

David turned the device over in his hands. Such a small thing, and yet it stood between life and death.

"Once you give the transfusion, that's not the end," Repesh warned. "You have to monitor for a reaction. And go too fast—" He stopped, watching David's face. "It's a lot, I know. Have you ever done a transfusion before?"

David shook his head. "I live with a nurse."

Repesh didn't look convinced. "Nurses are useful, but this is complicated. Does your friend even know how to cut into a vein if necessary?"

David hesitated. Did Ana know? Was he willing to risk that she didn't?

"I need a book," he said. "Something to—"

"A book?" Fitzpatrick scoffed. "He plans to learn medicine by reading a book."

Heat rose to David's face. Frustration. Desperation. A burning need to hit something. "We're wasting time," he snapped. "One of you should come with me."

Fitzpatrick shook his head. "Impossible. Someone has to protect what's left."

Repesh sighed, handing him a leather bag and a thick medical book. "Take these. Maybe your nurse friend can figure it out. If it works, come back. And return the book."

David nodded, already turning for the door. "Thank you."

He rushed out of the building and practically jumped on the horse, nudging it in the side to get it to run faster. The wind whipped through his hair, low hanging branches smacked his cheek and he could care less. The only thing on his mind was George. He'd wasted too much time talking. Now he had to make up for it.

When he reached the house, Melody sat on the porch reading by lamplight. He breezed past her, not bothering to tie up the horse. She'd handle it. Ana was in the living room when he came in the house, eyes blood shot. "Did you get it?" she demanded

David handed over the sack. "They said you'd have to cut into my vein."

"Who? Oh never mind." Ana waved the thought away. "I don't. I have sixteen-gauge needles." She grabbed his wrist, dragging him upstairs.

Pedro sat at George's beside, his fingers pressed into her narrow wrist as watched the clock on the wall. He looked up. "Her heart is slowing, but it's steady," he murmured more to Ana than David.

Ana took charge. "Go get the iodine, a couple of tourniquets, the sodium citrate and some sixteen gauges."

Pedro ran to gather the supplies. Ana turned to David. "You're *sure* you're O-negative?"

"Yes." He couldn't stop himself from staring at George. She looked so fragile in the bed.

"If you're wrong—"

He snapped out of the haze of sorrow and regret. This he could do. "I know my blood type." David pulled a chair close, rolling up his sleeve. "Like you said, she's dead anyway. Why not try?"

Pedro returned with the items needed for the transfusion. They worked in concentrated silence. Ana prepared the flask with sodium citrate, then felt for a vein on George. Pedro did the same on David before rubbing an iodine circle in the crook of David's arm. As the brownish-orange liquid dried on his skin, Pedro clamped the end of the tube the needle was connected to.

With bare hands, Pedro pulled back on David's skin. "You ready?" Pedro asked.

David nodded.

The needle pinched as it penetrated his skin. There was a flash of blood and Pedro slowly released the clamp to let it fill the plastic tube, dark red as it left his body. He then connected it to the Kimpton's tubing and removed the hemostat entirely. David watched as his red fluid drained into the flask and mixed with the sodium citrate. Ana taped the needle in George's arm and Pedro did the same for David. He then began pumping the silver handle above, adding pressure to the secondary tube set so the blood moved from the bottle and into George.

It was a long slow process. After about thirty minutes, or maybe more, he couldn't really be sure, Ana and Pedro disconnected them. Pedro wrapped David's arm and offered him a glass of non-alcoholic cider.

Ana placed another blanket over George and took her blood pressure. She smiled. "It's up. It's not great, but it's up, that's a start. A couple more transfusions and she might be out of the woods," Ana said.

It was something

"How soon can we do another transfusion?" David asked, rolling his sleeve down.

"Under normal circumstances, you'd have to wait at least eight weeks for the blood cells to replenish themselves. But in this case, we have to make an exception. She'll need another tomorrow. You should get some rest."

"I'll sleep here," David said.

Ana shrugged. "Pedro or I will be in here periodically to check on you both." She emptied the flask and carried it out of the room with her.

"You'll need to eat something. I'll bring you a sandwich," Pedro said following Ana out.

David lifted the sheets from George's battered body, his breath catching in his throat. She'd fought the motherfucker.

Ana had closed the worst of her wounds, stitching the gash on her stomach and covering it with white bandages that were already tinged pink. But the damage still screamed from her skin— purple and blue bruises blooming across her ribs, cuts lining her arms like war paint, scrapes scattered across her legs and knuckles.

His girl had put up a fight. She hadn't gone quietly. She never would.

Georgianna Harris was a fighter.

David pressed a kiss to the back of her hand. Cold. Too cold.

His fingers trembled as they brushed against hers, as if trying to coax warmth back into her lifeless skin. He'd nearly lost her. Almost let her slip through his fingers like smoke. He should have fought harder.

So many mistakes. But not arguing when she told him it was over? That was the stupidest.

He reached out, gently pushing back a tendril of her dark, tangled hair. God, her face.

Before, all he could see was blood. He hadn't let himself truly look at her, hadn't had the time. But now, in the dim light, the full extent of what had been done to her settled like a weight in his chest. The bruises. The swelling. The fresh cuts marring her features. Blood was still caked beneath her nails—evidence that she hadn't gone down without a fight.

David kissed her hand again. The tears he'd been holding back spilled over, burning hot down his cheeks. He let them fall freely, unchecked.

Then his body broke.

A great, heaving sob ripped from his throat, shaking him down to his bones. His shoulders curled inward, his chest tightening until it felt like he'd shatter under the weight of it all. He was crying.

Mourning.

His mother's face rose in his mind, unbidden and unwanted. She had asked for him. She had wanted to see him before she died, but he had been too busy chasing his next mission, too selfish to stop and be with her in her last months. Instead of sitting at her bedside, he had been in the Czech Republic, running from a ghost he hadn't even realized was haunting him yet.

At her funeral, his stepfather had only said a few words to him. "She asked for you, David. She begged for you. And you didn't come."

David swallowed the lump in his throat, staring down at George's pale, bruised face.

Maybe he deserved getting shot.

That's how he'd ended up in her ICU. A gunshot wound that should have killed him, but somehow hadn't. He'd been floating between life and death, unconscious for days. And she had been there.

His nurse. His angel. The first thing he remembered was her voice.

David exhaled shakily, brushing his thumb over George's knuckles. Come on, baby. Just one sign of life. One flicker. One twitch.

And then he swore he felt it.

A faint tremor against his palm.

His breath stalled. His eyes locked on her hand, waiting... begging... for it to happen again.

Move. Please, just move.

Pedro entered, juggling a syringe, a blanket, and a plate filled with carrots and a turkey sandwich. He set the plate down. "You need to eat," he said. "If you don't, you won't be strong enough for another transfusion tomorrow."

David didn't acknowledge him. Didn't let go of George's hand.

Pedro sighed, setting the blanket on the floor before moving to George's bedside. He counted her pulse, watching the clock. After a moment, he frowned and shoved the syringe back into his pocket.

"Her breathing's too slow for this," he muttered. "Ana says never give opioids if the count is too low."

David still didn't let go. He just sat there, gripping George's hand like he could tether her to this world if he held on tight enough.

There was so much death all the time. So much loss, so much moving on. But not this time. Not her.

His life had just stopped. And he was fairly certain it would be over if she slipped away.

Pedro hesitated, then spoke softly. "You really love her, don't you?"

David finally looked at him. Really looked at him.

The boy wasn't a boy anymore. He was harder, older. Life had carved its suffering into him, taking his childhood in exchange for survival.

"George..." Pedro swallowed. "She's a lot of things. But mostly, she's good. All of us think so. When my grandma got sick, she didn't hesitate. She gave her medicine, checked on her every day, fed us from her garden. When Ya-ya died, I knew I'd be okay. Because George was still here. And you..." Pedro glanced at him. "You two took care of me. Kept me out of the gangs. Showed me things. You and George are all I got left."

David wiped his face with his sleeve, exhaling hard. "I love her. And it's my fault. I should have..." He stopped.

What? What could he have done differently?

Nothing.

But still, he tortured himself with the thought.

After a beat, he let go of her hand, placing it back on the bed with infinite care.

"It's funny," David murmured, "how life works. How a series of random events collude to make one moment happen." He looked at Pedro, seeing for the first time a boy on the cusp of manhood. "Did I ever tell you how we met?"

Pedro shook his head.

David let out a breath. "I was in a coma. And she was my nurse. I never even saw her, but I knew she was the most beautiful woman in the world. She used to sing to me. I heard her voice in my dreams. She talked to me like she knew I was listening. I was asleep and falling in love with an angel."

Scalding tears burned his eyes again.

Flashes of their early days together filled his mind. The first time he saw her through a fever-induced haze. The first time she looked at him, really looked at him, and his heart stuttered in his chest. Her lips, soft and warm, tasting like the morning dew when they kissed.

"So how'd you find each other again?" Pedro asked.

David exhaled, glancing at the door.

"Trixie," he muttered, the name stoking his rage anew. She did this. "She's not a kid anymore," he murmured low to himself. Maybe she never was. Maybe he just refused to see Trixie as anything else. Because if he admitted what she was, what she'd done, then he'd have to kill her, too.

David took a slow, measured breath. "I needed medical care. A friend sent me here. George patched me up. Let me stay."

Pedro nodded.

"Eat," he urged, filling a glass of water at the sink.

David picked up the sandwich, took a bite. Dry. But he wasn't eating for taste.

He was fueling up.

In his mind, he ran through the names. The ones who had to die.

Trixie. Elliot. Aces.

He had decided on Aces, too. That fucker was somehow pulling all the strings.

David had played his part, let himself be used. But Aces had pushed one pawn too far.

As the night stretched toward dawn, David finally let exhaustion claim him. He dreamed of fire. Of smoke curling into the sky. Of flames licking the edges of a broken city.

It wasn't memory. It was a plan.

David was going to burn the city if he had to, and dance on the graves of his enemies.

Chapter Twenty-One

ANA DISCONNECTED DAVID FROM the last transfusion. She checked George's vitals, pressing her fingers lightly against her wrist before glancing at the monitors. Slowly, she smiled. "She's getting there. The baby is gone though. Too much blood loss to sustain a pregnancy."

David let out a breath he hadn't realized he was holding. Relief settled into his bones like warmth after a long freeze.

Ana turned back to him and began wrapping his arm. "You really didn't know about the baby?"

David flexed his fingers, watching as she secured the bandage. "I found the empty pill container. Figured she was pregnant and got rid of it. Didn't think she kept it. Especially after what you said."

Ana hesitated, looking down, guilt flickering across her features. "I'm sorry about that whole fucked-up night." Her voice was quieter now, raw in a way she rarely allowed. "You were right. I wanted George to be miserable. I couldn't stand the thought of her finally having everything when I was still so fucking bitter."

She let out a slow breath. "Then... I don't know. I let myself be happy with Melody, and now, I can see why she should be, too. That's life, right? It just keeps going. We move on with it. And George— she was willing to go against her better judgment and try to keep your baby. That says something, doesn't it?"

David exhaled through his nose, rubbing his thumb along George's hand. Her skin was less pale now, warmer. "I guess it does. What now?"

Ana shrugged. "She either wakes up so we can get some food in her, or she starves to death. Might wake up from the pain, though. I'm cutting off her pain meds to see if it jolts her."

David stroked George's arm, his exhaustion weighing him down like stones. "We get out of one part of the woods just to get stuck in another."

"Seems like it." Ana stretched, rubbing at the dark circles under her eyes. "I'm going downstairs to start breakfast. You coming down?"

He shook his head.

"I didn't think so." She smirked lightly, already heading for the door. "I'll send Pedro up with a plate."

David turned his head just enough to see her before she left. "I'm going out this afternoon. Don't know when I'll be back."

The word *if* lingered in the air like a ghost. He planned to come back. Planned to return to George and her smile.

But wasn't there an old saying about plans and making God laugh?

Ana simply nodded, then disappeared down the stairs to join Melody and Pedro.

After breakfast, David tried to sleep, though he knew better than to expect rest. He started in the chair by George's bedside, but at some point, he ended up on the floor, using a blanket as a mattress and his shirt as a pillow.

When he finally opened his eyes, the room was still and cool, shadows stretching long across the walls. George's quiet, steady breathing was the only sound that mattered. Music to his ears.

He sat up, rubbing at his face, tighter than he thought after sleeping the day away.

David got off the floor and kissed her forehead, then rested his head against her chest, listening to the rhythm of her heartbeat.

Under the soft glow of moonlight, she looked almost ethereal. Like some divine being made of silver and shadows. A sleeping beauty.

If his kiss could wake her, he'd believe in fairy tales.

Hadn't he been the Sleeping Beauty in this relationship once?

David kissed her mouth.

She tasted of dew, of something uniquely hers, something that had become a part of him. There was no memory of kissing anyone else that ever felt the same.

Because she was different... because he had never loved a woman before her.

She didn't wake.

David left her long enough to walk up to their room, fatigue trailing behind him like a ghost. The scent of her still clung to the space... something faint and warm.

He sat at her desk, fingers skimming over her pens, the smooth wood, the worn edges of her journal. Then he picked it up, opened it, and inhaled.

Her scent was still embedded in the pages, giving them life.

How many hours had he spent watching her write, her brow furrowed in concentration, lips slightly parted as she lost herself in thought?

Too many to count.

And now, this was all he had. A journal. A desk. A room that still carried the shape of her presence, though she wasn't there to fill it.

His fingers hovered over the pages, not ready to open it yet.

Not yet.

David picked up a pen, flipping to an empty page in her journal. There were some pages untouched. The cream paper waiting for someone to claim them.

A blank canvas for his soul. For the things he had never spoken aloud.

The sins.

The few triumphs.

The regrets that gnawed at him in the dark.

The black ink was a conduit for all his secrets, each one spilling across the page as he wrote. He let the words bleed out, not stopping to second-guess, not holding anything back.

Everything that had ever lived inside his head— every thought, every memory— he laid it all bare.

By the time he reached the last remaining pages, the truth of him was carved into them.

It was everything she'd ever need to know about him. *Unfiltered. Raw.*

All of it real.

He thought about flipping back to the beginning, reading her words... tracing the shape of her thoughts.

But what good would that do?

Maybe this was the start.

The start of them actually talking. Of knowing each other in a way they never had before.

David slid the pen between the pages, marking where his confessions began.

Then he stood.

The shower was hot, but it did nothing to shake off the exhaustion that had settled into his bones. He scrubbed the grime from his skin, let the water wash away the sweat, the dried blood, the weight of it all.

When he was clean, he dressed and went back to her.

George hadn't moved. Still unconscious, still lost somewhere beyond his reach.

David set the journal on the nightstand.

Then he leaned down, so close that his lips nearly brushed her ear.

"I love you."

It wasn't a plea. It wasn't a desperate whisper in the hopes she'd hear it.

It was a fact. One that no longer scared him.

He let the words settle between them, then turned and walked away.

Trixie wasn't home.

David let himself in through the back window near the fire escape, landing soundlessly inside. It was pitch-black, the kind of darkness that swallowed everything whole. He moved carefully, navigating from the back room to the storefront, only to stumble over her mattress on the floor. Sloppy.

She had a gun in here somewhere. He had to find it.

David combed through the apartment, checking the obvious places first. The gun was strapped to the underside of a small round table, right where he'd expect a paranoid lowlife like Trixie to keep it. He found knives, too, tucked behind the mattress, within easy reach. She'd been prepared for someone.

He dumped everything but the gun into a trash can in the storeroom and buried it behind a woodpile. No weapons. No escape.

The moment he heard the lock turn, he sat at the table.

Trixie stepped inside, alone, lantern in hand. The second she saw him, she startled, but only for a fraction of a second.

Then she smiled.

"David." Her voice was smooth, too smooth. "I've been expecting you." She set the lantern on a shelf, the dim light flickering shadows across her face. "How's George?"

"She's getting better." His voice was dry, empty.

Trixie moved to the counter, pouring herself a drink without taking her eyes off him. Rum. She took a long sip before setting the glass down and slinking toward the table, settling across from him like this was nothing more than a friendly chat.

She pulled a cigarette from a battered case, sticking it between her bruised lips. Courtesy of Elliot? Good.

David plucked the matches from the table, struck one, and lit her cigarette.

Trixie inhaled deep, exhaling a slow, luxurious plume of smoke. Like some old Hollywood starlet who thought she was untouchable.

"You've come to kill me," she said.

Just like that. No fear, no pleading, no hysteria.

One of her hands slid under the table, searching for the gun he had already taken.

David let her reach.

"That depends," he said, coolly. He pulled the hammer back on the revolver and rested it in his lap, his fingers curling around the grip. "You behave yourself, answer my questions, and I might reconsider."

Trixie's fingers twitched. She withdrew her hand, extinguishing her cigarette in a clay ash tray.

"I don't know what I can tell you that you don't already know."

David moved a round into the chamber, the metallic click shattering the silence.

"I wouldn't play games, Trix." His voice was low. Deadly quiet. "Who else was here that night?"

Trixie's eyes flicked around the room, searching for a lie. She had a tell: a twitch at the corner of her left eye whenever she thought too hard about a lie.

Her lips parted, but David beat her to it.

"Trixie." Just her name. A warning.

She licked her bottom lip. "Elliot Miller."

David stilled. He'd known it, though for George's sake, he hoped he was wrong.

Unfortunately, he wasn't.

The next question was the one he didn't want the answer to. But he had to ask.

"Did Elliot touch her?"

Trixie hesitated. "Touch her how?"

David took a slow breath, like it could brace him for what came next. "You know how."

Silence.

Then she rose, walking back to the counter. Not answering.

She grabbed the bottle and took a deep pull straight from it. Coward.

"I don't know," she said finally. "I didn't see after they took her."

David's fingers tightened around the gun.

He didn't remember getting out of the chair. But suddenly, he was standing.

Trixie turned back toward him, her voice sharp, slicing through the thick air like a blade. "She was a whore, just like me, you know."

David went still.

"She may not have sold her body, but she sold everything else. Favors. Deals. Hell, she fucked Aces to make sure he wouldn't turn against her." Trixie smirked, taking another drink. "Bet you didn't know that, did you?"

He had been at that meeting.

There was no sex.

Only whispered negotiations. Only survival.

Trixie saw it in his face. She knew she wasn't getting under his skin, so she tried something else.

"What do you care, anyway?" she sneered. "She said you two weren't together anymore. That you were moving on."

She slammed the bottle down, hard enough to make the glass rattle. "You and I—"

"There is no you and I, Trixie." David's voice was colder than the grave. "There never was. There never will be."

For so long, he'd seen her as just a kid. A girl who got a bad shake in life.

Now, he knew better.

She was just as bad as Elliot. A fucking demon.

David was on her. The gun hit the floor as his hands found her throat once more.

"You lured her here," he snarled, voice thick with rage. "Did you know what he was going to do?"

Trixie gasped, her nails digging into his hands, legs kicking wildly. David didn't let go. Didn't loosen his grip.

She managed a ragged breath. "Yes."

David's vision went red.

Trixie choked out a laugh, her nails clawing at his skin. "Elliot comes in here all the time. Even before his wife died, he'd come."

David didn't want to hear it.

She kept talking anyway. "He paid me to pretend to be her. Liked to call me by her name while he slapped me around. Loved to have me suck his dick while he moaned 'George.'"

The man was fucked in the head.

David's grip tightened.

"I asked him why once..." Trixie coughed, struggling against him. She wasn't getting out of this. Not this time.

"He said he wanted to imagine her while he did degrading things to me. Wanted to fantasize that my humiliation and pain was hers." Her eyes met his, a manic, gleeful glint behind them. "And you know what? I loved every minute of it."

David squeezed harder.

She gagged, her kicks weakening.

"The thought of Miss High-and-Mighty on her knees, getting spit on... turned me on."

That was it.

David bore down, watching as her bloodshot eyes bulged and her lips parted in a final, breathless gasp.

Her body went still.

If he held for just a few more seconds, he could end it right here.

End her.

But Trixie didn't deserve the time it would take to strangle her.

He let go, standing over her heaving, gasping form.

Picked up the gun. Aimed and pulled the trigger.

The shot was clean. A perfect kill.

A crimson floret blossomed in the center of her pale forehead, her eyes open with the ghost of something smug. David stared down at her for a moment, his mind already moving forward.

Elliot.

He could kill him tonight. End it now. But, George deserved to make that call. If she died, so would everyone on his list. Elliot, Aces, all of them. If she lived?

Well...

David could hardly wait to see the vengeful side of his girl.

For now, he'd bide his time.

Start a new project.

Keep her safe.

Besides, what if George needed another transfusion? If Elliot killed him, she'd have no one left.

His thirst for revenge would have to be satiated for now.

By the dead whore on the floor.

The plow horse was still tied up at the bottom of the fire escape, standing patient and still, unaware of the blood David had left behind. He mounted without a word and rode back to the house, the cool night air slicing through his clothes.

The world smelled like rain and dirt, of blood long since dried on his skin. Of death.

By the time he reached the house, dinner was already on the table. The scent of roasted chicken and mashed potatoes filled the space, warm and inviting was a stark contrast to the thoughts rattling around in his skull.

Pedro carved the chicken, glancing up as David stepped inside. "Are you gonna eat with us?"

For days, David had been holed up in that tiny room. Not eating much. Not talking much. His ass had probably worn a damn hole into the chair upholstery from how long he'd been sitting there.

He nodded. "Yeah. Let me just shower and check on George first."

The moment he climbed the stairs, his pulse picked up. Habit. He peeked into the room, exhaling slowly when he saw her. She'd turned in her sleep. Or someone had turned her.

He hoped it was the former. It meant she was coming to.

It also meant he probably wasn't the first person she wanted to see.

He didn't linger. A shower was waiting, and he was still half-covered in sweat and road dust.

By the time he joined the others at the table, they had already started eating. Three glasses of wine sat waiting, and as soon as he dropped into his seat, Melody filled a fourth and slid it toward him.

David took a sip, then set it down as Pedro piled his plate high with chicken, mashed potatoes, and broccoli. Ana added another spoonful of potatoes for good measure.

He picked up his fork and dug in, shoveling food into his mouth like a man who hadn't eaten in days. Because, really, he hadn't. Sandwiches and water were a pathetic excuse for meals.

It wasn't until the room went quiet that he noticed everyone was watching him.

David stopped mid-bite, swallowed the dry chicken, and chased it with a gulp of wine.

Melody poured him another glass. "Thirsty, huh?"

"Yes."

No one went back to their plates. No small talk. Just more staring.

David sighed, setting his fork down. "What?"

Ana shook her head.

Pedro shoved more potatoes in his mouth.

Melody rolled her eyes. "Fine, I guess I'll be the one to say it." She set her glass down with a thud. "Your girlfriend is upstairs in that bed after you found her bleeding out in an alley. You just found out she miscarried—"

"That he thought she aborted," Ana cut in, voice sharp.

Melody nodded. "Right. And now, after all of that, you're fine. Not a complete wreck, not brooding in the corner. You're talking in full sentences. So, what's going on?"

David inhaled, lacing his fingers together. "I'm still a mess. But I'm trying to hold it together for her. When she wakes up, I'll probably lose it again. But for now, I have to be strong."

Melody narrowed her eyes. "He has a plan."

Pedro furrowed his brows. "Plan for what?"

Melody waved him off. "Pedro, darling, the grown-ups are talking."

Pedro, in response, grabbed the bottle of wine and filled his glass to the top.

David wiped his mouth, sitting back in his chair. "I do have a plan." His plate was almost empty. He reached over, tore a leg off the chicken, and took a bite.

Ana raised a brow. "Are you going to tell us what it is?"

He needed something to do. A project. Something to keep himself occupied until George was well enough to talk about Elliot.

For now, that bastard better not set foot in this house.

"I'm going to build a gazebo," he said simply, still chewing. "And I'm going to cover it in wisteria." He glanced around at their blank expressions. "By summer, it'll be in full bloom, and she can sit out there and read."

Melody let out a bark of laughter. "A gazebo? You've got to be fucking kidding me."

"Nope." He took another bite. "Think I'll start tomorrow."

The silence stretched, heavy and confused.

He swallowed and met their stares. "Oh, and one more thing, don't tell anyone. Especially Elliot."

Ana frowned. "Why?"

David licked the grease from his fingers. "Because I don't know who we can trust." His gaze flickered to Melody. "Not even your father."

Melody didn't argue. Just shrugged. "I get it. He's not a bad guy, but he does like to jerk people around."

David finished his meal, pushed his plate away, and stood. Now that his belly was full, he intended to keep his vigil over George. No one would ever get close enough to hurt again.

George whimpered in her sleep. Stirred slightly. Ana must have cut down on the pain meds.

David sat beside her on the bed, reaching out to stroke her curls. She was warmer. That was a good sign.

Slowly, softly, he began to sing.

His voice was rough, worn, nothing compared to hers. But he sang anyway. Their song. The one she used to hum while she worked, the one that had become theirs before either of them realized it.

She shifted again, her breath evening out.

David kept singing, running his fingers through her hair, untangling the knots gently. She was so damn beautiful. Even now. Even battered and bruised, with shadows under her eyes and pain stitched into her skin.

As he reached the end of the song, he started over. And in the space between the chorus and the next verse, he whispered, "When you wake up, I'm taking you outside. And I'm going to show you something beautiful."

Then he started the song again.

Chapter Twenty-Two

PAIN COULD NOT EVEN begin to describe what she felt. George's eyes flew open as she cringed and grasped at her stomach. It was like a fire burned in her belly that couldn't be extinguished. She cried out and within moments Pedro was in the doorway.

"She's awake," Pedro shouted and came in the room. He took a syringe and vial off the bureau and filled the syringe with a clear fluid before coming to her bedside. "It's Demerol," he said as he injected her with it.

The pain dulled a bit, becoming more bearable. She relaxed against the pillows. The memories of that night pervaded her thoughts, soothed only by the dreams of David. She knew they were dreams because he was gone. She'd banished him from her life for telling her the horrid truth when she'd rather hear the beautiful lies.

Ana came in the room and smiled. "You had me thinking, for a minute there, that you were just going to go gently into that good night."

"Never." Her voice was raspy as she fought to formulate words and coherent thoughts. "What?"

"David found you. He brought you back." Ana sat on the edge of the bed. "He saved your life George."

"You..." George coughed. Water. That's what she needed. "Water."

Pedro ran into the bathroom and filled a glass. Ana helped George hold her head up to sip. The cool liquid soothed the scratchiness of her throat.

"I was going to do exactly what you've done. You were near death."

What George would've done was tried to make her comfortable, but wouldn't waste supplies or time on a hopeless cause.

"The idiot wouldn't let me," Ana continued. "He went and got the stuff we needed for a blood transfusion. Kept fighting for your life."

"The baby," George began the question, but if she'd been bad enough for a blood transfusion, she knew the logical answer.

"You miscarried it. There wasn't enough blood to sustain your life, let alone an embryo. The good news is there doesn't seem to be any permanent damage. You can try again if you want to later. "

George attempted to sit up. Her arms were too weak to provide much help in the task. Ana helped, rearranging the pillows behind her. "Where is he now?"

"He's out scavenging. Look, you should talk to—"

"Ana, no. I've said what I'm going to say."

"All right. I'm going downstairs to make some broth for you. We have to start getting food into that body of yours. Gotta have fuel for the engine." Ana got off the bed and went back downstairs.

Pedro picked up the journal from the nightstand, flipping it open before handing it to her. "You should do some reading. It'll help stimulate your mind."

George took it, feeling the weight of it in her hands. She knew this book. Knew the feel of it, the scent of ink pressed into paper. But the pages weren't hers.

Not anymore.

She flipped it open to the marked page, the pen still resting in the spine where he had left it.

David's handwriting stared back at her. Neater than she'd ever seen it.

> *My real name is David Alan Andrews. I was born May 4th in Augusta, Maine. My mother was English and remarried some rich English guy. My father was a fifth-generation dairy farmer.*

She read on, her eyes tracing each careful stroke of ink. A confession?

As his childhood unraveled across the page, her breath slowed. Then came his college years. His career. His life before her.

I was a top intelligence operative and frequently worked dual operations between Britain and the United States. I was trained to be an assassin and spy, so yes, I have killed people. A lot of them.

There are things I regret. Things I did just because it was my job. And you don't question the government when they say, 'Go to this country and take out this guy.'

I was lousy at relationships. Never had a real one before you. And to be perfectly honest, I didn't want one. I used to get what the guys called the three-month itch.

George tightened her grip on the journal, flipping through the pages.

There was so much.

His words stretched on, filling every remaining space. Every detail, every lie he had ever told, every reason why. He'd laid himself bare in ink, not just for her to read—but for her to know.

And then, the last page:

I know I don't deserve it, so I'm not going to ask. I just want you to know, I understand why you hid the things you did. It was for the same reasons I did.

I also want you to know that before you, there was no one. And I highly doubt there will be anyone after you.

Try to remember the good times, Miss Harris.

George sucked in a breath, her fingers tightening around the edges of the journal. *Damn you, David.*

Before she could stop herself, she tossed the book onto the floor beside the bed, as if putting physical distance between her and his words would stop them from carving their way into her heart.

The door creaked, and Ana entered, carrying a bowl of broth. She quirked a brow at the discarded journal but didn't comment.

"You going to eat," Ana asked with a smirk, "or am I going to have to force-feed you?"

George forced a weak chuckle. "I'll eat. I don't know how you've managed to run this place without me."

"It's all been going to pieces." Ana grinned, settling onto the mattress beside her. She raised a spoonful of chicken broth to George's lips.

George took a sip. It tasted like nothing. Warm and bland, settling heavy in her stomach. But at least it was something.

She tried to focus on the soup. Tried to ignore the phantoms circling in her head.

But the memories clawed their way to the surface.

The weight of her attackers...

The knife slicing into her skin...

The sound of her own screams, muffled by cold hands.

Her stomach lurched and bile burned the back of her throat.

"I have to..." She swallowed hard. "I have to vomit."

Ana moved fast, shoving a trash can into her arms just as George heaved. The broth barely hit her stomach before it came up again, sharp and acidic.

She coughed, wiping her mouth, her entire body trembling. "I'm sorry," she whispered. "It wasn't—"

"It's all right," Ana interrupted, already taking the trash can to the bathroom. Her voice was softer now. Gentle.

George let her head fall back against the pillow, exhausted.

Ana returned, the trash can now rinsed and set neatly beside the bed. "We'll try again later." She hesitated, hands on her hips. "Do you want something for the pain?"

George shook her head. "It'll make me throw up again. And the goal is to keep me hydrated, right?"

"Right."

Ana lingered. George could feel it— the uncertainty in her posture, the way her fingers fidgeted. She wanted to help. But there was nothing to do.

"Do you want me to sit with you?" Ana asked finally.

George shook her head. "No. I just want to rest."

Ana exhaled, rubbing the back of her neck. "Okay. Well, I'll bring more broth later."

She slipped out the door, probably relieved to be free of invalid duty. Ana was a good nurse, but she hated the waiting. She needed action, something to do with her hands.

George, on the other hand, had nothing to do but think.

And when she wasn't reliving that night, she was thinking about him.

His words.

His confession.

She hadn't left him because she didn't love him. She had sent him away because her love for him made her reckless. Made her stupid.

Loving David had allowed her to believe in something that didn't exist anymore. Hope. It made her forget the cruelty of the world. It made her want things she couldn't afford to want. So she had let him go.

Because if she had kept him, she wouldn't have been able to let him go at all.

George swallowed thickly and reached down, pressing her fingers lightly against the bandages wrapped around her abdomen. Beneath them, she could feel the raised stitches. The knife had gone deep.

She didn't remember the actual cutting. Just the moments before.

The look in his eyes. The sick thrill in his voice.

Elliot...

George clenched her jaw, her fingers twitching against the gauze. She needed to stop.

Outside, there was a sudden crash, followed by the rhythmic pounding of hammers. Construction?

George tried to lift her head, but the strain made her ache, every muscle in her body protesting.

She gave up and sank back into the pillows, breathing through the pain.

The dull throb in her body made it hard to rest, but she refused to take anything for it.

She was done being numb.

Eventually the combination of exhaustion and pain medication won and George fell asleep.

Shadows flickered on the wall, dancing in the lamplight as George slowly opened her eyes.

David was sitting beside her bed, setting a tray of food on the nightstand. He smiled, but the brightness of it never reached his eyes. Instead, silent tears slipped down his face, catching in the dim glow of the room. He wiped them away hastily, clearing his throat.

"Hi," he said, voice rough.

"Hi." Hers was barely a whisper.

"I brought you some soup." He reached for the bowl and spoon, hesitating. "Do you want help?"

She nodded.

David pulled the chair closer, his movements careful, deliberate. He lifted a spoonful of broth to her lips, and she took it, swallowing slowly, willing her stomach to keep it down.

Another spoonful. This time, the food stayed down.

Good.

"How are you feeling?" he asked.

"Like shit," she muttered.

David huffed out a quiet laugh. "Leave it to you to say what's on your mind." He picked up the glass of water and helped her drink before going back to the soup.

She hesitated, watching him carefully. There was too much to say. So much she wanted to tell him, but none of it seemed to fit.

Still, she had to start somewhere.

"David..." She swallowed. "I didn't go through with it. I didn't terminate the pregnancy."

His eyes met hers. No shock. No accusation.

"I know," he said simply. "Ana told me. You miscarried, though."

She nodded. "I'm sorry for not telling you sooner."

He shrugged, setting the spoon down. "There's so much more I have to be sorry for. I've lied to you from practically the moment we met. The only thing I never lied about was the fact that I love you." His voice cracked slightly. "Because I do. I love you, George."

She promised herself she wouldn't cry.

But here she was, tears spilling over, shaking as quiet sobs wracked her already aching body.

David put the bowl down and took her hand, pressing his lips gently to her knuckles. "Don't start that, please," he whispered. "I can't stand to see you cry." His tears fell onto her skin, warm and real. David was crying.

She'd never seen that before.

"My world ended when I thought I'd lost you," he murmured. "First you sent me away, and I could live with that. I figured I'd lurk in the shadows, making sure you were okay. It's not like I had much of a life." He exhaled shakily. "Then I found you. Ana was—"

"Only doing what I'd have done," she finished for him. "She was right, you know. There wasn't any use in wasting supplies on a corpse."

His grip on her hand tightened. "You aren't a corpse."

David climbed onto the bed beside her without letting go. She didn't want him to let go.

"You're here," he said fiercely. "I would've given every last drop of blood in my body and then some to save you. I can't go back, George."

She lifted her free hand and wiped at the tears streaking her cheeks.

"Please, Georgie..." He hesitated, like he'd just remembered that she hated that nickname.

But from him, it didn't sound so bad.

She let out a shuddering breath. "You can call me that. As long as I'm *your* Georgie."

David smiled, letting go of her hand only to cup her bruised cheek. The initial touch made her flinch, but then she relaxed into it.

"Always," he murmured. "Whether you like it or not." His lips found hers, soft and gentle, like a promise.

George was the one who pulled away first. "We have a lot to talk about."

David groaned. "You sure do know how to kill a romantic reunion, Miss Harris."

She smirked. "I'm laid up in a patient room and barely able to move. It's hardly romantic, Mr. Andrews."

He chuckled, sitting back. "Fair point." He ran a hand over his face. "What do you want to know?"

She studied him carefully, searching for the right words. "What happened to you? Before the hospital. Why wasn't there anyone to claim you?"

David's expression darkened. "I wrote it down. My—"

"You wrote down the facts," she interrupted. "I want the whole story."

David sighed heavily, shoulders dropping. "My mother was dead. My half-sister and I hadn't spoken since the funeral. And my dad... he was a drunk son of a bitch."

"What happened to him?"

He shrugged. "Probably put a bullet in his own brain. Fucking coward."

"David..." Her voice was low, careful.

He scoffed. "What? Any man that beats up a kid just because he can is a fucking coward. As soon as I was able, I got the fuck away from him. My mother never knew, because I was a brilliant liar. It wasn't her fault."

She took a breath. "What about friends?"

His jaw clenched. "Look, it's easy to say I didn't have any because of the job. But that's not the truth. I didn't want them. I kept people at arm's length because when you care about someone, it's harder to lie. Harder to put them in a little box and keep them there. And when you love them..." He trailed off, blinking hard. "When you love them, it's damn near impossible.

"I could've done so much more if I hadn't fallen in love with you." He let out a bemused chuckle. "Before, I never thought about the lives or the lies. Then there was you. And all I could think about was what you'd think of me. It scared the shit out of me that you might see me as a monster. So even though I wanted to tell you everything, I felt like I had to protect you... from me."

George reached out, rubbing her fingers against his thigh. Not sexual. Just comfort. "I know what you mean." Her voice was quiet. "I lied to you about the baby because I was scared. I used to be open. More transparent and hopeful. But then everything happened, and I shut myself off to survive.

"Then you came along." Her voice cracked. "And suddenly, there were possibilities again. It scared me. Every decision I'd ever made was for survival, and suddenly, I was thinking about a future that might never come."

David grabbed her hands, squeezing. "It's coming. A future is coming." His blue eyes went cold. "I know who did this to you."

So did she.

And it disgusted her.

The weight of Elliot's body on hers, his breath hot against her skin.

The other fucker who pinned her down.

She wanted their blood.

Not just their blood. *Their pain.*

David's voice was low. "I killed Trixie."

"Good." She didn't hesitate. "That little bitch lured me there. She knew. And I knew she knew the second that big fucker stepped out of the backroom."

His jaw tensed. "I killed him too." He met her gaze. "There's only one more."

"Elliot." She whispered it, like the name alone could summon him.

David nodded. "I'm going to kill him too."

"No."

He gave her an incredulous look, as if he expected her to want to forgive him.

But that wasn't who she was. George could never forgive and she didn't want. She wanted to feel the warmth of his blood staining her hands. To see the look in his eyes when he realized that not only had she survived, but it was her who was ending him.

"I want to do it myself." Her voice was like steel. "I have to."

David didn't argue. Didn't try to protect her. If this was what she wanted, he'd give it to her.

"I want Elliot to suffer before I end him," she said. "I want him to understand what it's like to have fucking nightmares."

"That's not you, George," replied David. But he didn't push the thought anymore than that. Elliot made sure that whatever softness she'd had, was snuffed out. David didn't fight her. He just met her gaze and whispered, "Tell me what you need me to do."

She didn't answer.

Instead, she pulled him into her arms.

And for that night, at least, the boogeyman stayed in the closet.

Chapter Twenty-Three

"No peeking," David murmured as he carried George down the stairs, careful with every step, his grip steady. The early evening air was warm, the scent of summer thick with wisteria as the vines draped through the slats of the gazebo.

He crossed the lawn, the grass soft beneath his boots, and stepped inside the wooden structure he had built with his own hands. *For her.*

He lowered her gently onto the bench, the one he had carved himself, and draped a blanket over her lap.

"Can I look now?" she asked, her voice light, teasing. A breeze whipped her hair across her face, and she wiped it away, but she kept her eyes closed.

"Not yet."

David's heart pounded. He swallowed hard, running a hand through his hair, adjusting the suit Ana had insisted he wear. He used to love wearing suits, but now? Now it felt like a costume. Unnatural. A relic from another life.

He hesitated. Should he sit beside her? Stand? Kneel?

In the end, there was only one way to do this.

He reached into his pocket, pulled out the ring box, and sank down on one knee.

The moment stretched, full of unspoken things, full of what-ifs.

Then he opened the box.

Inside, the ring gleamed in the soft glow of the lanterns he had strung up along the columns. The same ring he wanted to give her before.

Maybe this time... maybe this time, she'd say yes.

If not? He'd try again later.

David took a deep breath, let it settle in his chest, and exhaled. Everything was right.

"Okay," he whispered. "Open them."

George's eyelashes fluttered, then lifted. She blinked, taking in the scene—the wisteria, the lanterns, him.

She stared for a long moment, and David didn't rush her.

Then...

"Did you build this?" she asked.

Not exactly the response he'd been expecting.

She barely glanced at the ring in his hand, her focus on the gazebo instead.

"Yes," he answered, thrown off balance.

"I like it." She smiled softly, running her fingers along the wooden bench. "It'll be a nice place to sit in the summer. Maybe dance."

David blinked. What the hell was happening? He was on one knee with a ring in his hand, and she was talking about the damn gazebo?

Had the blood loss short-circuited her brain?

He cleared his throat.

"Well," she teased, "you have to actually ask the question if you want an answer." She glanced down at herself. "Though I'm not exactly dressed for the occasion."

He chuckled, shaking his head. "I asked you before," he said referring to the time he told her that he was going to call her his wife one day.

His palms were sweating. *Jesus.* "Georgianna Harris," he began, but she cut him off.

"Technically, you didn't ask before. And I never actually said no."

He gave her a look. "Are you gonna let me get through this?"

She waved a hand. "Just making sure we're clear on the facts."

David sighed. She was impossible. But, God, he loved her.

"You're the moon and the stars in my world," he said, voice steady, certain. "Without you, I feel lost and off-balanced. I need..." He stopped, shook his head. "No. I don't *need* you. I *want* you. I want you to be mine. I want to wake up every morning knowing that every night, I get to fall asleep with you all over again. I want yours to be the last lips I ever kiss. And when my time comes, I want you to be beside me."

She was so still, it was impossible to tell what she was thinking. Sometimes he hated that he couldn't always read her.

"I want to build a life with you, here or anywhere." He exhaled, his pulse thrumming. "I want—"

"That's a lot of wants," she interrupted.

He sighed. She was exasperating. Here he was, laying out all his hopes and dreams, and she was counting words.

But he loved that about her. Loved everything about her.

"I want to follow you into the dark and back into the light," he said. "Anywhere and everywhere. I just want you." His voice softened. "Marry me?"

George turned her head away.

Why?

David got off his knee, reaching out, brushing his thumb over the small, new scar on her cheek. Gently, he coaxed her back toward him.

Tears shimmered in her eyes.

He was making her cry again. Fuck. He was screwing this up.

"Georgie..." David's voice was soft as he tried to conceal the ever-growing panic that he was going to fuck everything up and she would turn him down.

"It's not you," she whispered. "It's..."

"The future." He nodded. "I know. Even if we only have an hour more, I'll take it. I'll take whatever time I can get with you."

His hand slid into her hair, his fingers tangling in the curls. "Marry me, George."

This time, it wasn't a question.

This time, he was telling her to let herself have this dream. To indulge in it. They could be careful. He wasn't asking to let go of all her apprehensions or to dream of a life that he knew terrified her. But he was imploring her to allow herself to have even the smallest sliver of joy.

Her lips parted, her voice barely audible. "Yes."

David froze.

"Yes?" he repeated.

She nodded. "Yes."

His breath hitched. His fingers trembled as he slid the ring onto her finger, where it belonged. The empty box fell to the ground, forgotten.

David cupped her face and kissed her. There was no hesitation, no restraint. His lips crushed against hers, devouring her like she was air.

She parted her lips, and he didn't hesitate, his tongue swept inside, tasting, claiming.

His hands traced down her body, feeling the thin fabric of her nightgown. Her breasts, perfect even covered, her nipples hard beneath the linen.

He moved lower...

Then he felt it.

The scar.

His fingers stilled against her abdomen.

George pulled away. Her hands pressed against his chest, pushing him back.

David didn't fight against her. Instead, he smiled reassuringly. "I saved your life," he murmured.

He took her hand and guided it down, pressing her palm against his right thigh. Against the scar.

The one that nearly killed him.

"You saved mine," he said.

Her fingers brushed over the fabric of his pants, tracing the place where his own wound had healed.

David leaned in, his voice nothing more than a whisper against her skin. "And you keep saving me, George."

He cupped her jaw, tilting her face up to his. "Don't you get it? The scars aren't ugly. They're not something to be ashamed of." His thumb traced the curve of her cheek, then lower, down her throat, over her collarbone. "They're proof," he said. "Proof that we survived."

His lips hovered just over hers. "And they're beautiful."

She kissed him softly on the cheek, lips warm against his skin. "I want to go inside."

David braced himself to lift her, but George shook her head, waving him off.

She was going to walk.

He didn't argue. He simply offered his arm, and she took it, gripping him lightly as they made their way across the yard, step by careful step.

When they reached the porch, she exhaled shakily. "Okay. You can help now."

David scooped her up, her body light in his arms, and carried her inside and up the stairs, past the familiar creaks in the floorboards, through the doorway of the bedroom that was theirs.

He set her gently on the bed.

George didn't hesitate. She reached for the hem of her nightgown, lifting it over her head and letting it drop to the floor. The blanket was pulled up in the next instant, covering her. Hiding her body.

David swallowed hard.

"You don't have to do anything, George," he said carefully. He wasn't asking for this. He wasn't expecting her to pretend things were back to normal, and he sure as hell wasn't going to pressure her. She had been through too much. She was still healing.

She took a deep breath and laid back against the pillows, saying nothing. Then, slowly, she peeled the blanket away, letting the light from the lamp illuminate her skin.

She was exposed.

Open.

Vulnerable.

David stood at the foot of the bed, his heart pounding. He could barely breathe. Did she want him? Did she know what she was doing to him?

His breath caught the same way it had the first time he'd ever seen her like this—like she was something holy. Like she was breathtaking.

"You're the most beautiful woman I've ever seen," he murmured.

George shivered under his gaze. "I want..." She hesitated.

David understood. She wanted to feel something besides the pain.

He slid out of his jacket, rolling up the sleeves of his dress shirt. Then came his shoes, his socks, tossed aside carelessly. He climbed onto the bed, positioning himself over her, close enough that she could feel the warmth of his body but not touching. Not yet.

He leaned down and blew a gentle breath over her nipple.

She gasped. The breath she had been holding escaped.

His fingers twitched at his sides.

That's what she wanted. Not just his touch, but his desire.

But he wanted her pain. He wanted to take it from her, to consume it, to bury it so deep that she never had to feel it again. He was strong enough to hold it all for her.

She reached for him, her fingers brushing his cheek.

David turned his head and kissed her palm. "Do you want me to?"

She nodded, silent, as if she didn't trust her own voice.

If she told him no, he would stop. If she showed even the slightest discomfort, he would stop.

He kissed the hollow of her throat, feeling the tremble of her pulse beneath his lips. She smelled different now. The aroma of soap and antiseptic clinging to her skin. She smelled clean, but still like her.

David's mouth found the swell of her breast, his tongue flicking over the hardened bud, teasing, tasting. Her breath quickened, and then a moan. Soft, but there.

Good. It was progress.

His mouth moved lower, down her stomach, over the fragile plane of her ribcage.

George seemed to hold her breath as he hovered over the scar. David stilled. The wound was still angry, still pink against her deep mahogany skin. His chest ached at the sight of it.

He kissed it and she exhaled, her body relaxing beneath him.

David kissed the scar again. And again.

Soft. Gentle. Reverently. Until he was satisfied that she knew it didn't disgust him. That he still wanted her. That he still loved her.

By the time he reached the apex of her thighs, she was ready. Her slickness glistened in the lamplight, her body calling for him. God, he wanted to take her. But tonight wasn't about him.

David dragged his tongue over her clit. George's moan was louder this time.

Yes. He wanted to hear more. Wanted to see it. Watch as pleasure took her apart.

He traced invisible words against her sensitive flesh, tasting, teasing.

George squirmed beneath him, her breath ragged. "Please," she gasped.

David closed his eyes. God, he wanted to give in. He wanted to free himself from the confines of his slacks and bury himself inside of her.

Not tonight. Tonight was for her.

He slid two fingers inside her, easing them in gently, feeling her warmth wrap around him.

She tensed. David waited, willing to take as much time as she needed. Then, as she relaxed, he pulled his fingers back to the very edge before thrusting them forward again.

George's hips lifted off the bed, chasing his touch. "More," she rasped.

He moved faster, his fingers thrusting deep, curling just right, hitting exactly where she needed.

Her moans grew louder. And her whole body shook, her breath catching on curses and gasps. Then she was over the edge, crying out his name, her body convulsing around his fingers, her pleasure blinding.

"Yes, beautiful, just like that." David watched it all. *Spectacular.*

She lay there, panting, glistening with sweat, completely spent. "Thank you," she whispered.

David slid his fingers from her, licking them clean of her taste. "My pleasure."

He pulled her into his arms, holding her tight as she trembled. There were tears on her cheeks, but for once, he knew they weren't from pain. He pressed his lips against her temple, breathing her in.

"David," she murmured.

"Hmm?"

"Do you..." She swallowed. "Do think you'd want to try? For a baby?"

David stiffened. It was a loaded question.

He wanted her. God, he wanted her in every way. But a child?

His mind flashed with a dozen possibilities, a thousand fears. What if something happened to her? But then, he imagined a daughter— one with her curls, her wit... her stubborn, unyielding will.

Maybe in another life.

David exhaled, pressing a kiss to her bare shoulder. He pulled the sheets up over them, tucking her into the warmth of his body.

"I already have everything I want," he said softly. "I'm good."

She didn't say anything, but he felt it.

The way her muscles unclenched, the way she melted into him. As though his answer was a relief.

Then a smile.

And that?

That was enough.

Chapter Twenty-Four

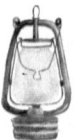

ANA'S DEFT FINGERS WORKED quickly, adjusting the vintage wedding dress with the precision of a woman who never let anything slip through her grasp. Melody sat nearby, needle in hand, carefully embroidering the final touches on one of the lavender bridesmaid dresses. The rhythm of their work filled the room, steady and methodical.

George, feeling restless, picked up one of the heavy sacks of old linen and made her way toward the back door, where Pedro was boiling laundry.

It was heavier than she anticipated. The weight dragged her down as she struggled to maneuver it down the stairs. She barely made it before plopping it just shy of its intended destination.

Pedro rushed over, taking the sack the rest of the way. "How are you feeling?" he asked, frowning as he adjusted the bundle.

"I wish everyone would stop asking me that," George muttered. "I'm fine, Pedro."

"David told me to keep an eye on you. Said to make sure you're not overdoing it."

She rolled her eyes. "Where is he anyway?"

"He went to look at a new horse." Pedro opened the sack, grimaced at its contents, and dumped the linens into the steaming pot. The scent of soap and damp fabric filled the air as he stirred the mixture with a long stick.

"So," he said, keeping his eyes on the swirling water, "what happens now that you two are getting married?"

George cocked her head, crossing her arms as she really looked at him.

"What do you mean?"

Pedro hesitated. "David says you might leave."

Her heart stilled.

She had agreed to exactly that. To start over. To go somewhere else. Somewhere where life might still exist in the way it once did. Where there were rules, stability... hope.

But Pedro wasn't just asking about them. He was asking about himself.

She sat on the tree stump near the chicken coop. Pedro hesitated, then dropped onto the grass at her feet. George reached for him, stroking his hair in slow, soothing motions.

Pedro had become part of her family, whether she'd meant for it to happen or not.

"You can come with us if you want," she said, still combing through his dark, unruly locks.

His shoulders slumped with relief before he even had a chance to respond.

"Are you really leaving?" His voice was quiet, hesitant. "Ana said once that you'd never leave."

"I had different priorities then," George admitted. She had different reasons to stay. "But I can't stay anymore, Pedro. Not now."

He was silent for a long moment, thinking. Then, softly, "I don't suppose you can. You and David... you could never have a real life here. Too much has happened."

George let out a slow breath. "The house is a tomb," she confessed. "I know it doesn't seem that way, but there are too many ghosts here. Too many memories I can't shake." She paused. "I think I stayed out of guilt."

Pedro's brow furrowed. "Guilt for what?"

She exhaled. "For surviving."

There it was. The truth.

She survived when so many others hadn't. She'd made choices that left her standing while others fell. She had clung to life the way a drowning woman clings to driftwood, and she'd done it without looking back.

And then there was Ana.

They were better now. Friends again, even. But their bond had become an endless cycle of friendship and hate, of comfort and wounds that would never heal. They were both stuck, repeating the same mistakes over and over.

One of them had to leave.

For both their sakes, it had to be George.

Pedro turned, shifting onto his knees. Before she could react, he hugged her.

It was sudden and startling.

Pedro didn't hug. He didn't like to be touched... not since his grandmother died. But now, he held her tight.

George froze for a moment, then let herself lean in, wrapping her arms around his back. He smelled like sweat and yard work, but she didn't care. The kid was having a breakthrough.

Pedro pulled back but kept his hands on her forearms, his grip firm. "If you hadn't survived," he said, earnest and steady, "neither would I. You saved me, George. You brought me into your home, taught me something useful, gave me a family." His voice wavered. "You survived because you were meant to."

She hesitated, then placed her hand over his.

"I survived because I don't know any other way," she murmured. Then, softer added, "But David wants more now. A life. I think I want that too." Her thumb traced small circles against his skin. "And I want you to be part of it."

Pedro's face split into a wide grin.

"Anywhere," he said. "I still have a lot to learn. And Ana's over it. Says I talk back too much."

George laughed. "You do. But I'll teach you what I know."

Pedro stood, dusting off his pants. "I should finish the linens before Ana comes back and throws a fit."

George pushed herself up from the stump, wincing as a dull ache spread across her middle. She ignored it.

If David found out she was still having pain, he'd never leave her alone.

"Did David say when he'd be back?" she asked.

Pedro shook his head.

"Tell him I ran over to Sal's to get some seed?"

Pedro raised a brow. "You taking a horse?"

She nodded. "It's only a couple blocks east. I'll be fine."

She made her way up the stairs and into their bedroom, trading her dress for trousers and suspenders, rolling the sleeves of David's oversized shirt so they wouldn't swallow her hands. The loose fabric didn't irritate her wound, which was more than she could say for most of her clothes.

Then, she went to the supply cabinet.

Her fingers hovered for only a moment before she plucked a vial of morphine sulfate from its place and slipped it into her pocket.

She didn't need it, yet. But it was better to be prepared.

The barn was quiet, save for the soft rustling of hay. David had taken one of the horses, but the quarter horse was still there. Good.

She wasn't strong enough to lift a saddle, so she didn't bother. Instead, she tossed a few blankets over its back and secured the reins. Leading the horse outside, she climbed onto a bale of hay and swung a leg over its back. The quarter horse huffed, shifting under her weight. George inhaled deeply, gripping the reins tightly. It was taking more out of her than she anticipated.

She was fine.

She could do this.

George rode west, toward the grimy underbelly of downtown. Toward the filth and rot. David would be pissed when he found out.

He'd get over it.

There were scores to settle. A few more pieces to knock over before she could even think about something as ridiculous as a happily ever after.

The streets were alive with the kind of quiet tension she'd grown up with; the kind that hummed beneath the surface, that clung to people's backs like a second skin.

Eyes followed her.

It had been months since anyone outside the house had seen her. David made sure of that. *Too risky*, he'd said. *Elliot will find out.*

She hoped he did.

By nightfall, he'd know she was alive. And he'd realize she was pissed.

The battered fountain in front of Aces' hotel stood like a relic of a time long gone. George dismounted, using the crumbling ledge to steady herself before her boots hit the pavement. She tied the horse to the stairwell, adjusting the reigns, giving herself a moment to breathe. Then, she made her way inside.

She forced herself to move with confidence. Aces had to see her, not the woman left bleeding in an alley.

Not a victim.

A hairy girl greeted her at the bottom of the stairs. "He's in a meeting," she said, already leading the way to Aces' private lounge. "Help yourself to a drink. Bartender's sick."

The lounge was a shrine to excess. Decadence built on the blood of others. She understood it— hell, she'd thrived in it once. Played God with a flick of her wrist. Believed she had power. Believed she could tip the scales however she pleased. But she knew better now.

The only difference between her and anyone else was that she knew how to play the devil when she had to.

And she played very well.

George stepped behind the bar, fingers trailing over glass bottles filled with liquid richer than gold. Patron. Grey Goose. Bombay Sapphire. The real thing. Not the bathtub poison the desperate drank.

Which one would pair best with her special ingredient?

She heard his swagger before she saw him.

"George," Aces greeted, a broad grin stretching across his face. "Imagine my surprise. I'd heard the worst. But here you are."

Here she was. Smiling back as if nothing happened and this was just a social. A hollow thing.

"Thanks, Aces. I was just about to make myself a drink. You want one?" She gestured at the two glasses she'd pulled from behind the bar.

"Don't mind if I do." He pushed open the terrace doors, stepping into the sun.

She poured his first.

The vial of morphine emptied in a breath, clear liquid blending seamlessly with the martini. Grey Goose. Two olives. Clean. Smooth.

She poured herself something different. Something she actually wanted to drink.

George joined him outside, offering him both glasses. Aces took a sip of the screwdriver, frowned, then swapped it for the martini.

Good.

She sipped her own, watching him over the rim of her glass.

"Aces," she murmured, "why'd you stop me from killing the other faction leaders in the beginning? Wouldn't it have been easier if it was just you?"

He smirked. "It would've. But it'd also have been less interesting."

Of course. They were all toys for his amusement. He was like this in the old days too. Aces lived for drama in the hospital. He'd sometimes wind up other staff just to watch them stumble about.

George let her smirk mirror his.

"You always did like strategy games," she mused. "Chess was your favorite, if I recall."

"It was." Aces gestured to a board set up near the koi pond. "Want to play a round?"

She sat opposite him. Black.

They played in silence. He studied her moves with care; she played recklessly, fast and thoughtless.

He chuckled when he took her rook. "You never think ahead."

She shrugged. "I was never one for chess."

They continued until he lost interest, turning instead to his record collection.

George stood, moving back toward the bar. She emptied her glass in the sink. "You were always right about me," she said.

Aces looked up. Finished his drink.

She turned to face him. "I liked the game we played. I liked being feared. I liked knowing people thought I was unpredictable. A necessary evil. It kept me safe. But I let them think I got soft. That was my mistake. I fell in love. Started pretending I could have something else. Something more. And the moment I did, they stopped fearing me."

At least enough for Elliot to feel emboldened that no one would hurt him if he killed her.

She smiled. "You used to give me such good advice, Aces. But you should've never talked me into stopping."

His expression flickered with something akin to interest? Or maybe understanding?

"If you're implying I—"

"I'm not implying anything," she said. "I'm telling you. There was only room for one person at the top. And you wanted that spot. You got it."

Aces' brow furrowed. And then he understood.

There had never been two kings. Just a king... weak and vulnerable.

And a queen.

George moved quickly, grabbing his shirt and pulling him into a kiss. It caught him off guard. He hesitated. Just for a second. Unsure whether to pull her in or push her away.

That second was all she needed.

She counted his breaths. Slowing as the morphine was took hold. His grip loosened and his eyelids fluttered.

She could leave him now to slip away quietly. Let the poison lull him into a painless, forgettable death.

But that wouldn't do.

That wouldn't protect Ana. Melody. Pedro. David.

No.

They needed to see. People needed to understand that even someone like Aces could be brought down.

She whispered against his lips. "Checkmate."

Then, she drove her foot into his.

Aces stumbled and she shoved him. Hard.

His body tipped over the edge. Next came his scream, shattering the air—high, sharp, panicked. Somehow she thought it'd be faster. Quieter.

It wasn't.

Fifteen floors down, he hit the asphalt with a sickening crunch.

A woman screamed.

Doors in adjacent buildings opened and people spilled into the streets. They gathered and gaped, forming a commotion around the lifeless pharmacist. Slowly, some looked up. And George made sure they saw her.

Then she left as if returning home from her rounds.

No regret.

By the time she reached home, a small, satisfied smile played at her lips. Melody was going to lose her mind. Aces was a criminal, but he was still her father. Ana would have to choose.

But George wasn't going to force her too. She'd done what she had to. She was willing to face the consequences.

At least they would be safe.

She dismounted, barely stepping inside before David was on her, checking her for wounds, for blood.

"Where have you been?" he asked.

She met his gaze. "I think you already know."

David sat on the closed toilet while she undressed in the bathroom, turning on the shower.

"I heard someone pushed Aces." His voice was careful. "People think it was you."

She stepped under the hot spray. The water felt divine as it cascaded down her body. Between the horse and Aces, she'd overdone it.

"It was," she replied.

Silence.

"I was going to do it." He didn't seem upset or angry with her. Just taken aback that she had beat him to it. Especially in her condition.

She shut off the water. "And what? Let me watch? Let you fight my battles?"

David frowned.

"If I let you do this for me," she said, "I'd stop respecting myself. You would stop respecting me." She grabbed a towel. "And then you'd stop loving me."

"I would never—"

"You look at me like I'm going to break," she said softly.

David swallowed hard. Then stood and stepped closer, pulling the towel off. His fingers were gentle as he ran them over the still discolored scar on her abdomen.

"You almost did." His voice was wrecked. "I almost lost you."

"But you didn't." She lifted his face, forcing him to see her. "He didn't break me, David. Only you could do that."

His eyes darkened. "Elliot—"

"I'll get him first." Her lips curved into a slow, sharp smile. The kind that said behind these lips were sharp teeth.

David kissed her forehead. "You should get dressed. Preacher's coming soon."

She smirked. "I suppose I can't be late to my own wedding."

He smiled at her, chuckling softly to himself. "What am I going to do with you, Miss Harris? Guess we'll be heading out at first light."

She nodded. "Pedro too."

David shook his head, an amused grin on his face. "Wouldn't dream of leaving him behind. I'll get him to start loading the truck and hitching up the trailer. Looks like we won't have a decent wedding night after all."

Chapter Twenty-Five

DAVID FIDDLED WITH HIS ring, the gold catching the light of the flickering lanterns strung around the yard. He stood near the preacher, murmuring something in a low voice, his expression at ease.

When he caught George watching, he smiled. It wasn't one of those bright, easy grins. It was something softer. A smile just for her. The grey suit fit him too well. It clung to his broad shoulders, the fabric a little too heavy for a summer evening, but damn if he didn't look devastating. It was unfair, really.

This man. Her husband.

Her David.

She let herself admire him for just a moment longer before slipping into the house to find Ana.

Inside, Ana was smoothing the last bit of icing over the lopsided wedding cake. It'd probably taste like shit, but it was the thought that counted.

Ana glanced up, taking in George's appearance. "You look nice in that dress. The white lace suits you."

George smirked. "I'll take that as a compliment." She hesitated. "I need to talk to you."

Ana didn't look up. "You should be outside. Mingling. Keeping your new husband company."

"Ana..." George's voice was quiet.

Ana sighed, setting down the spatula, finally facing the conversation she'd been avoiding.

"I'm really leaving tomorrow," George said.

Ana's brows knit together. "I don't understand why."

"Because it's time." George folded her arms. "You and I... we've been caught in this loop for too long. We can't move forward with the other one still here." She let out a slow breath. "And when Melody finds out what I did, she's not going to want me around."

Ana stilled. "What did you do?"

"I killed her father."

The silence between them felt charged as if both of them were running through scenarios and possibly coming to the same conclusion.

Ana's mouth parted slightly, then snapped shut.

"I pushed him over the balcony of his hotel," George added, her voice measured, steady.

"Jesus, George." Ana wiped her hands on her apron. "You realize what you've done?"

"I know exactly what I did," George said.

Ana's eyes glossed over, her cheeks flushing as she blinked back tears. "You knew this would mean I'd have to choose."

George nodded. "And there should be no competition. Choose her. Always choose her."

Ana broke. She stepped forward, wrapping her arms around George tight. It was a rare thing, Ana hugging her first.

"What am I going to do without you?" Ana's voice wobbled.

George squeezed her back. "Go on living. Do something amazing. Keep this place running, probably better than I ever did. Maybe learn to cook?"

Ana playfully swatted her arm, chuckling. The laughter was a welcome reprieve from the tears.

George felt her own tears welling up. Damn it. She wiped them away quickly.

"I was just a crutch," George admitted, her voice raw. "A reminder of what we lost instead of what we could build. You deserve more than that."

Ana pulled back, swiping at her own eyes.

George forced a small smile. "It was always going to end, Ana. One of us would leave. Or one of us would die. I just always thought it'd be you leaving me."

Ana let out a soft, broken laugh. "I think I knew that too." She sniffed. "So why does it hurt so much?"

"Because endings always do."

They'd been holding each other back. Clinging to the past and the grief that colored every corner of their lives. Every time they rebuilt their friendship, they'd found new ways to tear it down again.

This was mercy.

"Thank you," Ana whispered. There were too many things wrapped up in those two words. Thanks for their friendship. Thanks for their survival. Thanks for this. It was catharsis.

A commotion outside snapped them out of their sentimental goodbye.

Then a sharp curse.

George ran out to the yard with Ana right behind her, just in time to see David swing. His fist connected with Elliot's jaw with a sickening crack.

"You sick son of a bitch," David snarled. "How dare you come here?"

Elliot staggered, nearly hitting the ground from the force of the blow.

When she returned outside, David and Elliot were still facing off.

She stepped onto the porch. Aiming. "David," she said, her voice cutting through the chaos, "stop."

He froze. His chest rose and fell too fast, his knuckles bloody. His eyes... God, his eyes. He was ready to kill Elliot, and nothing would stop him.

Elliot staggered to his feet.

A small figure darted from the crowd, gripping George's legs.

Abigail.

George ran a hand through her niece's hair. "Go inside with Ana, sweetie." She pried the girl away.

Ana took Abigail by the shoulders, ushering her inside before she could witness what was coming.

Melody had appeared, standing near the edge of the yard, her gaze bouncing between George, Elliot, and David.

Elliot wiped the blood from his mouth. "George," he said, his voice dripping with feigned relief. "Thank God it was just a rumor. I heard you were attacked. I went looking for your body, but I couldn't find it. Then this dick wouldn't let me in to see you." He gestured toward David, shaking his head like a disappointed parent. "How come you didn't tell me you were getting married?"

George cocked the gun. "Because you weren't invited."

He smirked. "I don't see why not."

"You know damn well why not." She growled, keeping the shotgun trained on him. If he even twitched in a way she didn't like, she wouldn't hesitate to put him down.

Elliot sighed dramatically. "Speaking of people who weren't invited—did you hear about Aces?"

George didn't blink.

"A shame he couldn't be here today," Elliot continued. Mocking. "Of course, you probably already knew that."

Melody's face twisted.

"What do you mean?" she asked.

Elliot grinned. "He's dead." He let the words settle, watching Melody closely. "Word is some woman pushed him off the terrace at his hotel. But if George was so sick she couldn't leave the house, well..." he trailed off, raising a brow.

Melody's gaze snapped to George.

Her father was dead. George had killed him.

And Melody knew.

She probably even knew why in hindsight, but it didn't change a damn thing. George had killed her father.

"Elliot you have three seconds to get off this property. You leave alone and you never come back," George said.

"I'm not leaving without my daughter," Elliot replied.

"You don't deserve your daughter. How can you look her in the eye after what you did?"

It wasn't until people started whispering that George remembered there were a crowd of partygoers who had no idea what happened to her. They'd kept it a closely guarded secret.

"And what did I do?" Elliot was smug, like he knew that George would never tell. He was probably betting on her pride she wouldn't want to relive the embarrassment and shame of being too weak to protect herself in front of the world.

She didn't. She wanted to bury it deep. But more than that, she wanted the whole world to understand what a fucking weasel he was.

The images were still garbled in her head— a vivid nightmare. George needed time to get there. To find the courage to talk about what happened to her.

"You know why I told you your plan needed work? It wasn't because it sucked. It was pretty decent. The problem was you. You expected everyone to fall under one leader, you. You're a coward and a tiny wannabe dictator. But you never want to get your hands dirty and you never want to deal with the fallout of your actions." She took several deep breaths, then with all the vitriol she felt, she said, "That's why you had that other guy hold me down while you raped and sliced me open. You ran instead of making sure I was dead."

"George..." David's voice was soft. "You don't have to do this."

"Yes I do." George returned her attention to Elliot. "You didn't even have the fucking balls to show your face. I only knew it was you because of shitty cologne that you insist on wearing. You should've finished the job, Elliot. You should have slit my throat."

Elliot's mouth curved into a cruel smile. Tears made a silent trek down her cheeks and all the fucker could do was smile.

"I always wondered what you were like. And you were a real hell-cat. It made everything that much sweeter," he said before turning to David. "How does it feel to know that you're fucking my sloppy seconds."

David lunged at Elliot, tackling the smaller man to the ground. They rolled around each hitting the other, each attempting to maneuver the other, trying to get leverage. The other guests murmured and whispered as they hurriedly moved out of the way of the two men rolling n the grass and mud.

Elliot got the upper hand, pinning David down with his hands wrapped around his neck. David struggled, his legs moving furiously as he tried to fight against strangulation. His face reddened from the lack of oxygen and stress.

George took a deep breath. She tried to get a good shot; if she missed she'd hit David.

One, two, three...

She squeezed the trigger. The shot gun went off with a deafening boom. For a moment all she heard was white noise. She blinked hard and fast several times, trying to clear her eyes of the tears.

Elliot's body fell forward. Everyone stilled. George's breath caught in her throat. What if the shot hadn't been good and it went through Elliot and into David. Dear God, don't let it hit David.

David rolled Elliot's body off him. With the gun in hand George ran down the steps and dropped to her knees beside her husband. She touched the cut on his lip. "You're bleeding."

He felt his mouth, looked at the blood and shrugged. "I've had worse. A lot worse."

"You're not hurt?" she asked.

"I'm okay. How about you?"

She smiled. "I will be." George turned her attention to the guests. "Party's over. I strongly suggest you all go home."

One by one, the guests filed out of the yard. By morning, everyone would know George had been raped and nearly killed. They'd also know she murdered Elliot and Aces. The remaining faction leaders would jockey for top positioning and might even decide to finally see her for the threat she was.

She wouldn't be there. David had made sure the truck had enough gas in it and in the red cannisters to get them a good distance away before they needed a refill, even pulling a trailer with a couple of horses, a pig, and a goat.

David got to his feet and helped George up. The dress was ruined with grass stains. It didn't matter. He was alive.

Melody walked over to them. Before George could register her hand moving, Melody slapped her in the face hard enough that it felt like the blow came from a closed fist.

She deserved it and worse.

Melody's stare was hard and fiery. "I can understand why you went off the deep end, but I'll tell you this: I want you gone by morning. If I ever see you in this house again, I swear on my father's grave, I'll kill you." Her voice was tight as she issued the warning, then she stormed past them and into the house, allowing the door to slam behind her.

George went inside while David dragged Elliot's body toward the barn. She climbed the stairs and went straight to her bedroom. So many memories, so much work had been accomplished in the wee hours in this house and now it was all gone. She loaded the most important books, a few records, the victrola, and her journal into a couple of plastic boxes and covered them with lids. She and Ana had already split basic medical equipment and supplies, ensuring that she had the bare minimum she needed to set up a practice somewhere else.

Anything else, she'd have to loot like she'd done in the beginning.

Pedro came by and, without a word, took the boxes downstairs. George changed into more practical clothes— a pair of pants, a lightweight shirt and a small jacket. It got chilly at night, even in the summer and with an uncertain destination, she needed to be prepared.

She left the pretty lace dress on the bed. Maybe Ana could repurpose it for something useful.

George climbed the stairs to the attic.

Ana was playing with Abigail in the middle of the floor. It was the best place to protect the girl from the scene outside. George smiled as her niece counted the spaces in Chutes and Ladders. She fought the tears that were coming.

Abigail may not have been blood, but she did love that little girl. She'd been there for Abby's birth, all her birthdays, and she'd held her hand while the child cried over her mother.

Now George would have to do it again. Despite what a prick Elliot was, he was always a decent father.

George sat next to Abby and stroked her hair. She kissed the blonde strands and memorized her scent. She couldn't fight the tears anymore. They came and she tried to blink them away. "Abby, I have to talk to you," she said.

Abigail turned. "What's wrong Auntie George?"

She struggled for a moment, trying to think of what to say. What would even be appropriate.

George decided half-truths were best. "Your daddy had to go away. He had to run an errand and he's going on a journey."

"What kind of journey?" she asked.

It was better to let the little girl think her Dad was some kind of hero than the slime he was. George couldn't force herself to steal this child's innocence with bitter truths. No. Let the adults shoulder them.

"He's going to find a way to fix the town. He heard a story that there was a man who knew how to fix everything and make it the way it used to be. He's going to find that man."

"When will he be back?" Abigail asked with all naivety of a child.

"I don't know, Sweetie. But it's going to be a long time and I know he wants you to stay here and help look after the younger kids. You gotta be brave, my girl."

George glanced at Ana, who was quietly weeping, then she returned her full attention to Abigail.

She took another breath, then continued, "The thing is, I'm going away too. Ana's going to look after you while your daddy and I are gone."

"When are you coming back?" Abigail started to cry.

George scooped her up in her arms. She didn't want to let her go, but she had no idea where she was going or what lie ahead. It was too dangerous for a little girl like Abigail. Staying with Ana was the best thing for her.

"I'm not coming back, Sweetie. There are people out there who need me, just like there are people here who need you." George choked on her tears and kissed Abigail again. "You have to be brave and you have to be strong for me."

George got to her feet. Abigail clung to her, begging her to stay. It was heartbreaking, but George finally let her go.

She handed Abigail to Ana. "Take care of her. She needs a mom more than ever now. You were the best one I ever knew."

Ana studied Abigail for a moment, then did what George knew she'd do. She held her like a mother trying to sooth her child.

David and Pedro waited by the truck for George as she came out of the house. A blue tarp covered their belongings in the bed of the truck. David reached for George and kissed her tear streaked cheeks.

"What did you do with the body?" she asked.

"We took care of it," David replied, his tone one of finality.

Ana came running out of the house with a box in hand. She must've passed Abigail off to Melody. "I packed you some food and supplies. I know Pedro had gathered some earlier, but I wanted to make sure you had enough. There's some seeds too and a couple of saplings needing transplanting." She handed the box off to Pedro. "You don't have to go, Pedro. You have a home here."

He gave Ana a quick hug and took the box. "I want to go with them. They're the closest I have to parents. I want to stay with them."

George hugged Pedro tight and he let her. She had a son. She'd known him since the early days of the black out and gotten used to him hanging around. It never crossed her mind that he'd adopted them as much as she and David had him.

She'd found a family of her own.

"We'd better get going while there's still some light. I think we can drive all night, put some distance between us and Minneapolis," David said. He opened the driver's side door.

"Yeah. You guys better get going," Ana hugged George once more. "You take care, okay?"

George closed her eyes and savored this last goodbye. "You too. Don't let this place fall to pieces. I've worked too hard to maintain it."

Ana chuckled and dropped her hands to hold George's. "Yeah, because I'm so helpless."

George shook her head. "Goodbye, Ana."

"Bye, George."

They lingered like that for a moment, basking in the bitter-sweet end of their friendship and alliance.

George got into the truck and sat sandwiched between Pedro and David. She put on her seatbelt as David started the beat up old truck.

"Where to?" David asked, shifting the truck into gear.

"I don't know. Someplace warm," she said.

"I've always wanted to live in California," replied Pedro, rolling down the window to let the breeze in.

"Funny thing, Kid, that's where I'm from," George replied smiling.

The truck began to move forward. George turned in her seat to look out the back window. Ana was standing on the porch waving. George watched her until they turned the corner out the driveway, and she could no longer see her.

"You're really from California," he said.

"Yeah. I'm from this town called Half-Moon Bay. It's a artsy community. We had an artichoke farm just outside of the main part of town." She thought fondly to her childhood, before her father had remarried and moved the family away from the farm to the Midwest. "As a kid, I'd ride my bike to the beach just to watch the small fisherman's boats."

"Can we go there? Can we go to California?"

David smiled and put his arm around George. "We can go wherever you want."

He began to hum *I'll Be Seeing You.*

As dusk faded into night, George watched the stars. They were so pretty, gleaming in the distance, dancing against the sky like ballerinas on silk. Her future was uncertain and whether they'd make it to California remained to be seen.

But she knew one thing: she had David and Pedro.

It could be enough.

And no matter where they ended up, they would be home.

Book Club Discussion

Welcome to the book club guide for *Last Light of Home*. This novel explores not only a post-apocalyptic world shaped by survival, scarcity, and power, but also what it means to trust, to heal, and to love in the ruins. The following questions are designed to help readers unpack the emotional complexities of the characters and the broader moral questions the story raises. Use these prompts to spark conversation, reflect on character arcs, or explore themes that echo our own world

Discussion Prompts

1. George and David don't follow the usual romantic script. How does their relationship evolve differently than typical love stories? What makes their dynamic feel real, earned, or even painful at times? How does survival shape or distort their ability to love?

2. What does this moment reveal about emotional connection in extreme circumstances?

"You're here," he said fiercely. "I would've given every last drop of blood in my body and then some to save you."

3. George faces impossible moral decisions. What lines does she cross to stay alive, and how do those choices haunt her? How would you have acted in her place?

4. How do George, Ana, David, and Pedro form a new kind of family? What defines family in a post-collapse world?

5. In a world built on barter and scarcity, who holds the power and who gets exploited? How does George navigate authority, especially with Elliot and Ana?

6. How does emotional vulnerability become a form of resistance in this world? Who heals first, George or David, and why?

7. What role does hope play in George's journey? Is she capable of imagining a future beyond mere survival?

8. What makes George and David's romance feel realistic and earned? How does their relationship grow differently than conventional love stories?

9. David defies the usual "alpha male" trope. How does his emotional openness shape the relationship and story?

10. In a barter economy, how do trust and loyalty become a currency of their own? What does George learn about giving and receiving help?

Afterword

I finished writing this book in 2012, when the United States felt like a different place. At the time, I shelved it, convinced that this dystopian story was too bleak... too far-fetched for the world we were living in. But in the years since, we've witnessed global destabilization, a pandemic, and a series of constitutional stress tests that have exposed deep fractures and growing mistrust in our governance and democracy.

When I revisited this manuscript— one of many old works that had never seen the light of day— I was struck by how poignant, even prescient, it felt. What once seemed too grim now felt eerily relevant. And yet, despite its darkness, this story is, at its core, about hope.

George's world is harsh, but as she navigates its challenges, we see hope take root. Love, family, and the quiet act of building something real in the face of uncertainty—these are the things that sustain her, Ana, David, and Pedro. By the final line, the glimmers of hope that were absent at the start shine through.

I hope you enjoyed this tale, but more than that, I hope you always remember to seek out the light in your own world— even when everything else seems dark.

- Sophia Luxe
  2025

Acknowledgements

A book is never just the work of the writer. The words and characters may be ours, but there are always invisible hands along the way— offering sounding boards, support, and feedback, forming an unofficial and invaluable motley crew that keeps the whole thing running.

To my husband, thank you for making sure this writer stays fed, watered and caffeinated; for doing your best to support me, even when that means listening to all the hot tea about people who don't actually exist.

To Sarah, somehow, we found each other, and now you've become my right hand, my left hand, and on more days than I care to admit, my entire brain.

Erin, thanks for humoring me. Often. Frequently. Probably more than is reasonable.

And finally, to the readers: if this is your first book of mine, thank you for giving me a shot. If it's your second or third, thank you for sticking with me.

About the author

Sophia Luxe, spinner of tall tales, caffeine enthusiast, and playlist sorceress, lives in sunny Southern California with her husband, human child, and their three chaotic fur children. She writes with one hand and sips Red Bull with the other, usually while curating mood playlists that range from indie folk to K-pop to "songs that make you feel like a villain." When she's not deep in a Word doc, you'll find her lost in a book, probably muttering "just one more chapter" for the fifth time in a row.

Find her on the web:
   Website: www.sophialuxewrites.com
   Bluesky: @sophialuxe.bsky.social

Also by Sophia Luxe

The Wicked Series
These Wicked Deeds
These Wicked Desires